THE HOME MAKERS

THE
HOME MAKERS

A Novel by

Ivy Strick

Taplinger Publishing Company
NEW YORK

First edition

Published in the United States in 1979 by
TAPLINGER PUBLISHING CO., INC.
New York, New York

Copyright © 1979 by Ivy Strick

Library of Congress Cataloging in Publication Data

Strick, Ivy.
    The Home Makers.

    I. Title.
    PZ4.S9168Ho   [PS3569.T694]   813′.5′4   78-20706
                        ISBN 0-8008-3923-4

"**H**EY, AIN'T THAT FRANK in the road, Neil?"

"Where, Arthur?" Neil shaded his eyes with a stiff hand.

"Check your glasses, Art. You're getting blind as a bat," Jamison hooted. "That feller's half Frank's size and all scrunched over, and besides, didn't he drive that caravan thing of his, Neil?"

"Can't you just say 'camper,' Jamison? It's just a camper." Neil sighed and watched with the others the methodical progress of the stranger on the road. The man was overdressed for the mild weather in grimy castoffs, a bum. He had a sack slung over his shoulder and his eyes cast down, searching his path for scraps and parts of things and lost coins. Something glinted on the ground and he snatched it up, indifferent to his audience, and stowed it in his bag. Neil longed to know what he'd found.

"I asked special for a blanket and never got one," Arthur complained.

"Never got his blanket! Look what he's wearing already," Jamison invited the men. "Is that what you chop wood in up in Canada, Art?" Jamison rocked vigorously, chuckling, his crooked hands jerking in his lap.

"Nebraska, Nebraska, I told you a thousand times. I swear he says that Canada thing just to get my goat." Arthur huddled lower in his rocking chair, huffing and wagging his head.

"Here, take my blanket. I feel warm today." Neil gathered the thin material in his spotted hand and passed it over across a new man, Reese, who appeared to be dozing. He turned his attention back to the road, fixing his eyes on the point where Frank's camper would first be visible coming around the hairpin turn. It seemed to Neil that he'd been gone a long time. That was probably a good sign.

"Hey, Neil," Jamison called down the row of chairs. "How come Frank don't just build you a house hisself, being so particular and so handy at everything, huh?"

Neil shrugged and grunted noncommittally. Frank had in fact

5

built several houses back in Belle Plaine but it would have been pointless to mention this to Jamison.

"Hey, you ever seen this house, Neil?" called Arthur.

"No, but I'm sure it's fine if Frank picked it."

"All the time he took to find it, he could've built one up from scratch, right, Neil?" Jamison cackled and rocked himself.

"Well," Neil sighed, "from what he told me, I think this one is pretty nice." Actually, it wasn't so much what Frank had said as the rare glint of excitement in his eyes.

Neil strained sideways to get at a fat cigar in his jacket pocket. He heaved himself out of his chair and dragged it to the end of the porch, complying with a rule in effect since he'd taken up the habit, a difference of two yards.

"Do me a favor and blow it in my direction," called Reese, whose laugh ended in a fit of phlegmy coughing.

"God, man, don't you have a handkerchief or something?" Jamison's lip curled as he looked away in disgust.

"Listen to who never coughs or spits," Charlie piped up, peeping out of the folds of a great blue comforter. He jerked his shiny head around, collecting grins and nods of agreement.

"Just don't get Reese started again," Jamison muttered.

There was a delicious aroma wafting around from the kitchen windows. The food at Springer's was nothing to complain about. The menu was varied and nutritious, the portions ample. Since it was Sunday, the men were awaiting the main meal of the day, served early enough to allow Idabelle her church service and half-day off.

"Smells like chicken," said Arthur.

"Frank's gonna miss dinner, Neil," Jamison called out happily.

"Don't worry about Frank's dinner," Neil answered. It didn't make much difference, he reasoned to himself. If the news was bad, Frank would be in no mood for dinner, and if it was good news, he might take Neil down the highway to the new seafood place.

"Hey, Neil, who's gonna do your cooking and cleaning and what-all when you two move into your house?" Jamison rocked excitedly. "You boys won't be having meals like we got here, you know, and the laundry all done up, everything . . ."

"Frank's a pretty fair cook, I recall." Neil cleared his throat and took a billowing puff of his cigar.

Jamison hooted and slapped both knees. "Well, don't that beat all! Damn me, I should've guessed it! Is there anything he can't do, this grandson of yours?"

"He don't pick on people all the time," Charlie shouted from his blue cocoon.

"Well, damn, what did I say now? Was I picking on you, Neil? If I did, I'll apologize."

Neil shrugged in annoyance and squinted out at the bright dusty road before them, his eye on the turn.

"I notice Jamison's got nothing to say about Frank to his face," Arthur taunted. "But behind his back you get real brave."

"Brave! Why brave? I got no beef with Frank. He's a quiet sort of feller. Don't say nothing to me and I don't say nothing to him. And all I said was he can do anything. That's a compliment, Art."

"Yeah, yeah, we all heard enough, Jamison," said Charlie.

"Well, *now* I'd like to know who's picking on *who?*" he whined. "Aw, I'm gonna go wash up." He pushed himself out of the deep rocker and shuffled down the row, steadying himself on the porch railing, a look of injury erasing his usual sneer.

"So, Neil, what are they gonna make of that check, you think?" Charlie craned forward to peer over at Neil's calm profile.

"Nothing wrong with that check," Neil replied. "Certified."

"Yeah, but no offense, to look at Frank, them old baggy overalls, a kid's haircut and everything, they just might wonder is all. He don't look like no rich man is all, to plunk down the full amount. No offense."

"Now, hold on, we had a guy back home," Reese began, "kept about a hundred dogs in his yard and dressed in dirty old clothes and never had a phone or electricity or anything, and when he died they found a million bucks under his floor. So you never know. No offense to Frank."

"Look, Frank worked hard from the time he was about fifteen

7

and saved up his money," Neil wearily explained. "Never frittered it away like other young fellas, drinking and raising hell. So that's, what, twenty-two years of saving up. And it's nothing to be ashamed of. If they don't want to take a certified check from Frank, then the joke's on them cause the money's there." Two bright spots burned on Neil's cheeks as he turned back to the road.

"You're right, Neil, the joke *would* be on them. I didn't mean nothing," said Charlie.

Campbell Road was still deserted, shimmering in the hot sun. It wound down a steep hill from Springer's at the top to the wide Pacific Ocean below. All of Nelson Beach was visible from the long shaded porch: the neat modest houses turned this way and that to sit comfortably on the hillside, the highway cutting through the tiny business district, the honey-colored ribbon of sand.

"Anyway, you could always come back here if it don't work out with Frank," said Reese confidentially.

"It'll work out fine." Neil felt a quiver inside as he spoke; if Frank got the house, everything would be different.

"You know, you're lucky, Neil," said Arthur. "It's good to be with family. That's the best. Back home, I had a sister I lived with the last ten years, and then she had a stroke and I came out here. Seven years younger than me . . ."

"I'm sorry." Neil had heard this before.

"Not too many young people care about the old folks or want to have them around. You're real lucky, Neil."

"I know," he said. Still it was funny the way Frank turned up, full of these secret plans which seemed somehow to center around Neil.

His cigar was only half smoked when the dinner bell chimed prettily in the hall. He stubbed it out on the underside of the porch rail, dropped it in his pocket, and rose carefully, stretching his neck and back. He held the screen door open for the other old men while taking a last look down the road.

"GRAMPS."

Neil stirred on his bed and turned his head, tortoise-like, to look over his shoulder. Frank filled the doorframe admirably, blocking the light from the hallway. A sheaf of papers was folded in his hand. He got the house, Neil thought.

"So it's settled then?" Neil rolled over and sat, planting his bare feet in the shaggy mat. He rubbed his bleary eyes and saw by the bedside clock that his nap had been a short one. He still felt heavy from dinner.

"I got stuff to do first," Frank muttered. "Settle up with her, get some boxes for our stuff."

"You mean we're moving today?" Neil tried to work some saliva into his mouth. He wished he could see Frank's expression or draw him into the room.

Frank gestured loosely with the papers. "There's furniture comes with the house." He turned and lumbered down the stairs, shaking the floor with every step.

Neil sat a moment longer, trying to digest the news, and then began to move around the cluttered room, taking inventory of his possessions and marveling that Frank could buy a house and move them in, all in the same day.

He saw that the packing wasn't going to be much of a job. He had some clothes from Belle Plaine that were too warm for California but too good to throw away, some new clothes bought here, toiletries, his whittling stuff. He had never figured on getting his own place when he left Belle Plaine and then he'd never figured on Frank turning up either. But he was always a funny one, thought Neil, the quiet type.

He stepped over Frank's rolled mattress to peer into their closet and into the chest of drawers beneath the window. His large-knuckled hands plucked at the stacks of shirts and underwear. There was a packet tied with a string of yellowed, disintegrating letters written by his wife some fifty years ago. It was a long time since he'd opened them, knowing the paper would crumble in his hands, but he still recalled random passages clearly: "I detest this wretched holiday and can't think why I agreed to it when all I do is swat away the horse-flies and tick off the days till my return. Auntie and Uncle terribly old-fashioned, call you my fancy-man. You should like that." And, "Mother no better, we fear we're going to lose her despite our efforts. Wish you could be here, my Darling, you comfort me so. Kiss Baby Em for Mama and think of me." It wasn't often that they were parted, he and Mamie, but those times were filled with the gushing girlish letters that remained her style always and he had saved every one.

Packing would be a simple matter of placing their neatly folded clothes in Frank's boxes. Neil sat on a camp chair by the window with the packet in his hands and waited for Frank, feeling again the quiver of excitement inside. After a short time, he heard the unmistakable footfalls down in the hall and then felt them on the stairs.

"Did you see Charlotte, Frank?" asked Neil.

"She went into town. I left the money."

Frank's arms were full of nested cardboard cartons, probably more than were needed for the task. He spread them out on the bed and began to empty the drawers and closet into them.

"I'd sure like to say good-bye to Charlotte. She was awful nice to both of us. Ida, too," Neil sighed.

"Ida's in church."

"I know." Neil took a deep breath. "Frank . . .?"

"What." Frank turned a face like a blank wall toward his grandfather.

"Never mind." Neil lost the desire to reason with him.

In minutes, Frank was done and ready to go. He made his first trip out to the camper with the largest box. Neil straightened the bedspread under the others as best he could, and shut the gaping closet door and drawers. He looked around the small room and tried to summon memories of the past year, but everything was happening too quickly. He drew a blank, hardly knew how he felt.

Frank continued his methodical removal of cartons, announced his last trip, and clutching the letter packet to his chest, Neil followed his grandson down the stairs and out to the porch.

The crazy yellow camper, Frank's proud creation, hummed

and sputtered in the dusty road. It had been built on the chassis of an old Chevrolet, with the back chopped away and a little round-cornered house set in its place. The front seat, the windshield, and the hood were intact.

The other old men were napping in their rooms and there was no one to wave good-bye. Frank fitted himself into the driver's seat and revved the motor. Neil stepped out into the warm sunshine.

"THAT WAS GOOD, FRANK," said Neil, wiping his mouth.

He recalled the time back in Belle Plaine when Emmie was laid up with hepatitis and Armand was still in high school and Frank took over all the cooking for the family. At first he had to rely on Emmie's cookbooks and personal recipe file, but before long he was improvising favorite dishes and inventing new ones. They all put on a few pounds that winter.

"You finished?" Frank wiped his hands on the drooping seat of his overalls.

"I'm stuffed. It was a good dinner. Well, I guess I'll take a walk down to the beach in a few minutes. Want to come, Frank?"

"No. I'm gonna finish the tile." He lumbered over to the doorway to what used to be the porch and was now part of an expanded living room, and lowered himself to the floor.

Neil could see him from his chair at the table, laying down squares of linoleum in the new area. He'd done all the work himself, evenings, building the new walls, knocking down the old, setting in the glass-louvered windows that faced the ocean, painting inside and out.

After a few minutes, the old man took a cigar from the humidor, pulled on a light jacket, and set off down the road. The air was refreshing, the sun hung low over the water, and the beach appeared temptingly empty from the hill.

As he passed through the quiet street he could see into lit windows around him: families still at dinner, women washing up at the sink, the blue winking of television sets. He reached Center Street where the highway slowed for a few hundred yards before

11

continuing along the coast. That was the whole of the business district: the bank, the grocery, the drugstore, tailor, funeral home, saloon, and so on.

Neil's mouth watered for the cigar but he resolved not to light it until he reached the beach. He hurried down Center to the gravel-and-tar parking lot. The sun was just kissing the waves as he crossed the square to the railroad ties along the far edge. There were couples sitting close together in the few remaining cars, using the excuse of the sunset to linger. He sat on the dark, sharp-smelling wood, unlaced his sturdy shoes, and peeled off his socks, tucking them well into the shoes, then rolled his cuffs above his hairless ankles. Under his feet the sand was still warm in contrast to the cooler evening air. It felt good.

Now he fished out the cigar and bit the end off, and the tobacco on his tongue brought forth a gush of saliva. He lit up with great blue clouds of smoke and rose, leaning well forward before straightening his knees. With the cigar clamped between his teeth and the shoes dangling from his hand, he strolled across the littered sand to the water's edge.

The ocean was cold as always when he tested it, dabbing his toes in the wavelets, but his real interest lay higher up on shore: a foot-wide strip that snaked along the waterline, composed mainly of dried seaweed but also containing the shells and beach grass and dead sea creatures which intrigued the old midwesterner. He walked beside the ribbon toward a spit of black rocks, the end measure of his evening walk. He rarely glanced out at the magnificent display in the sky and wore his magnifying glasses the better to peer into the tangled debris at his feet.

His first find of the evening was a long twisted stick of driftwood that turned out to be handy for stirring the sea trash when something caught his eye. There were dozens of small orange crabs, belly up, missing most of their legs, crushed cans and wrappers, and shells and stones that showed every color when wet, dull pink and gray when dry. The pungent smoke spared him the odor of decay and he walked unhurriedly, puffing out his chest with satisfaction.

He spotted several bits of glass, the only souvenirs he usually kept from his walks, and pushed down on the stick to stand up after pocketing them. The stick was a help and he thought of smoothing over the knobby end and whittling the narrow end to the shape of a cane. By the time he reached the black rocks, he had found two pieces of anonymous white glass, one imperfectly sanded, a piece of green Coke bottle, and a bit of amber beer glass. Only twice so far had he uncovered the rare cobalt of the old Noxzema jars. It was a shame, he decided, about soda cans and plastic jars and the whole ecology thing that discouraged people from throwing their empties out to sea.

There was a lot of sea junk piled up where the rocks jutted into the water, and he squatted on his heels to search through it when he was startled by a strange voice. The cigar dropped from his teeth as he looked around for the speaker.

"I know you," croaked the voice again.

Neil followed the sound this time and identified a bundle of rags resting on a ledge above as human. He retrieved the half-smoked cigar and brushed sand off the soggy end but it had gone out.

"You took me by surprise," Neil answered pleasantly. "I didn't see you there."

"You live in the yellow house, with the farmer."

Neil relaxed, chuckling at the description. He had been a farmer almost all his life, Frank never, yet Frank's chosen uniform of baggy overalls, pressed blue shirts, and bowl haircut made him look more the part.

"I guess you *do* know me," Neil said. "But it isn't nice to spy on folks." He shook a finger at the grimy little man.

"Maybe I am a spy!" he cried gleefully. "Maybe that's what I am!"

They laughed together, then smiled awkwardly. Neil wiped a tear from the corner of his eye. The sun had dipped below the horizon and the light was fading fast.

"Well, I guess I'll start back," said Neil. "Good-night to you, then." He looked back at the deserted parking lot.

"Got any money?" Wily blue eyes sparkled out of the weather-worn face.

"Sorry, I don't." Neil smiled vaguely and turned away, hurrying toward home.

FRANK BECAME AWARE of muffled sounds outside his bedroom window and opened his eyes. The curtains were drawn and he could see only a sliver of the starry sky without disturbing them. He lay still and listened, and at first it seemed that he was hearing the shrubbery brushing against the house, but then the sounds moved away toward Neil's window.

The bedsprings creaked in the old man's room and the next thing Frank heard was the flush of the toilet down the hall. He pulled on a flannel robe and went out to meet his grandfather.

Neil was bleary-eyed and startled to see Frank looming suddenly out of the dark. "Having trouble sleeping . . ." he whispered.

Frank wasn't sure if it was a question or a statement and he grunted noncommittally.

"Well, give it another try . . ." Neil said, and moved past to his doorway.

"Wait." Frank still didn't know which of them Neil was talking about. He pushed the bangs off his forehead and frowned. "Did you hear something just before?"

"Uh, might have. Sounded like a dog maybe. Maybe somebody taking a shortcut home."

"It's four o'clock, pretty late for folks to be out."

"Well, what do you think? A burglar or something?"

"I don't know. Maybe."

"What should we do, do you think?" Neil attempted to mirror Frank's concern.

"I'm gonna take a look outside. Stay here."

Frank winced in the harsh light of the kitchen and dug around under the sink for his flashlight. Neil stood uncomfortably by, unable to help and feeling weaker now that he knew the exact time. He began to despair of getting any more sleep that night.

"Want my slippers, Frank? The grass is gonna be wet out there." He slipped off his corduroy scuffs and Frank grunted and stepped into them, his heels hanging well over in the back.

He shuffled outside to the driveway and listened for a moment, cocking his head, before snapping on his light and swinging it around at the trees and bushes as if it were a weapon. He crept around to the backyard and examined the ground beneath the bedroom windows. The weeds there might well have been trampled, but despite his air of authority, Frank knew little about tracking and couldn't make out whether the intruder had two legs or four, or if it meant them any harm. He glanced around at the neighboring houses, but every one was dark. As far as he could tell he was alone.

Neil was sitting at the kitchen table, resting his head in his hands. "See anything?" he asked, looking up with hollow eyes.

"Nope," said Frank. "But I guess I'll get me a shotgun tomorrow."

"Sure, why not?" Neil quickly agreed. They had always kept an array of guns at home, for hunting and protection.

"Want some cocoa?" Frank muttered. He became a blur of activity and Neil's face brightened as he watched.

He whipped out the enameled pot, two mugs, dark bitter cocoa, sugar, milk, spoons, reaching for things with both hands in an economy of movement, as quick and sure and organized as a veteran short-order cook. One hand poured the milk and returned the carton to the icebox, the other began to stir. He added measures of cocoa and sugar, and a sweet rich aroma filled the room. When the mixture was thick and hot, he divided it into the mugs and topped it with canned whipped cream and a sprinkling of the gritty bitter chocolate.

Neil gratefully took his mug from Frank, warming his hands against the crockery and inhaling the vapors. "Real tasty, as usual," he said between sips.

Frank grunted acknowledgment and drank grimly, thinking about the shotgun he would buy and wishing he had his old one from home.

"Think you can sleep now, Gramps?" he asked at last.

"I don't know, Frank. This cocoa'll help some, but it's hard, you know, when you get old." Neil slurped the bitter dregs and sighed deeply.

"We could stay up, play some cards," Frank suggested. He

15

brought the mugs to the sink and rinsed them under the tap.

"No, no, never mind. I think I'll sleep," said Neil. "Tired enough, for sure," he added with more confidence than he felt. He stood slowly, favoring his stiff knees, and saluted brightly from the doorway.

" 'Night, Frank," he said.

" 'Night, Gramps. Don't worry."

Neil closed himself in his room and climbed back into bed. He closed his eyes and saw the words floating in space: "You know how they say you don't feel the heat, it's so dry and all? What rubbish! I feel about to expire every moment I'm out of doors. But Em is coming along beautifully, getting so big and strong you won't know her. I wish you'd let the Devil take the corn this once and join us, but I know, I know, don't scold. Love you, Dearest . . ."

Frank's eyes began to burn in the light. He switched it off and wandered into the new room, completed at last. It was a vast space, the old living room and the porch combined, and furnished so far with just two old rockers that had come with the house. They were set side by side, facing the louvered windows as though still on the porch. He drew one around so he could rest his feet on it and sat quietly, watching the black ocean and the outline of the town and the growing dawn.

"Now I can't get this here waffle iron to heat up at all!" Idabelle dealt the thing a wallop with her broad brown hand and sadly wagged her head.

"Well, don't hit it, for goodness sake! That never helped anything. Let me take a look." Charlotte Springer edged Ida aside and stared fixedly at the grill of the appliance. It was flooded with batter and cold as a stone. She flipped the switch energetically, as if to catch it off guard, and sighed. "Oh, dear, if only we had Frank."

"Mister Frank was the last one tinkered with that."

"Why? What was the matter with it?"

"Only one side was heating up. Now both sides is dead."

16

She stood solidly at her employer's elbow, defending her territory, to Charlotte's growing annoyance. Her round, smooth arms were folded firmly across her enormous bosom, her trunklike legs securely planted.

"Well, then, we'll just have to have something else for our gentlemen this morning. It doesn't matter. You could make pancakes out of that batter, couldn't you?"

"I could make 'em," Ida drawled, "but they wouldn't be good. I beated that batter special for waffles."

"Well, do it anyway," Charlotte said crisply.

Ida wagged her large head again and stooped to draw out a cast-iron skillet from under the counter. She knocked it into Charlotte's ankle, causing her to step back but not yet leave the kitchen.

"I can make 'em," she muttered again, "but they won't be good."

Charlotte caught herself staring again at Idabelle's hips as she moved about the room. Their girth was astonishing in itself, but it was the apparent weightlessness of the dimpled flesh that intrigued Charlotte; it was as though the woman existed in a different field of gravity. She bent suddenly to check the contents of the oven, affording a rare view of her torso-less hindquarters.

"What have you got in there?" Charlotte asked, breaking her reverie.

"A pan of muffins, Missus," Ida answered grudgingly.

"Muffins *and* waffles?"

"Pancakes."

"But it amounts to the same thing. It's all starch, all carbohydrates. Don't you see? It doesn't make a rounded meal."

"These here are *corn* muffins," Ida wearily explained. "And them pancakes was supposed to be waffles what have a nice crispness to 'em."

"The texture has nothing to do with it. It isn't rounded. Look, where's your protein? What about fruit? Do you understand? You have all grain products there." Charlotte waved disgustedly at the stove. "I see I'll have to organize this myself."

Idabelle rolled her eyes toward heaven as Charlotte rifled first the pantry, then the icebox. Her lips were slack with extreme boredom and her arms were still folded in passive resistance to any change in her menu.

"Now! Here are some perfectly good eggs. That's all we need, Ida. Soft boiled for everyone. There are at least two dozen here. And use that egg timer I bought so we don't have any accidents." She pushed a crockery bowl at Ida's stubbornly folded arms.

"I thought them eggs was gonna be for Mister Frank's angel cake." Her dark eyes narrowed accusingly.

"Please, Ida, no more arguments today. I'm worn out already and it's still morning." She set the bowl on the counter and clapped her palms together, ending the matter. "We'll just order more eggs, all right? I have an order for Muller's anyway. But right now I want my guests to have some protein with their breakfast. And give them some orange juice, for heaven's sake—there's a ton of it in the freezer. And no more nonsense, please." Charlotte pivoted in what she imagined to be military style and marched out to the porch.

Idabelle snorted and mumbled to herself, "No more nonsense, *please* . . ."

She bent to get the pot out of the cabinet and, from this vantage point, noticed that the waffle iron's plug was dangling out of the socket. She plugged it in and watched the batter begin to bubble over the surface of the grill. Humming sweetly, with a grin of utmost satisfaction, she replaced the bowl of eggs and gave her batter a few more strokes.

E MMIE HEARD A CAR pulling into her yard and leaned over the sink to peek through the curtains. She recognized Willa's old green Dodge and wiped her hands on her apron. She watched from the door as Willa stepped carefully in the new fall of snow which seemed already to have formed an icy crust.

"I don't want to mess up your floor," Willa apologized, stamping her boots on the cement step.

"Oh, here, I'll get something." Emmie took a plastic garbage bag from under the sink and spread it before the door. "Goodness, it's freezing." She shuddered.

"Ten below last night. It's not supposed to go up past zero today," Willa sighed. She unwound her scarf, removed her woollen coat, and sat with Emmie at the kitchen table.

"So, how's your mother getting along, Willa?"

"Oh, well, thanks for asking. She's a little better, I guess. But it takes a long time when they're old, you know. The doctor says not to expect miracles."

"She was never a very strong woman, your mother."

"That's true."

"Oh, I got some muffins baking! I almost forgot." Emmie rose and peered into the oven. "They need a few more minutes to brown, I guess."

"Heard anything from Frank yet?" Willa asked halfheartedly.

"Not one word! But that boy was never one for letter-writing. Pop sent another card, day before yesterday. Let me see if I can find it. The kids might've made off with it." Emmie bustled into the hall and ransacked a Popsicle-stick letterbox.

"You think Frank is liking it out there?" Willa called.

"Hold on, I can't hear you. Oh, here it is." She returned waving a scallop-edged picture postcard. "I told you they bought a house, didn't I?"

"You said he was *looking* for one. You never said bought one." Willa was crestfallen.

"Oh, I thought I did. Well, anyway, Pop says they're all moved in. So here's this one—he writes 'All well here. Hope you are same. We are settled in. The living room is all finished. Frank sends regards. Love, Pop.' "

"Is that all? Let me see the picture."

Emmie handed it over. "I wonder what they did in the living room. Muffins smell good." She snatched them out of the oven with a gloved hand. They were brown on top, dotted with purple. "Want to try 'em with me? I tried some canned blueberries I found in the store. They were awful small. I don't know if they taste any good." She shrugged.

"Thanks, I'll have one, but just don't offer me seconds after

19

that. I'm almost the same size as Ma now, got to watch out."
Willa forced a chuckle and patted her midriff.

"Oh, you're still young. You don't need to worry. It's when you get to be my age . . ." Emmie loosened two muffins and brought them over on saucers with a tub of margarine and a knife. "We could use some coffee with this," she murmured, and set a pot on the stove to reheat.

"So, don't you know any more about this house or anything? I mean, it was so strange when Frank just picked up and left like that, didn't you think?"

"Well, he was always my quiet one, you know. Makes his own plans and never thinks to let anyone in on it."

"But he was never that close to your dad when he was home," Willa persisted. "I mean, I just wondered *why*."

"Oh, those two always got along fine." She thought for a moment and shrugged. "He just got this idea to go be with Pop. I think it was when he started building that camper. Remember he was working every night out in that drafty garage? Well, I think he was already planning to leave back then." She poured the hot coffee and brought over the mugs and a carton of milk.

"But what did your dad think of him showing up?"

"He never said. He just sends these picture cards with an itty bitty space to write."

"But how do they manage, just the two men together?" Willa pressed her finger into the soft crumbs on her plate and licked them.

"Oh, Willa! Frank can do anything around the house that I can, most things better. Don't worry about *that*. He can cook and clean and fix everything . . . I never had no cause to worry about him taking care of himself, not that boy."

"But he's *not* a boy still, Em. I mean he ought to think about getting married, having his own family," Willa blurted out. "I mean, don't you think?"

Emmie could have pointed out that Willa herself was the same age as Frank and also unmarried. She hesitated for a moment. "Well, sure, I'd like to see him settle down with someone nice, but it ain't up to me to run his life for him. He'll find someone when he's ready, I guess. So for now, he wants to be with Pop. Nothing wrong with that.''

Willa's face was flushed when Emmie looked up from her plate. "Well, I just . . ." She broke off. "What's he doing for work, Em? Same as usual?''

"Gee, I don't know. I suppose. He never could take to regular hours. Anyway, between the two of them, they can't be hurting for money.''

"Did you send him my regards, like I said?" asked Willa, subdued.

"I sure did," said Emmie. There was the sound of a car motor in the yard, breaking the heavy winter stillness, and Emmie trotted to the door to see who it was. "Armand's home. I hope nothing's wrong,'' she fretted.

"Maybe I'll write him myself. I could maybe crochet him one of my pot holders. You think it would be all right?''

"I don't see why not.''

Armand parked the Buick next to Willa's car and stamped up to the house as though he were mad at the ground. He wore a quilted nylon parka over his suit and the suit jacket hung out below like a little skirt. His slicked-back hair was gathering snowflakes.

"Where's Marcia?'' he grumbled as he came through the door.

"She went over to her mother's, I think. Why are you home so early? Anything wrong?''

"Aw, there's some big blizzard coming this way so we shut down for the day, that's all. Business is dead anyway. I gotta call Marcia and get her to run by the school for the kids and get her butt home before it comes down. Howdy, Willa,'' he added, remembering his manners. "I advise you to get along home, too, before long. 'Scuse me.'' He hung his scarf and parka on a peg by the door and trudged into the living room.

"Oh, well, I guess I'll shove off then, if we're in for a storm. Ma will worry.'' Willa sighed and heaved herself out of the chair. "So, do you think it would be okay if I wrote to Frank?''

"Oh, sure. I think that'd be nice," said Emmie. "But he's not one for writing himself so don't take it personal if you don't get a letter back." Emmie began to clear the table while Willa bundled herself up. "You know, I can't recall ever getting a word on paper from that boy, and I'm his own mother."

"Well, maybe I'll send along a pot holder, too. I don't guess he'll be needing any more scarves out there." She forced a nervous laugh and let herself out. "Bye now. Take care."

"Drive carefully," Emmie mouthed through the window.

"Now where's that boy?" she muttered to herself, hurrying into the hall.

He was lying on the living room sofa with his feet on the arm, mussing the antimacassar, holding a magazine five inches above his face. He was still wearing his suit. He turned to the doorway with a look of intense boredom.

"Willa go?"

"Just now. How come they closed early, dear?"

"I told you, there's this blizzard, and business stinks anyway. Nobody in their right mind buys equipment now. All we get in is warranty work. The service boys got their hands full, but the salesmen are going nuts. I don't know how much more I can take, standing around all day in this goddamn suit." He sat up suddenly, tore off the jacket, and flung it across the room.

"If it's so terrible . . ." his mother began.

"You know that Sharpe makes us stand up the whole time just in case somebody happens to drop by? So's we look like we're ready to do business or some such bull. I ain't cut out for this, no way." He flopped back down and glared at the ceiling.

"If you hate it so much, you should look for something else," Emmie suggested softly. "I mean, you always have your home here and we're not in a pinch. If you hate the store, then find something you like better."

"Yeah, like what?" he asked disgustedly. "I don't know nothing else. I can sell heavy equipment only 'cause I used it myself, but that don't make me no salesman. I never been handy like Mister Bluejeans there—"

"Now, don't you poke fun at Frank. He never did nothing to hurt your feelings, did he?"

"All right, all right." He sighed and held the magazine over his face again, his mouth set in a hard, bitter line.

"I don't like you making fun."

22

"Will you just forget it?"

But Emmie couldn't stop herself. "And you weren't very nice to Willa just now, either," she scolded.

"Well, what does she want here, anyway? Missing our boy? I thought we saw the last of her when old Frank moved out." He flipped the glossy pages angrily and never looked up.

"Oh, Armand, I feel sorry for her. And I like to have her drop by for a visit. It gets lonesome here, so I wish you would be a little more pleasant to her. Will you try, dear?" she pleaded, shifting her weight uncomfortably in the doorway.

Armand made no response beside the irritable page-flipping. Emmie walked wearily to his crumpled suit jacket, laid it carefully across the chair, and left the room.

"Dear Frank," Willa wrote. "Hi. How are you? We are all fine here. Mother broke her hip last month (maybe you heard from your Mom?) and it's taking a long time to heal. But her spirits are good. When she says she is a burden to me I tell her that she took care of me when I was helpless (a baby) and now I'm returning the favor. I guess maybe it's like you and your Grandpa. Except he is not sick like Ma. Anyway, we were supposed to have a storm here today but there was nothing much yet, only a few flakes. I bet you don't miss our weather much out there. It must be heaven to have sunny weather all the year round. I can hardly imagine. Maybe when I retire (from what?) I'll move out west too. I was over visiting your Mom to say hi and she showed me a picture card of the beach out there. I am planning to crochet you a couple of pot holders out of rug yarn which I'll mail you soon. I got the pattern from Jo Anne Hardy, JW's sister, and I hope you can find a use for them. Well, this old blizzard looks like a bust. We all miss you here. Every time something goes wrong in this ramshackle place Ma starts hollering, When is that Frank Diggory coming back? But we don't miss you for that only! Give your Grandpa my regards and Ma says hello to you both.

"Your Friend Always,
"Willa"

Willa read over her letter and it seemed all right. She set the pad

23

and pen on her night table and switched off the frilly-shaded reading lamp. Her eyes were tired and her throat ached a little. She curled up on her side, covering her ear with the quilt, and snuggled into the soft mattress. The tightness in her throat began to relax and she drew up the hem of her nightgown and warmed her hand between her thighs.

IT WAS LATE, almost two-thirty, and Roscoe would have to be getting up for work in only five more hours. Still, he knew better than to stay in bed, cursing in the dark, yanking the covers around. He pulled on a cotton kimono and selected a bottle of Scotch from the liquor cabinet by the light of the moon. He kept his special glass there too, the last of a set, a wedding present. He brought the armload of supplies to the porch, the bottle and glass, the ice bucket, and a jar of salted nuts.

He deposited the things on a low bamboo table and stretched out on one of two aluminum, plastic-webbed chaise longues. He poured his first drink and made a concerted effort to relax, gazing into the murky night penetrated here and there by shafts of moonlight. He could make out the shape of the hedge beyond his porch and past that, the rounded comical silhouette of the caravan next door.

His thoughts turned, as he knew they would, to his wife, and once again he reviewed and debated the role he had played in her death. As always, the sticking point was his failure to insist on a procedure that might have prolonged her life while violating her beliefs as a Christian Scientist. He had sadly bowed to her will then and spent interminable nights since going over the same ground. He tried to urge his thoughts back to the time he called "B.C."—before cancer—hoping to find some pleasure in his memories, but blame and longing and loneliness inevitably won out these sleepless nights.

The liquor occasionally helped Roscoe to put Marianne's suffering in a mildly humorous light. He recalled her plump solemnity, the certainty of God's will that made her positively smug in her hideous pain, self-righteous to the end. He poured another shot over fresh ice and snuggled lower on the chaise. A heaviness began to creep over him that held out the promise of a few hours' oblivion. He closed his eyes and breathed in the scent of his roses mingled with brine, wafting on the breeze.

Startled by the creak of door hinges nearby, Roscoe sat up and strained to see some movement in the night. The next moment, he discerned the scurrying form of a man moving from the absurd camping vehicle to the bushes behind his neighbor's house. He stood to get a better view with his heart racing at the show of stealth and possible evil.

He pulled his robe close and tiptoed around to their driveway and up to the kitchen door. He took a deep breath and rapped smartly on the glass until a hulking giant with a smoldering expression towered over him in silence.

Now that he was seeing the man in pajamas, Roscoe realized with surprise that until this moment he'd never seen him in anything other than denim overalls. He might have wondered if this was the same man had it not been for his eccentric childlike haircut and his stature.

"Sorry to bother you," Roscoe began in a hoarse whisper. He cleared his throat nervously. "I was just now sitting out on my porch, you see, and I saw a suspicious character on your grounds, at least he seemed so to me. He came out of your trailer thingy, I believe, and then ran round the back of the house." Roscoe waved vaguely, indicating his porch, the camper, the house.

Frank made no response; he seemed to be puzzling over something.

"Well," Roscoe shrugged, "I just thought I had better let you know. Just in case it was anything. Sorry if I disturbed you and all. Good-night then." He forced a polite smile and backed away.

"Where're you from?" Frank asked unexpectedly.

"What, do you mean originally?" Roscoe drew near and looked up with amusement. "Devon, England. But I've lived here in California, oh, more than twenty years now. You can still hear it, eh?" He relaxed a bit in the stony presence.

"What did you say, something about seeing somebody?" Frank was still muzzy with sleep and shy before the foreigner with his fancy printed robe.

"I say I saw a fellow sneaking about, just before, and I thought he might be up to no good. But he seems to be gone now." Roscoe peered around. "I guess it was a false alarm."

Frank stepped back into the blackness of his kitchen and returned to the step with an imposing shotgun dangling at his side. "Gonna look around," he mumbled as he brushed past.

Roscoe followed, feeling adventurous yet safe behind his armed and powerful neighbor. They toured the small yard in Indian file, encountering nothing unusual, and then turned back to approach the camper.

Frank listened outside it with his head cocked, then swung open the small metal door and stood aside. When no moving target emerged, he crept in, head ducked low, pointing the gun before him.

Roscoe followed eagerly, curious to see the interior of the vehicle. He found it neat and cozy, with walls that appeared to contain all sorts of foldaway equipment. It was just tall enough for Roscoe's host to stand erect, but the scaled-down table and benches, the frilly curtains covering the porthole windows, the oval rug tacked to the floor, made Roscoe think of a child's playhouse.

Frank noticed at once that the bunk bed had been disturbed but, more important, there was the stale odor of urine emanating from the tiny stall by the door; his toilet had been used under the mistaken impression that it was in working order. He glared angrily around, looking vainly for the culprit, the gun still half poised.

"Well, I wasn't mistaken," Roscoe chirped. "You've had a visitor."

Frank scarcely noticed the slight Englishman as he tried to think what his next step should be.

"Well, I shouldn't worry if I were you. It was just a tramp, it seems," Roscoe went on. "Just looking for a place to sleep. Anyway, he won't be back tonight, don't you think?" Roscoe stepped out onto the gravel and gazed around.

26

Frank eased himself out the little door and slammed it possessively shut.

"I guess you'll want to keep it locked from now on," said Roscoe.

"No."

"No? Then what?" Roscoe was beginning to feel a chill. His bare feet were wet, his pajama cuffs as well.

"Gonna wait for him in there tomorrow night."

Roscoe looked at the large square hand clutching the gray muzzle of the gun and gulped. "Listen, friend," he began, "I have a thought. Why don't you come over to my place tomorrow night and we'll sit out on my porch there and keep an eye on your house and all. It's a perfect view. And that way you could trap this fellow inside and find out what his game is without anyone getting hurt by accident. What do you say?"

"Well," Frank hesitated, glancing across the low hedge to the offered lookout and uneasily back to his own place, "I don't want to leave Gramps alone."

"But we'd have a perfect view of your house, better than if you were waiting inside there—you can see the door and the back of the house," Roscoe urged. "I really think you'd do better to trap this fellow inside than to lie in wait for him."

"I don't know." Frank stared off into the dark, over Roscoe's head, frowning.

"I would be glad to wait up with you and be of any help. I've been having a touch of insomnia anyway. Please consider it. My name is Roscoe Small, by the way. Pleased to meet you at last." He smiled and reached for Frank's empty hand and shook it, thinking how delicate and soft his own hand must feel in Frank's.

"Frank Diggory," Frank murmured. "Maybe I'll come. Around eleven. 'Night." He turned and lumbered toward his door.

" 'Night," Roscoe echoed.

"HEY, POPS. YOU! I got a job for you." A bartender hailed the derelict and sniffed with distaste as the man drew near.

"You got something for me?"

The bum didn't look so old up close; it was his stoop, his weathered skin, the hair that seemed to be pepper and salt one moment and sandy blond the next that gave the impression of age. Azure blue eyes shone out of his coppery face with disconcerting intelligence.

"There's a mess of empty crates in the cellar," said the bartender, inhaling through his mouth. "Haul 'em out to the alley back there and I'll give you a bottle. Deal?"

"Scotch whisky?" The blue eyes turned crafty.

"Not my good stuff, but yeah."

"Got a deal . . . got a deal . . ." The bum mumbled as he followed his new employer around to the cellar door and down the crooked steps into the dark. He seemed old again, muttering to himself, resigned to a stint of labor.

The bartender yanked a greasy string, switching on the naked bulb overhead. Empty crates and cartons were stacked against one stone wall, paper supplies and beer kegs were against another.

"I want all this brought around back to the alley," the bartender said, then left the man to his work.

First he searched the small dank room for anything that might be of use but wouldn't be missed. He found only a rusted nail clipper in one spider-webbed corner and pocketed it automatically. Behind a heavy sealed carton he saw a dead rat with its head partially ripped away and it made him gag.

He carried the crates three and four at a time up the uneven steps and around to the back of the alley. He tired quickly and had to rest, light-headed, between trips. After a while, the cellar was cleared. He switched off the bulb and felt his way upstairs.

He wandered through the alley to the back of the bar, where the

28

kitchen door stood open to catch the sea breezes. Inside, three black men were bumping around in the tiny space.

"Hey, old man," called one of the cooks, "want a real job? Come on in here, I'll teach you to cook. You like that?"

The three men laughed at the bum's angry scowl.

"What do *you* think? Do I look like a fool?" He turned and spat in disgust. "Working all day in a itty bitty hot kitchen . . . a hellhole . . ." he muttered.

The cooks' laughter died and they went back to their frying and grilling, trying to ignore the indignant bum blocking their air.

"A man would have to be a *fool* . . . Real job, huh!" he went on, swaying like a snake and narrowing his surprising eyes until one of the cooks handed him a thick hamburger to shut him up.

He ate quickly, leaning over in the alley so that the grease would drip on the packed dirt and not on his already grimy shirtfront. After this hasty meal, he presented himself at the front door, waiting patiently to be noticed. The bartender followed the alarmed stares of several customers and rushed out with the promised bottle in a twisted paper bag.

"If you come back in a week I'll have more for you, buddy," he said. "Okay?"

"Do I look like a fool? Week in, week out, huh! A man has to be crazy . . . that's right . . ." He tucked the bottle inside his filthy jacket and stalked away, deeply offended.

He headed for the black rocks at the end of the beach and settled himself on a dry sandy ledge with his bottle secure under one arm and a splendid sense of well-being. He dozed there, smiling faintly, until the sound of car motors revving in the parking lot brought him slowly to consciousness.

He was dazed in the twilight and clutched wildly for the bottle which had slipped down the rockface but rested unharmed in the sand. Now that he had the beach to himself, it was time for a drink, a drink and a leisurely rummage through the trash baskets ranged along the edge of the parking lot.

He found a quarter first thing, glinting on the black tar, and it seemed like a good sign. From the baskets he rescued an unopened box of pretzels, half a buttered roll in a plastic bag, a wet but clean sock, and a warm flat beer that he drank fastidiously, tipping the stream into his open mouth. He searched the entire lot for more lost change, found none, and rambled back through town to his hideaway, the basement of a long-vacant shop.

He stowed the food in a plastic garbage bag that hung from an overhead pipe to keep it from the rats, then began the climb up the winding road past the neat little houses where families were sitting down to supper, bickering, gossiping, watching shrill comedies on television sets. It was dark outside and he felt comfortably hidden and took his time.

When he reached the yellow house, the farmer was cooking supper for the old man—some kind of steak it looked like. When he tired of watching, he crept into the funny little camper, working the door cautiously, and stretched out on the high soft berth. He took a few pulls on his bottle and slept a good long while.

He woke himself by some internal alarm and saw through the porthole window that the house was dark and the moon had risen, a fat crescent, high in the sky. He left the camper and scampered around to the rear of the house.

He first checked the farmer's room, still and dark, then stepped into the bushes under the old man's window and tapped the glass with his horny fingernail. Before he had to tap again, the lined pink-and-white face appeared, groggy but smiling, between the curtains. The old man raised the window slowly, carefully, until there was space enough to slip through a thick meaty sandwich wrapped in a paper napkin.

He was creeping back through the shadows to the warm berth when he saw a stranger coming up the gravel drive, hammering on the door as if to wake the dead. Then the farmer appeared with a huge gun, looking to blow someone's head off.

The bottle was back in the camper, he realized, and he felt a black rage at himself and all the world as he started back to the cold damp basement in town. He kicked at trash cans and gates and stones along his way, anything to create a racket and express to the snug, sleeping citizens his bitter disappointment.

30

"OH, BROUGHT YOUR OWN TONIGHT," said Roscoe. He rose politely as Frank climbed the porch steps. They had waited and watched together for two nights already, but he was still awkward in Frank's presence.

The bamboo table was stocked with two glasses, the ice bucket, a bowl of pretzels, and a new bottle of Scotch.

"Found this in town," said Frank. He held up the plastic jug of hard cider, dangling it from his finger. Under his arm was tucked the heavy tool kit.

"Ah, let's have a look. Is this what you fellows drink back home?" Roscoe squinted at the label, turning it toward the moonlight.

"I don't know. Some folks, I guess. I like it better than that there." He jerked his chin at Roscoe's supply and crossed the porch to peer into the darker shadows there. The shotgun was revealed under his other arm. Roscoe hated the sight of it, oily gray and lethal.

"Why don't you stow that thing and take a seat," said Roscoe. "You know, Frank, it's just possible we scared that fellow off for good that first night."

"He'll be back."

"Not necessarily. We may have seen the last of him. I, for one, would not be disappointed."

"Well, anyway, I'm gonna fix that switch like I said. Bought you this new one today." Frank dug around in the sagging front pocket of his overalls and pulled out the plastic-and-metal device. "Watch my house when I'm inside," he said.

Frank easily found his way down the dark hall to the bathroom; the layout of Roscoe's house was the same as his own except for the placement of the porch. He opened his tool kit and laid out the work light, then searched the kitchen for a fuse box.

When he failed to find it in the back of the utility closet or in any other likely spot, he gave up and lit the hall light. He knew he

31

could replace the switch without cutting off the current—he'd just have to take care not to complete the circuit with his screwdriver or his hand.

He unfastened the plate around the switch and unscrewed the switch itself. He pulled it out from its hole in the wall, carefully straightening the thick, insulated wires. The worn-out switch had its screws on either side of the box, while the new one had them together on the same side. Frank unhooked the wires and bent them wide apart. One of them tingled between his fingers, reminding him to go slow. He loosened the screws on the new switch and attached the dead wire first. As he was about to hook up the remaining wire, he checked the switch and flicked it to the off position, avoiding a nasty shock. With the screws well tightened, he fitted the whole thing back in its little nook, screwed it to the wall, and repositioned the plate over it.

He snapped the new switch on and off and it lit unhesitatingly each time; no more jiggling to get the thing in just the right spot only to be plunged into darkness in the middle of taking a leak. Roscoe had feared that the problem was something buried deep inside his walls, but Frank knew from experience that the switch was simply worn out, that the bathroom switch was always the first to go.

He packed up his screwdriver and work light, buckled the leather straps that held the long steel box shut, and lumbered back to the porch, shaking the house with his steps.

"It's fixed then?"

"Yup. Told you it was just worn out."

"Frank, I really appreciate it. Will you let me pay you for the parts at least?"

Frank waved away the small cost and sat on the edge of the empty chaise. "Guy in the hardware store asked me if I wanted one that clicked or one that didn't," he said.

"Which one did you get?"

"A clicker." He settled uneasily on the flimsy plastic webbing. "See anything yet?"

"Nothing unusual. Frank, are you warm enough? There's a bit of a chill tonight." Roscoe was curious to know if his companion even owned a jacket or sweater.

"This don't bother me," said Frank. "Back home we don't call this cold."

"Of course. Tell me that name again? It keeps slipping my mind." Roscoe reached over to the ice bucket and filled his glass; he had sociably delayed his first drink until Frank's work was done.

"Belle Plaine."

"Ah, French, isn't it?" Roscoe poured himself a generous shot, then filled a glass with ice for his guest.

Frank took it reluctantly, stared at the cubes with dissatisfaction, and poured his cider in resignation. He sipped quietly, fondling the gun muzzle at his side, while Roscoe tried to think of things to say.

"Ever been married, Frank?" he asked finally.

"Nope."

"I was. I was married once. My wife passed away several years ago. Christian Scientist, you know," he confided.

Frank didn't know and frowned slightly.

"Tell me about that new job you have, Frank." Roscoe tried again, speaking softly.

"Job? No, it's just a couple days' work. I work for myself." Frank seemed to bristle in the dark.

"Well, what I meant to say is, what exactly are you doing?"

"Oh. Just knocking down a dividing wall and replastering. Putting up this shelving system when they get the plans. In the new variety store down Center."

"I suppose what I really want to know is how you acquired all these different skills. Myself, I was never handy at all. But you, you can do anything with your hands. I admire that. How did you get so good at it, Frank?" He tossed back the rest of his drink and poured himself another.

"How did you get good at what you do?" Frank had finished his glass of cider and was swirling the remaining bits of ice around to help them melt.

"I'm not so sure I am!" Roscoe chuckled softly. He was a vice-president of the Nelson Beach First Federal Savings Bank. "You see, I don't happen to have any special talents, Frank, and I could never see myself as a shopkeeper or I-don't-know-what. I have a decent education and the bank was the best thing available to me at the time. I did well enough there to advance to the point where I do very little good and even less harm. I don't really need the money now, just myself, but I'd be terrified to stop. I don't think I'd take to retirement the way your grandfather does. In any case, that's a ways off.''

"Terrified of what?'' Frank swallowed his ice water and filled the glass with neat cider.

"Oh, it doesn't matter. I'm just rambling on. I think I'll take a look at your handiwork and use the facility.'' His wink was lost in the dark.

Frank heard an exclamation of joy from within and ducked his head shyly. Suddenly a movement caught his eye at the far end of his house, impossible to make out at that distance. He grabbed the shotgun and vaulted the porch railing, landing low and catlike on the wet grass. With his gun pointed, he moved swiftly around the hedge to his own ground, clinging close to the side of the house in the deepest shadows. He crept sideways, leading with the long gray muzzle, and then he heard the unmistakable crunch of gravel on the front path. He waited around the corner and held his breath till the sound was repeated, then sprung out into the open, planting his feet, the gun raised to his shoulder.

"Good Lord, boy! Put that thing down!'' Neil scolded with a hand over his heart. He sank down on the doorstep and waited for his blood to stop pounding.

"Gramps, what are you doing out here?''

"Let me catch my breath, Frank.''

"What do you got behind your back?'' Frank asked, craning around to see what Neil concealed.

"A sandwich. Good Lord,'' the old man sighed.

"You were walking around eating a *sandwich* in the middle of the night? Gramps, are you feeling okay?'' Frank waited stubbornly for his answer with a puzzled frown.

Neil stroked the white stubble on his chin and gazed around him and sighed a few times. He looked up at the hulking silhouette of his grandson against the blue-black sky and saw that there was no way out.

"Well, Frank," he began wearily, "I woke up and felt kind of hungry and so I made me a sandwich."

Frank was far from reassured. "But you were taking it outside, Gramps. Did you know you were outside?"

"Now you're making me mad, Frank! I think I'll go eat this here and go back to bed, if you don't mind. Here, help me up, son." He reached for Frank's arm and took a big bite of bread and meat before going inside. "Nice night," he mumbled, spraying crumbs. "Fog cleared."

"Frank, where are you?" Roscoe's hoarse whisper preceded him around the corner. "What happened? Did you see something?" He looked excitedly from Frank to the gun to Neil and back again.

"Oh, my grandson here nearly did away with me, is all," Neil explained. "I'm just gonna turn in, Roscoe. Hope you boys catch your prowler before you kill some innocent bystander." He let the screen door slam behind him.

"Frank, this is too dangerous. We have to stop. Imagine if you'd hurt your grandfather by accident . . ." He let his words sink in and tried to read Frank's expression. "I really do think we had better give it up. Better to inform the police and let them patrol the area, perhaps. Don't you agree, Frank?" Roscoe bobbed anxiously in front of him, peering at his broad scowling face.

Frank pushed the bangs off his forehead. "I'll get my tools back in the morning," he muttered.

"All right. Fine. I'll leave them just inside the front door. Good-night then." Roscoe whistled a nervous trill and disappeared into the gloom.

Frank went inside to his room, tore off his clothes, and flung them away. He threw himself down on the bed and his eyes welled up and his dark chin crumpled. He waited, with his fists in tight balls, for sleep to come.

FRANK BLINKED DOWN from the doorstep at the woman as if she were a total stranger. She was not. She stepped back, flustered.

"I . . . uh, I just stopped by on my way to town to bring you fellows a little casserole. Ida made more than we needed and I just thought I'd bring you by the extra. It's Neil's favorite. . . . Anyway, here it is." Charlotte Springer pushed the covered dish at Frank's dangling arms.

He continued to stare mulishly, stock-still.

A bright blush spread upward from Charlotte's starched collar. "You could return the dish any old time, no hurry about that," she chattered desperately, looking every which way but at Frank's indifferent eye, and wondering how she would ever rid herself of the dish if he refused to take it.

"Who's there, Frank?" called Neil from somewhere inside.

"It's me, Neil, hello-o," she called back with relief.

Neil hastened to the door with his knobby hand outstretched. "Well, what a nice surprise! Come on in. What have we got here?" He indicated the casserole as he guided her past Frank.

"It's your favorite, oyster stew." She was almost giddy with gratitude and allowed herself to be drawn into the remodeled living room.

"That's mighty thoughtful of you, Charlotte. We been missing some of them fine meals of yours, haven't we, Frank?"

Frank was squinting past them to the sun-flecked ocean and winced but didn't speak.

"Well, we do our best," she said with a giggle.

Neil found Charlotte's girlish embarrassment enchanting; she seemed less the manageress now than in her own home and he found himself wishing that he was a much younger man.

"Anyway," he began, "it sure is nice to see you, dear. I kept meaning to come up and visit, but then with one thing or another, getting settled in here . . . anyway, we're glad to see you, right, Frank?"

Neil indicated that she sit and he took the other chair himself, clamping his hands on his bony knees, gently rocking. His freckled arms protruded sticklike from the rolled shirtsleeves and looked particularly frail to Charlotte. She reminded herself that he was in remarkably good shape for a man of eighty-four.

"What a wonderful room! So large and light," she exclaimed, gazing around.

"Frank did every bit of the work himself. See, it used to be kind of a narrow room and didn't get the sun on account of the porch. So Frank knocked down that wall and pushed the whole thing out, and with these windows all opened it still has the feeling of a porch. That door there used to go from the porch right into the kitchen and it was all painted shut and stuck, remember, Frank?"

"It's lovely. It *is* like a big porch. Frank," she said bravely, "what are you planning to do with all this space, if I may ask?"

"Yeah, what *did* we decide, Frank?" Neil watched with growing discomfort the inexpressive back of his grandson, then waved a hand airily. "I don't guess we settled that yet. Anyway, it's real nice to sit here and watch the ocean and town and everything. We're in no rush about anything. I guess we'll put in more furniture one of these days."

"Well, I better put this in the icebox or it'll go bad, I'm afraid. You know seafood," she added cheerily.

Charlotte rose with her dish just as Frank crossed the room and she was afraid for a moment that he intended to block her way to the kitchen door, but then he lifted a long tool box off the floor and stalked out the other way.

"Here we go." Neil took the dish and led her into the kitchen. "Don't mind Frank, Charlotte. You know how shy he is. Just hard to get to know is all, he don't mean nothing by it," Neil assured her. "I guess he had to go off to work."

They couldn't find room at first in the refrigerator for the oval dish. Charlotte was surprised and then embarrassed to see how well stocked they were. She had imagined the typical near-empty bachelors' refrigerator but here were fresh fruits and vegetables, the leftover butt of a ham, half a home-made chocolate cake, cold cuts, cheese, a pan of cornbread. Someone in the house, she realized, was as competent a cook as she or Idabelle and her offering seemed pointless. She helped Neil make room on a shelf and disposed of the casserole at last.

"Goodness me! What in the world . . .!" She pointed at the shotgun leaning in the corner by the door, drawing back with an expression mixed of fascination and alarm.

"Oh, that." Neil waved it away. "We been hearing strange noises. Frank thinks it's a prowler or something, so he got that gun, that's all." He shrugged pleasantly, puzzled by her reaction.

"But a great big thing like that! I'd hate to hear of any accidents."

Neil laughed dryly. "Yeah, I know. But, Lord, everyone keeps guns where we come from. Nothing special."

"Where I come from, too, but not in Nelson Beach. We're just a sleepy little town."

"Well, anyway, when you grow up around guns like me and Frank you don't have the kind of accidents you're thinking of. Don't worry, really." Neil took her elbow and steered her back to the living room, away from the troubling sight.

"Tell me, how are the old fellas back at the house? I keep meaning to drop by."

"Oh, they're all fine. Squabbling as usual, but fine," she said, smiling. "Neil, I wish I could stay longer but I'm on my way in to Muller's. My account is a little confused. Boring business but it has to get done." She smoothed her dress over her plump hips and waited to be shown out.

The talk of business reminded Neil of his first impression of Charlotte Springer, capable, independent, self-assured, and he compared that image with the blushing woman flustered silly by Frank. He looked curiously at the skin around her eyes and her neck as he escorted her to the door and realized she was younger than he'd thought, probably no older than Frank. Of course, most people took Frank for *younger* than he was, Neil reflected, on account of the haircut and overalls and all.

"Well, Charlotte, I hope we'll be seeing more of you soon. And really, don't mind about Frank. It's just his shyness," Neil confided.

"Okay, bye for now." She started down the path to her car.

"Oh, and thanks for the stew," Neil called after her.

"You can heat it in the dish it's in," she called back.

N EIL SAT AT THE EDGE of his bed, woozy from his afternoon nap. He rubbed hs eyes and stretched his back and checked his watch. His bladder began to nag and he shuffled down the hall to the bathroom.

Outside, he heard the screech and slam of the metal mailbox in the front yard, and he walked out into the caressing warmth of the afternoon. He unfastened the box's hot clasp and reached in to find a postcard and two envelopes.

"Hey. Old man."

"Oh, it's you." Neil spotted the familiar heap of rags across the street, leaning against a spindly palm. "Just call me Neil, okay? Sounds friendlier."

"Okay, Neil. Is the farmer around?"

"Frank? He's out working." Neil shaded his eyes to get a better look at the raggedy man. "What do you like to be called?" he asked.

"I like to be called Mister Callahan," he replied, cackling convulsively.

"Oh, all right, if you want to be formal." Neil glanced at his mail. The postcard was from Emmie, then there was a letter addressed to Frank in a curly feminine hand, and the last was a phone bill.

"Hey, Neil," called Mister Callahan, "did I miss lunch?"

"I already ate, but you're welcome to come in and I'll fix you something. Follow me." Neil waved him over and started up the driveway to the kitchen door. He stepped high and carefully on the rutted gravel, without looking back to see if his invitation had been accepted.

Callahan hesitated. He brushed off his greasy jacket and wet his lips as he watched the progress of the old man. At last, the growling in his stomach won out over his fear of the farmer and he trotted to catch up.

The screen door sprang shut as he reached the step and he

stared into the neat homey kitchen with longing. Neil was leaning into the open icebox with an intent expression. Callahan watched him seize a covered pot and was reassured that the invitation had been in earnest. He scratched the screen for attention and attempted to smell himself, impossible in the briny breeze, to see if he would offend in the closed room.

"Door's open. Come on in, Mister Callahan. I promised you a meal." Neil waved again, an exaggerated gesture as though coaxing a timid child.

Callahan sidled through the door and kept close to the wall, as far from Neil as the space permitted, till he reached the table. He crouched in his chair, gripped the arms, and grinned balefully, twinkling his surprising blue eyes at Neil, challenging him in some way.

Neil continued to putter around in the business end of the kitchen, locating a saucepan, its lid, a large spoon; stirring the food, adding a dribble of water, scraping it out onto a plate; serving it with a cloth napkin and a flourish.

"A little warm in here, don't you think?" Neil asked, cranking open the window, his nostrils quivering slightly.

Callahan's grin faded and he lowered his eyes to the steaming plate of macaroni with meat sauce.

Neil sat down across the table.

Callahan took up the fork in his hard brown hand, then threw it down. He shook out the napkin and tucked it into his greasy shirtfront, and again picked up the fork only to drop it in exasperation.

"Hey, Neil," he rasped, "you ever seen a hungry man eat?"

"Oh, you'd rather be alone, sure. I'll be down the hall here. Sorry," Neil said, backing out the doorway.

Callahan smelled ripe even to himself indoors, and he felt his face flush invisibly under the tough coppery skin. His mouth was flooded with saliva and he bent low to the plate and shoveled in the hot food, barely chewing or tasting it. As he ate, he wondered idly if there was any alcohol in the house. He wondered if the old man would give him cash.

The screen door opened and he looked up from his meal in

horror as first the long toolbox and then the farmer himself passed into the room. He sat motionless, counting his heartbeats.

Frank deposited the box on the counter and wiped a dusty palm across his glistening face. Then he slowly turned and his eyes met Callahan's and his jaw dropped in astonishment.

Callahan jumped up with a pitiful whimper, knocking over his chair, and cowered in the farthest corner from Frank, shivering, wetting himself as Frank moved forward. His eyes darted to the living room door and he made a mad dash for it.

Frank stood bewildered in the kitchen, listening to the intruder crashing around in the living room, then in the hall, and at last out the front door.

"Gramps! Gramps!" he shouted, stumbling down the hall and almost colliding with the old man.

"Frank, what the hell is going on?"

Frank was only mouthing words in his confusion. He shook back the dark bangs and tried to organize his thoughts. "Gramps! I just saw him—it *must've* been—sitting right there!" he sputtered.

"Oh, Lord. He didn't even get to finish. Poor fella's scared to death of you, Frank."

"What are you talking about?" Frank's voice rose as he struggled to understand.

"I'm talking about poor Mister Callahan."

"*Mister?* I didn't see no misters here."

Neil righted the chair and sat at the table with a sigh. "He's just a poor soul, Frank, that don't mean no harm at all. Sorry, I should've told you before."

"Told me *what?* Just back up a minute. Is this Callahan the guy that's been prowling around here? The guy me and Roscoe was sitting up trying to catch?" He squinted at his grandfather in disbelief.

"Now don't get in an uproar, Frank. Sit down a minute and let me talk and don't get all fired up. Now, this is the whole thing: I see him on the beach sometimes and we talk, and sometimes he comes around here and I give him something to eat, a sandwich or something. It ain't like we can't spare the food," he wheedled.

"But he's the guy slept in my camper. He's the one used my toilet out there," Frank argued. He stood stubbornly in the middle of the floor, his hands balled up in fists.

"He'll never do it again. You got my solemn word on that."

"But *why*, Gramps? A dirty old bum . . . ?" Frank couldn't believe his ears.

"I told you, he's just a poor soul that I take pity on and I help out. Also he's kind of funny. I think maybe he don't have all his marbles, but he wouldn't do no harm at all. He's just getting along the best way he knows how, Frank."

Frank tried to puzzle out what, if anything, was being asked of him. "You give him food, you say?"

"Food," Neil said firmly, "and a place to sleep if he wants it."

"But he's dirty," Frank complained. "It's disgusting. I don't want him stinking up my camper."

Callahan's odor still hung in the air.

Neil brightened. "I'll get him cleaned up, Frank. Don't you worry about that. You won't recognize him when I get through."

"I don't want to recognize him."

"And I'll make sure he understands about the toilet. He won't be any trouble at all, you'll see."

"Wait a second. What about drinking? I don't want him if he's a drunk, Gramps."

"Well, I never personally saw him take a drink so I don't know for sure, but I never given him liquor or money, son, just the food I told you about. I guess I'll give him some old clothes, just stuff we don't use. Leave everything to me."

"Well, as long as he don't drink, I guess. . . . Look, is he gonna come in the house here?" Frank looked uneasily around the room.

"I sure doubt it. Especially after today!" Neil laughed and Frank softened his expression. "Oh! I nearly forgot. You got a letter from that sweet little Willa Peterson. I left it on top of the icebox. I guess you broke a few hearts back home, Frank."

"Naw, she was just a friend."

"Well, open it up, son. I'd like to hear some news from home, if it ain't too personal, that is."

"I'm gonna wash first. I cut my arm with a rasp."

Dear Frank,

I write to you with some sad news which perhaps you heard already from your Mother. Last week my Mother passed away from pneumonia that set in after her hip injury and we buried her. She suffered a lot in the end with her breathing and delirious and all, so at least now she is out of her suffering and at rest. I miss her a lot now, with nobody to take care of and all alone in this big old house. My brother Burt and his wife came down for the funeral but couldn't take off much time from work and he invited me up north to visit any time but I don't know. Those kids of his do wear me out I must admit. Anyway, I guess I could take a trip now or anything I want with nothing to tie me down so don't be surprised if I turn up in California one of these days. But seriously, your Mother has been real sweet to me in this hard time and I'm real grateful to her. Anyway, the time goes slow now with no one to look after and I miss Ma an awful lot. Sometimes I wish I was kinder when she was still here but everyone says I was a good daughter to her and I just hope it's true. But enough about my problems. How are you and your Grandpa doing out there? A woman here visited San Diego which I know is a ways south of you and had the time of her life and came home all tan. It must be real nice. You know what? I never saw the ocean in my life, just the Great Lakes which is almost like the ocean since you can't see across to the other side. I am enclosing a bookmark that I made from a pattern that we got at the church and sold these at the fair to raise money. But this one is special for you and I hope that you find a use for it.

Your Friend Always,
Willa

NEIL HAD A FULL BELLY and a fat cigar in his pocket when he set off toward the beach with purposeful steps. As he walked the road he reviewed in his mind the things he had to say and tried to find words that wouldn't offend.

He arrived at the beach earlier than usual. There were still a number of stragglers on the sand, folding blankets and towels, repacking picnic baskets, collecting pails and shovels and children.

Neil sighted down to the spit of black rocks, peering over his glasses, but failed to discern a human form at that distance. He removed his shoes and socks and walked along the firmer sand near the water's edge, only glancing at the debris at his feet, intent on the rocks ahead.

When he reached the spit, he walked its length and saw no signs of life.

"Mister Callahan!" he called, cupping his hands against the wind. "It's me, Neil. Can you hear me?" He waited with his head cocked to hear an answer over the persistent pounding of the surf.

He reached for the slippery edge of a jutting rock and stepped onto a low little ledge. He felt with one foot for a higher step, found one that seemed secure, and moved his grip higher up on the face of the spit.

"Mister Callahan! Are you there? Please answer me if you can hear!" he shouted.

He suddenly felt he was losing his grip and tried to step back to his first position but missed the footing and tumbled onto the sand. He lay there in his panic like a turtle on its back, too startled to help himself.

"Now look what you've done!" Callahan scrambled over the crest of the spit, surefooted on the terrain, and squatted at the old man's side. "Look what you've done, Neil. You could have hurt yourself," he said, fixing Neil with his azure gaze and forgiving smile.

Neil calmed himself, realizing he was unhurt, and sat up with effort. He tried to brush the sand from his back, feeling foolish.

"I was looking for you," he said between breaths. "I just came to tell you that I talked to Frank about everything and you don't have to be afraid of him any more."

"Afraid? Afraid! Why would I be afraid of Paul Bunyan with that portable cannon he totes around!"

"Paul Bunyan, you say? By God, you're an interesting fella,

44

Mister Callahan. That's what I like about you," Neil chuckled. Face to face, with some sunlight left, he noticed that Callahan was scarcely older than Frank, forty or so at the most.

"I'm not interesting. I got the same feelings as you, you know. I ain't a circus act." He held his chin high. "Just what the hell do you want, coming down here after me?"

"Well, I just . . . I came here to say if you like that camper we got, it's okay for you to sleep there. Frank agrees and he promises he won't bother you. That's all." Neil spoke hastily; it wasn't going the way he planned.

"I asked you what you want?" Callahan persisted.

Neil fidgeted with his jacket and inadvertently felt the cigar in the pocket. His mouth watered as he imagined the comforting smoke, but he couldn't very well light up without having a cigar to offer his companion.

"Why put it like that?" he answered unhappily. "It's not that I *want* anything from you. I don't. What could you be thinking I want? I'm just offering you a place to sleep and the food would be regular if you want it. Take it or leave it." Neil was offended and perplexed. He tried to pull himself up against the damp rock face but Callahan laid a leathery hand on his shoulder.

"Hold on there, Neil," he said gently. "Are you telling me that there ain't a thing in the world that I gotta do in exchange for all this soft life you're offering?"

Neil sat back on the sand which was growing cool. "Well, there are one or two things, but it won't be too hard on you, I don't think." He paused and noted a look of bright attention in the luminous eyes. "First thing, that toilet in the camper don't work. It needs a special hookup, so you can't be using it, okay? You can come in the house if you want or make your own arrangements, but whatever you do, don't use Frank's toilet." They smiled together in the thickening dusk. "The next thing is you gotta give up that filthy outfit you got on. Frank won't stand for it in his camper. Now, I got plenty of nice things that we don't ever use that might fit you. You just pick out what you like. But you gotta stay clean if you want to sleep in there, okay?"

"Ha! Is that all? You probably think I'm attached to these here garments, but I tell you no lie—I can't stand my own stink inside of a room. I would be most honored and grateful to wear my benefactor's castoffs.''

"There's one thing left—alcohol. Frank won't stand for no drinking in his camper. I personally don't give a hoot whether you drink or not, and I figure you probably do, but don't do it in the camper and don't ask me for booze 'cause I gave my word on that.''

"Put your mind at ease, Neil. I never will." He grinned at the old man, then took a deep breath and sat up straighter. "Now I got a few words to say. I didn't much enjoy being rousted by the farmer with that blunderbuss of his and I'm trusting you, Neil, to keep me informed of his whereabouts. And let's have a little knock on the door before coming into the trailer. *And* I plan to come and go as I please, *when* I please, and don't owe nothing to nobody. Understand?''

"I do. You'll have your privacy, I promise. Well, I guess I'll be starting back now. . . ." Neil struggled to his feet and dusted off the seat of his pants. The light was fading quickly. "Well, be seeing you," he said.

Callahan grinned like a death's head in the gloom.

Neil turned and set off across the sand. When he was a decent distance away, he drew out the cigar and lit it gratefully. The thick orange ember was the only spot of light on the lonely beach.

"HELLO, HELLO," called a melodious voice. "Anyone home?"

"Oh, Charlotte! Come on in. It's open." Neil waved to her down the long hall from the kitchen and watched her approach.

She wore a flowered shirtwaist with a tight bodice and a wide skirt. She was blushing already and the pink of her skin looked lovely against the blue-and-lavender dress. She seemed to grow younger each time Neil saw her.

"I didn't recognize your voice at first. I guess my ears ain't what they used to be.''

46

"Oh, you! You're sharper than every one of my guests and not a one is over seventy-five, I believe."

"In a month from Friday I'm gonna be eighty-five years old. Makes me feel like a real antique if I stop and think about it." He escorted Charlotte to the table, gripping her plump elbow. "I was just finishing my coffee. Can I get you a cup?"

"Please, I'll get it myself. Just point me in the right direction."

"The percolator's right behind you and there's mugs in the cupboard up there."

Charlotte poured her coffee and joined Neil at the table.

"Oh, this is nice and strong," she said, adding another spoon of sugar.

"I hope it's not too strong for you. This is the way I like it, myself. Frank don't care much for coffee but he makes me a pot before going off to work."

"Then he's not home," she deduced.

"Just left. Doing a little job down at the bank last couple of days. Well, it's not so little, I guess." Neil scratched his head, then smoothed the white waves over his pink skull. "He's putting in these bulletproof thingamajigs in all the tellers' windows. They pay a good piece of money for that," he added proudly.

"Well, why not! They have it all! Anyway, I'd like to know who's going to stick up a bank in *this* sleepy little town."

Neil wondered idly if the bank held a mortgage on her house. "Tell me, Charlotte," he began, "how did you come to own that boardinghouse in the first place. I've always been curious."

"Oh, it's no secret, but there *is* a story to it. I don't know if I ever mentioned I'm from Wyoming originally . . .?" She raised her eyebrows and Neil nodded his head. "Well, my mama passed away when I was very small, I hardly remember her at all. So there was just me and my three big brothers and my daddy together on the ranch. He has a pretty big place out there, real nice spread, as we say. Anyhow, I had an Aunt Rose, my great-aunt she was, and she was afraid I'd grow up a tomboy, rough and I-don't-know-what, out there alone with the men. Every summer she had me come out and stay with her and that was her house. She lived there all alone, just her and a colored

47

girl. I kind of liked those summers and looked forward to them even though it was pretty hard to be as ladylike as she wanted. Then, when I was about twenty, Aunt Rose took sick and I came out to take care of her, but she passed away and left me the house and a little money. Well, by the time I buried her and paid the taxes and all, that money was just about gone and I couldn't see how to keep the place up without any income. So that's when I took in my first boarders." She sighed and smiled.

"Hey, I bet that took guts," said Neil.

"Yes, you know, eighteen years ago, for a young girl to be taking in men boarders was not considered too respectable. I had to be very careful. Folks around here like to talk when they have nothing better to do. But at least the house was mine and I intended to keep it." She looked proudly defiant. "It gave me my independence. Of course, my family tried to get me to come home, but I did what I wanted and stayed on."

"I'm just surprised you was never snapped up by some fella. . ." Neil chuckled uncomfortably as his voice trailed off.

"I have nothing against marriage," she answered airily. "I just never met the right man. You know, in a town like this, most of the young people can't wait to move off to the cities and the people that move in are families or retired people. Oh!" she cried, jumping to her feet. "I completely forgot! The main reason I stopped by is to give you a little something, for you and Frank. I left it out in the car. I'll be right back." She trotted down the hall and out the front door. She returned breathless, pressing one hand to her breast and concealing the other behind her back.

"One of my gentlemen, a new one you didn't know, had to go into a nursing home last week and he left a lot of stuff behind for anyone who wants it. Well, when I saw this, I immediately thought of you two country boys." She held out the gift, a double album set of "Bill Monroe's Greatest Hits." "We haven't got a record player at my place anyhow and I thought you might have some fun with this."

"Oh, this is nice. Thanks for thinking of us, Charlotte." Neil stood and kissed her lilac-scented cheek. "The Monroe Brothers just happen to be Frank's all-time favorites. He's gonna be real pleased with this."

"Well, I'm glad. But I better shove off now. I got a load of errands to do out at the mall and it gets so crowded by noon."

Neil set the album aside and walked her to the door.

"Charlotte, maybe you'd like to have dinner with us one night this weekend. Frank's a pretty fair cook, simple stuff, you know, but plenty of it. I'll find out from him what's a good day and give you a call, okay?"

"Oh, that would be fun. I'll look forward to it. Bye for now."

Neil waved to her from the front step as she cruised off down the road and wondered how he could get hold of a record player by the end of the week.

"**W**HY WON'T HE TELL YOU his name, Gramps? Ask him again. Tell him what it's for."

"I did tell him, son, but he's a little, you know, eccentric."

"Crazy, you mean."

"Listen, if you don't want to do it for him, then do it for me."

"But it's gonna look terrible, Gramps," Frank complained.

"It won't look so bad. Nobody'll even notice, I bet."

Frank shook his head in disgust and set up his sawhorses in the near-empty living room, spacing them two feet apart. He took from the hall closet a nicely weathered one-by-four, salvaged from a recent job, and measured off three twenty-inch sections. He sawed along the penciled lines, then smoothed the edges with a sanding block.

He swept up the sawdust and settled himself at the kitchen table to draft the letters of the three names, first roughly on paper, then onto the plaques:

NEIL HORNER
FRANK DIGGORY
MR. CALLAHAN

It took nearly an hour of lip-biting concentration to get the letters drawn and spaced and centered just right on the boards. Next, Frank took out a wood-burning tool, purchased for this project, and began the painstaking process of burning and graving the letters into the wood.

When the lettering was done, he opened a little bag of screw eyes and bent half of them open with his needlenose pliers. He screwed them into the top edges of the plaques and screwed the closed ones into the bottom edge. He linked tops and bottoms together and squeezed the screw eyes closed.

Neil watched from the window as, out front, Frank screwed two closed eyes into the horizontal post under the mailbox and attached the free-swinging plaques. Frank stood back to take a look and Neil hurried out of the house.

"That looks real fine, Frank. Them letters look professional!" Neil admired the result of Frank's labor with a feeling of personal satisfaction.

Frank cocked his head and frowned, focusing on the "MR."

"Hardly notice the Callahan thing, myself," Neil said brightly.

Frank grunted and strode back to the kitchen.

"Want to eat, Gramps?" Frank took four hard-boiled eggs, an onion, a jar of mayonnaise, and a stalk of celery from the icebox.

"Sure do!" Neil patted his small round belly. "Thanks for the sign, Frank. Makes me feel real good to see all our names out front like that."

Frank snorted in reply, still rankling from the Callahan thing. He shelled the eggs under the faucet, chopped the onion and celery, and mashed it all together with dressing and salt and pepper. He spread the egg salad thickly on two rolls and added a handful of potato chips to each plate.

"Want a tomato?"

"Sure, fine." Neil could see the mailbox and the swaying plaques from his chair if he craned his neck.

"Milk or juice?"

"No, nothing. Oh, Frank! We got a present." Neil noticed the album on the chair beside him and handed it over.

"Where'd it come from?"

"Charlotte came by this morning and brought it over. One of the old fellas went into a nursing home and left this behind and Charlotte thought we might get a kick out of it. Don't you think that was nice?" he prodded. "She's really a sweet woman, that

Charlotte. Pretty, too, I think. If I was your age, Frank . . . Well, that's the way I used to like 'em, not too skinny, just right. And redheads are good luck. Anyway, I got a funny feeling she's partial to you, Frank."

Frank's head was bowed and Neil couldn't see his face, just the smooth dark bangs.

"What are we supposed to do with this?" Frank grumbled, sliding the album away from him.

"Well, I never had the heart to tell her we got no victrola either. But I was thinking it might be fun to get one, you know? I always did like music," he mused. "Specially the old-time stuff."

"Buy a record player for this one album?"

A blob of egg salad dropped out of Neil's roll onto his clean khakis and Frank jumped up, scowling, for a paper towel.

"I told her we would have her come to dinner one night this weekend," Neil went on bravely as Frank swabbed his thigh.

"What the hell does she want!" Frank exploded, aiming the wadded paper at the sink. "Why don't she leave us alone?"

"Damn me, boy! If you aren't the stubbornest, most pig-headed—Damn! How many friends do you *got*?" Neil rose and threw his sandwich down on the plate. "Well, how many?" he shouted.

Frank blinked back at his grandfather, paralyzed with emotion.

"Boy," Neil went on, "I'm gonna tell you something you should've learned for yourself by now. A man needs friends in this world. You can't make it alone. Do you hear me?"

Frank barely nodded. His mouth hung open.

"Now, I invited Charlotte to supper because she's showed both of us a lot of kindness and she's a fine woman who has the misfortune of being sweet on you. Now, if you want to shame me, you just go on acting like a—like a damn jackass!" Neil was red in the face, sputtering.

"I'm sorry, Gramps," Frank murmured, staring down at his hands, twisting his fingers together. "I'm sorry," he croaked miserably, and stumbled out of the room.

Neil's heart was pounding against his ribs and he breathed deeply to try to calm himself. He felt a wave of agonizing pity for Frank, but still, he thought, the boy's got to learn. If Frank were

51

small, he would have shaken him by the shoulders till his teeth rattled. Things were different here than on the farm. What will happen to him, Neil wondered, when I'm gone?

He had no appetite left. He puttered around the kitchen, still shaken, piling the half-empty plates on the counter. After a short time, he heard the front door slam. He went to his room to lie down, reproaching himself for his temper and doubting his chances of dozing off.

N EIL AWOKE TO THE HONKING of a car horn somewhere in the street, an irritable sound. Then a series of sharp knocks on his own front door had him up on his feet, dizzy, rubbing his eyes in the darkened room. He tottered down the hall, smoothing his hair and rumpled clothing before opening the door.

Outside on the path stood the town's only cab driver, looking dull and overheated. Neil didn't know him by name but recognized him by his peaked cap and sunglasses.

"You Neil Horner?"

"Yup, but I didn't call for a cab." Neil looked past him to the road; there was no vehicle in sight.

"No, I got something for you. I'm in your drive." The man pointed around the house with a wide sweep of his arm.

"Well, let's go through the house. Come on in." Neil led the way to the kitchen, perplexed.

"Just hold the door open," the driver instructed. "I can handle the rest."

Neil held the screen and watched the driver swing open the trunk and lift out two large brown cartons. He stacked them in his arms and brushed past Neil into the house.

"That's not all. There's two more," he said, shaking out his arms.

He opened the rear door of the cab and slid out two smaller boxes. He deposited these with the first two, in the middle of the kitchen floor, mopped his forehead with a cloth, and squinted down at the old man.

"Frank said you'd have cash around, said you could pay the three bucks."

"Oh, of course." Neil reached for the jar in the cupboard where Frank kept emergency money and handed the driver a five. "Keep the change," he said shyly, "for your trouble."

"No, that's okay, Pop. The fare's enough." He made change and added, "Frank's a pal."

"Oh, yeah?" Neil brightened. "How do you know Frank?"

"Oh, he did a valve job for me last week. Garage wanted sixty bucks, but Frank gave me a good price. Taught me something about my motor, too." He fanned himself with the cap and looked out toward the driveway.

"Did Frank mention what he got in them boxes, or who it's for?"

"No, he didn't say, but I picked 'em up from him at Music Masters so I guess it's a stereo or something, but he didn't tell me nothing about it."

"Okay, then. Sorry to keep you. And thanks."

Alone, Neil examined the cartons and found only serial numbers and cautions to handlers on the outsides. He cut through the tape on one of the cartons with his penknife and removed a piece of Styrofoam to reveal, wrapped in heavy plastic, a sleek, modern turntable. Then he heard a familiar scratching on the screen door.

"Is that you, Mister Callahan?" Neil called.

"Is *he* there?" came the hoarse whisper.

"No, the coast is clear. Come on in."

The door opened slowly and a transformed Callahan strutted into the room. "Well, Neil, am I fashionable enough to join your household? Say something." He sniffed at his armpits and closed his eyes dreamily. "Fresh as a schoolgirl."

"Wow! You look wonderful, like a new man. I bet I wouldn't know you if I passed you on the street. It's amazing—you even got a face under there."

Callahan wore one of Frank's blue shirts, the frayed collar swimming around his scrawny neck, and an immaculate but dated heavy tweed suit of Neil's. It was a trifle short in the sleeves and pants legs when Callahan stood straight but it fit him well in the shoulders and waist and crotch. His wild, matted hair had been cleaned and tamed somewhat and the man did smell like nothing so much as a bar of soap, a bar that Neil had tucked, along with a cheap razor, inside the bundle of clothing.

"Come and look at what Frank bought us," said Neil. "You know anything about putting together these new complicated types of phonographs, Mister Callahan?"

"You think I can't read directions, same as anybody? I'm no fool," he added, squatting to examine the turntable. "I can read and write and do arithmetic, too. Huh!"

"That's fine. I'm glad to hear it. Let's unpack all this stuff, then, and try and put it together before Frank gets home. It would be some surprise to have it set up and working already when he comes in," Neil chuckled.

"And when would that be, while we're on the subject?" Callahan glanced nervously at the door.

"Well, to tell the truth, I don't know for sure, today. But you know this house. If he comes in the front door, you just scoot right out this door here, and if he starts coming in this way, you scoot out the front. See? It's no problem."

"Huh! I just about get my head blown off and it's no problem."

Callahan sat on his heels and watched Neil cut the tape on the other boxes. They uncovered the amplifier next and then the two large speakers. They found a bundle of wires and a hopelessly thick instruction book in the bottom of one carton.

They carried the pieces into the living room, where the two lonely rockers faced the ocean, and set to work scanning the dense diagrams. They soon gave up on the book and studied instead the connecting wires, color-coded and labeled with little L's and R's, and, in short order, they had it all hooked up. The only difficult part was getting the delicate needle to stay in place in the arm; it popped in and popped out again the way Neil had it. Callahan jiggled it into position, following a picture inside the needle's box, and it stayed put.

"Well, after all this work, we only got one record, but it's a real good one. I'll go get it," Neil said happily.

He hurried to the kitchen and Callahan stood watch at the

window. The glass louvers were shut and he cranked them open until he felt the salty breeze on his weathered cheeks, tender after the recent shave.

Neil returned with the album and removed one of the records. The stereo set was spread out on the bare linoleum along the back wall. Neil knelt by the turntable, and set the record on it.

"Look at this, they even got a speed to play seventy-eights. Lord, it's been a long time since I saw one of them. My wife had a bunch once . . . I don't know what happened to them."

He reached over to the receiver, turned on the power, and started the turntable. At first, the music came from one side only, but Callahan found the balance knob and then improved the tone by tuning the treble and bass. They pulled the rockers around from the windows to face the speakers, and sat down to listen.

"This Paul Bunyan's record?" Callahan squirmed and cackled. He began to mimic the pronunciation of certain words, "flare" for "flower," "yer" for "you're," "whah" for "why," and so on. Neil continued to rock contentedly while Callahan perched on the edge of his seat, jittery and rebellious, smelling himself from time to time.

Neil surprised himself by remembering every tune as it played. The record was scratchy and worn, but it was cheering to hear the old songs again. Neil closed his eyes and his knobby hands jerked in his lap. His feet tapped quietly. "Hear that? That's the claw-hammer style," he said. "I used to play like that."

They heard the slam of a door, then felt the floor tremble under Frank's heavy step. Callahan jumped up and looked wildly from the hall door to the kitchen door and back again, unable to choose his escape, panicked and further confused by the music.

"The front door, Cal! Hurry!" Neil cried, caught up in his friend's fear, forgetting that there was no real danger.

Callahan disappeared down the hall and let the door slam behind him.

"Gramps . . . ?"

"In here, Frank," Neil called from his rocker.

"You got it working." Frank stood in the doorway smiling shyly at his shoe tips.

"Sit down and listen with me. This is a great record, Frank, got all my old favorites. You remember this," he coaxed. "Listen to that banjo. Listen to Bill on that mandolin."

"Can't sit yet, Gramps. I got a mess of stuff to put away. I'll listen from the kitchen."

"What're you up to now?" asked Neil, heaving himself out of the chair and following Frank.

"Tell Charlotte she can come tomorrow or the day after if she wants." Frank's back was toward Neil. He emptied bags of groceries into the icebox and cupboard as he spoke.

"Well, that's real fine, son, real fine. What're you planning to cook?"

"I got a turkey here, make that cornbread stuffing, sweet potato pie, fruit compote for desert. . . . They sure got good fruit out here."

"You never got to can the stuff," Neil added. "It grows all year round."

"You know what I saw in the market today? Sugar cane," Frank said. "I didn't even know what it was till I seen the sign." He met the old man's shining eyes and turned back, embarrassed, to the bags.

"Guess I'll turn over the record," said Neil.

"You gonna call her?"

"I could . . . or you could go up in person and return that casserole dish for me. I never got around to it yet."

Frank accepted his sentence with a sigh. He folded and stacked the bags in the pantry and took the dish down from the shelf.

"OH, HELLO, NEIL. Is Frank about?" Roscoe was outfitted in immaculate gardening clothes, holding a pair of shears in one gloved hand. He grew the most beautiful roses in town and called them by strange names that Neil had never heard before.

"He went up the hill. Should be back in a few minutes. You can come in and wait for him, see what we just got." Neil led the way to the living room.

"Well, I suppose I could wait a few minutes." He imagined that Neil was going to show him some new piece of furniture and was puzzled for a moment, seeing the same two rockers. Then the stereo set sprawled across the floor caught his eye.

"Ever see one with so many parts?" Neil asked proudly. "Me and Mister Callahan put it together ourselves."

"You and Callahan, eh? You know, this looks like an excellent piece of equipment. Did Frank select it himself?" Roscoe knelt before the amplifier to admire the elegant control panel.

"Yup, he picked it out this morning. And look here, we got this record set." Neil handed Roscoe the empty jacket and started the machine. At the first twanging notes of the mandolin Neil was beaming, unable to keep still.

"You fellows like this country and western stuff, do you?" asked Roscoe, wincing slightly. "I happen to have several records that Marianne was particularly attached to, more of this sort, if you're interested. I'm not mad about it myself, to be perfectly honest."

"It sorta grows on you. You gotta give it a chance." Neil sat and rocked to the rhythm. His expression was dreamy.

"Just let me pop next door and see if I can't dig out those records for you," said Roscoe, dashing out the door.

Neil's eyes closed and the old memories crowded into his mind—Mamie moving slowly around the steamy kitchen in the summertime, singing softly to baby Em while she worked. And the socials back when they were still courting—part of the time he'd play banjo with the boys on the little platform and watch his girl whirl around the floor with the other fellas, then he'd get his chance to hold her himself, outside in the moonlight. And there was Mamie crooning to Emmie when she woke frightened in the night with a storm beating down on the roof. When he was a young man, not many folks in Belle Plaine owned victrolas, but most had upright pianos, whether or not anyone in the house could play. They'd buy sheet music at the five and dime and learn to pick out favorite songs on fiddle or guitar or banjo. That was a long time ago.

Roscoe trotted back with an armload of records.

"There were more than I realized. Look here." Roscoe took

the other chair and read off the names as he handed the records to Neil. "Jimmie Rodgers, looks quite old, the Original Carter Family, watch the cover, it's coming undone. Fiddlin' John Carson. You like fiddle music, Neil? Another Jimmie Rodgers, Hank Williams, Roy Acuff, Hank Williams again, Ernest Tubb, The Stoneman Family, The Stanley Brothers, Bob Wills and His Texas Playboys, more Ernest Tubb, Ramblin' Jack Elliot, and last but not least, Carl T. Sprague: The Original Singing Cowboy."

"Well, well. There's some good stuff here. I know Frank is especially fond of the Carter Family. Yup, I can see we're gonna have a fine time with this record player."

"Yes, well, I'll see Frank later, I suppose . . ." Roscoe stood and edged toward the door.

"Aw, come on. Sit here and listen with me for a little while. Give it a chance." Neil patted the seat beside him. "These boys practically invented bluegrass music."

"Well, maybe a few minutes, but I really just popped in to tell Frank that the pay voucher went through at the bank. If I don't see him today, tell him he can pick up the check any time. Or I could bring it home with me Monday, if he'd like. That's really why I came by. Could you give him the message if I miss him today?"

"Sure. Now sit still a minute."

Roscoe squirmed in his chair while trying to keep a pleasant and attentive expression frozen on his face. He had given this music a chance before, for Marianne, and he still detested it, though he wouldn't say so to Neil. There were certain bluegrass tunes he didn't mind. They reminded him of old English folk ballads. But the majority of the stuff sounded comical at best, witless and vulgar at its worst. He twisted his lips into a painful grin and drummed his fingers as he waited out his few minutes.

"Gramps?"

"In here, Frank. Come look what we got," Neil called.

"She's coming tomorrow, Gramps," Frank mumbled in the doorway. "Hi, Roscoe."

"How are you, Frank?" Roscoe asked, rising with relief.

"Look here," said Neil. "Roscoe brought over some old records he had. There's a good Jimmie Rodgers, two of 'em, and the Carter Family, Bob Wills, Hank Williams, and some others I recall less well."

Frank had something concealed behind his back and he brought it out—another record album in a flimsy jacket.

"Idabelle gave me this," he said. "We got to talking about music there in the kitchen and it turns out that her church here is famous for their choir. They made this recording and they sell it to raise money, but she made me take this for free."

"Well, well. We're gonna have us some record collection if it keeps up like this," Neil laughed. He studied the grainy photo of the choristers with their long white gowns and featureless dark faces.

"Let me put it on." Frank took the record back from Neil and settled himself on the floor by his stereo.

Roscoe cleared his throat and inched nearer the door.

"Frank," he said, "I just stopped by, actually, to say that your pay voucher cleared and the check is waiting for you."

"Oh. That was fast."

"Well, I pushed it through. By the way, this is an excellent machine you've got there. One of the best makes."

"Oh, the record player, you mean? I told Ralph at Music Masters to pick me out something good. It sounds good, too, don't it? Almost like you're there."

"Well," Roscoe knit his fingers and stretched. "I really must push off. My roses need me. I'll let myself out."

The warm harmonies of the gospel singers followed him down the drive.

"DONE WITH LUNCH, Gramps?"

"Yeah, thanks. Oh, I'm in your way."
Neil rose as his empty plate was whisked away.

"Gotta start fixing stuff for dinner," Frank muttered.

Neil went to his bedroom closet and took out the long stick of driftwood he'd saved. He turned it in the light, noting the interesting swirls and gnarls all down its length and the intricately marked bole on the thick end. The wood had already been smoothed by the ocean, but Neil had the idea of emphasizing the natural grain with his whittling. He foresaw many pleasant hours of carving and polishing ahead of him.

"Frank," he said at the kitchen door, "can you find me my whittling tools? They're in a cigar box and I didn't see it since we moved."

Frank tried to hide his annoyance. His hands were deep in a bowl of buttery cornbread crumbs, tossing in the egg. "Whittling tools?" he echoed.

"You know, I had them little carving knives in that box. . . . Remember I carved them little animals up at Springer's? Remember I did part of a twelve-link chain once?" The stick was tucked in the crook of his arm. "It busted on me."

"That's when you said it hurt your arthritis."

"Well, I figure it this way, Frank," Neil began.

Frank ran his hands under the tap and wiped them on his thighs in resignation. "Yeah, what?"

"If I stopped doing every little thing that hurt my arthritis there wouldn't be a heck of a lot left. But if I keep on using my hands they won't freeze up on me. I seen fellas' hands just freeze right up so they could never use 'em again. So can you find me my box, Frank?"

Frank brushed past the old man and knelt in the hall, rummaging around on the closet floor.

"You mark my words," Neil went on. "Everything hurts when you get to be my age. It ain't pleasant but it's a true fact. Almost eighty-five. Lord knows I got little enough to complain about compared with most folks. I been real lucky, got my own teeth, see pretty good, don't hear too bad, get around on my own steam. But, son, if you start telling me something's gonna hurt, well, I just gotta laugh because *everything* hurts more or less. It's a true fact of life. Yup, old age is—"

"Is this it?" Frank shook a cigar box that was pinned shut.

"Hey, you found it!" Neil reached eagerly for the box and hurried into the living room with Frank at his heels.

"What're you gonna whittle?"

"Oh, well, this here's a stick of driftwood I found down on the beach. See, I'm gonna smooth over the top and sorta pretty up the rest of it and take it with me on my walks. Look at all the designs in the natural grain of it. I'm just gonna sharpen up the designs that're already there, then polish it up real good."

Frank squinted doubtfully at the stick. "You're talking about making yourself a cane," he said slowly.

"Yeah, I guess."

"You just said you can get around okay."

"I know what I said, Frank. But this stick helps me to straighten up if I bend over for something or when I sit. It helps me."

"Soon you won't be able to do without it, Gramps."

"Son, you're not listening to me," Neil sighed. "I know I can walk good. There's no argument about that, but that's not what this is for. Why don't you go ask Roscoe if plenty of English gentlemen that can walk perfectly good don't carry canes. Anyway, Frank, I take your opinion in a lot of things, but I'm planning to carve this stick, and I'm planning to take it on my walks, and that's that."

Frank stood by the door with his huge hands hanging at his sides. He watched Neil settle in a rocker, lay the stick across the arms, and work the pin out of the box lid, then dump the odd little knives into his lap, and put on his magnifying glasses. Without another glance at Frank, he began to sharpen the blades on a flat white stone.

"I just thought . . ."

"It doesn't matter. It's okay," Neil sighed. It scares him to see that I'm old, he thought to himself. He wanted to smile at Frank, but Frank was gone when he looked up. He soon heard him in the kitchen making the dinner preparations.

Neil whittled for a while, then dozed. His dreams were punctuated by the sounds of cooking. He awoke groggy and confused in the twilit gloom and then he recalled that company was coming. He held his watch close to his face and saw that he'd have to hurry to be ready for Charlotte's arrival.

He dressed himself in fresh gray slacks and a white long-sleeved shirt. He added a favorite sky-blue bow tie that showed up his eyes and the snowy whiteness of his hair. He went over his cheeks with the electric razor and slapped on some sweet-smelling after-shave, then wet his comb and smoothed the wavy hair over his pink skull. He clipped a stray hair out of one nostril and, feeling pretty snappy, went to see how Frank was doing.

No surprise, Frank was wearing the soft baggy overalls and Neil noted unhappily that there was a large grease stain on the seat. He reminded himself that Frank's blue shirt at least was clean, starched stiff as a board, and that he too had shaved a second time. He tried to be satisfied.

"I just wish we had a nice tablecloth," said Neil.

"The table looks okay."

Frank had taken care in setting it, with crescent salad plates and the wine glasses, everything neat as could be.

He pulled the turkey out onto the oven door. The skin was crisp and golden brown all over. Frank draped it with a tinfoil tent and shoved it back. He took out the sweet-potato pie, dotted the top with miniature marshmallows, and returned it to melt the little puffs. There was a bottle of white wine, bought at Neil's insistence, chilling in the icebox. Frank's bottle of cider stood ready on the counter.

"You know what would've been nice?" Neil asked dreamily. "Candles."

Frank snorted. "What time is it, Gramps?"

"Time, already. Seven-oh-five. Maybe I'm running fast."

They heard the gravel crunch in the driveway and Frank chose that moment to amble to the bathroom, shutting himself in with a slam.

"Hello-o," Charlotte called through the screen.

"Come in, come in." Neil hurried forward to hold the door for Charlotte, whose hands were full with a bottle of wine and a covered cake plate. "What have we here? Oh, you shouldn't have bothered. You're our guest! Frank made us a beautiful meal. He's just washing up."

"Well I'll just set this in the fridge to chill," said Charlotte. She opened the door and her face fell as she spotted the other bottle.

"The more the merrier." Neil patted her arm. "If we don't drink it all tonight, we'll just finish it another time."

Charlotte flushed deeply as Frank shambled into the room.

"Say hello, son." Neil jabbed an elbow into Frank's side.

"Hello, Frank," said Charlotte.

"Charlotte brought us a nice cake for dessert," Neil said to Frank with a meaningful look.

Frank grunted and frowned at the cake under its clear plastic cover.

"I guess we can start," he said at last.

"Hold on there, son. Let's offer our guest a glass of wine first. Charlotte?"

"I'd love some. Thanks."

She sat at the table, perching on her chair like a dainty full-bodied partridge, glancing brightly around. Neil hovered by Frank's elbow as he uncorked their wine with the corkscrew of his pocketknife.

"Well, here's to good friends and good food," said Neil, clinking his glass against Charlotte's.

"Hear, hear. You're not joining us, Frank?"

"Frank never had no taste for wine," Neil jumped in. "Don't that turkey smell like heaven? Frank here is quite a cook."

"It smells wonderful." She blushed and took another sip.

Frank looked immense in his kitchen; the appliances seemed out of scale, and the dishes and utensils looked like toys. But Charlotte noticed that he handled himself well, using both hands to arrange everything on platters and put on the finishing touches.

"Well, it looks just beautiful, Frank. I might have to ask for some of your recipes," she exclaimed. "My Idabelle can never get the turkey right. Either she bakes the thing to death and it gets all dried out and stringy, or she leaves a cover on the whole time and the skin is just like rubber. You know, I think she likes to try my patience on purpose sometimes."

"She's taking me to church tomorrow," Frank said unexpectedly.

"Church!" Neil wiped his mouth and stared. "That's a new one!"

"To hear some singing," Frank muttered in explanation. He took the seat opposite Neil.

There was an extra plate at Neil's side, and after Charlotte was served she watched curiously as Neil filled the extra plate with white meat, stuffing, sweet-potato pie, salad, a warm roll, and

63

gravy. He handed this across to Frank, who grudgingly covered it with a clean dishcloth and set it on the cement step outside the door.

"What in the world . . . !"

"We have another guest." Neil smiled at her astonishment. "Friend of mine, Mister Callahan, sleeps out in the camper, takes his meals out there. He's a little eccentric."

Frank snorted.

He began to eat with his head lowered to the plate, his eyes strangely blank. Charlotte sneaked peeks at him, at once attracted and repelled by his behavior.

"Plate gone yet, Frank?" asked Neil.

Frank leaned his chair back on its hind legs and squinted into the dusk. "Nope. Still there," he answered.

"Well, I guess I'll just run it out to the camper, then. I never can enjoy my dinner when another fella's is getting cold." Neil crumpled his napkin on the table and went outside.

Frank heaped his plate with seconds of everything and dug in again. Charlotte imagined that she hadn't seen a man eat so much so fast since maybe her dad.

"So you and Ida are striking up a friendship, Frank?" Charlotte began lightly.

"Just going to church, hear some music."

"It reminds you of home, I suppose."

"No." He frowned at his plate and slowed his chewing.

"I just thought, maybe . . . Well, I guess not."

"There!" Neil said brightly. "Now I can enjoy my food. And Mister Callahan says to say thanks for dinner."

Frank snorted and pushed his plate away. He crossed the room in three strides and grabbed the cider jug. He poured a wineglass full and sipped silently, staring at the darkened window.

"More wine, Charlotte?" Neil winked over at her.

"Oh, not for me, thanks."

CALLAHAN HAD HAD A REWARDING DAY. First he did a few hours' work cleaning out the cellar of the bar and earned a bottle of booze. Then, when he went over to the beach, a car full of teenagers almost ran him down in the parking lot, hooting and honking, and left him a six-pack of beer on the pavement before driving off. Callahan could hardly believe his eyes, but he picked it up and it was full and cold, and he wished the boys would come back and take another swipe at him—it was easier than hauling crates.

His mouth watered as he hurried with his prize to the rocky nest at the end of the beach. There he enjoyed two of the beers while watching the sun's slow descent. When it was dark enough to be on his way, he stood shakily and did a few steps of a jig, whistling that crazy hillbilly music, and fell back on the still-warm sand, laughing and hiccupping.

He stashed the remaining beers in his new hiding place, a dank, wooden shack that used to be a refreshment stand, now rotting and padlocked near the parking lot. There was a broad loose plank that could be swung aside, leaving enough space for a man to wriggle through.

He started up the hill just ahead of the fog. It felt good to climb into the soft warm berth in the camper and have a right to be there. His bottle was tucked away under the front car-seat; he kept his promise and never drank in the camper, but he needed to know the bottle was nearby.

He lay in the dark and his mind drifted all the way back to the time in Philadelphia, to the wife and kid and the payments on everything. He was too young, never got his bearings. At first he tried to tell her he wasn't ready. Then he started staying out nights, and when he came back she'd fix him with this look, like she was his mother, not his wife. It only made him stay out more, that look, until he met up with some hobos one night and drank with them and they showed him how to jump a train. He stayed drunk for three or four days. By the time he sobered up, there was nothing around but scrub and cactus as far as the eye could see. At first he thought it was just a lark—he'd go back soon.

"I wasn't always a bum," he said aloud.

But I don't ever want to be any good to anybody any more, amen, he thought to himself.

"Mister Callahan?" There was a gentle rap, rap, rap on the door.

"Come in."

"I just wanted to bring you your dinner. It was getting cold out on the step," said Neil. He uncovered the plate on the little square table and watched Callahan slip down from the bunk. "Never can enjoy my food when someone else's is getting cold." He grinned pleasantly in the gloom.

"I wasn't always a bum, you know."

"You're not a bum. You're my friend." The old man winked and turned away from Callahan's pained expression, hurrying back to his bright kitchen.

Callahan could see them moving around inside the house, momentarily blocking the light from the windows. He sat at the table and pulled over his knife and fork and the heaping plate. He tucked the cloth into his shirtfront and chewed some of the food. It seemed to have no flavor and he was unaccountably angry. For one crazy second, he thought he'd like to throw the food all over the camper, really make a mess, and leave there for good. Instead, he took his bottle and his rage outdoors and immediately felt better under the wide starry sky.

He crept close to the house, hid himself in the shrubbery, and felt better still. He could hear them talking, chattering away, unaware that they were overheard, and it made him giddy with excitement. He heard a woman's voice—too young for the old man, but too old for the farmer. He wondered what she was doing there and drew nearer the window. He took a pull on his bottle and welcomed the liquid fire deep in his throat.

He listened especially to the woman and soon decided that she was as foolish as any of them. He rose slowly, quietly, till he was on his toes with his fingers and nose hooked over the window ledge. He could see the three of them, the farmer in his overalls,

66

the old man with his back to the window, and the plump silly woman flirting shamelessly with both men. Callahan was pleased by Frank's reaction, cheered him on in his indifference, and toasted him with a long warming drink.

He sat back on the hard packed dirt, leaning against the house, and let the voices float past him, listening only to the tones, one high and nonsensical, another low, gruff and infrequent, and the middle one friendly and appeasing.

Then they moved to another part of the house, and after a few minutes' silence, Callahan was startled by the twanging strains of that agonizing hillbilly music. For some reason, it seemed to choke him up and sting in his eyes. One moment he'd be mocking it, and the next he'd feel an unspeakable misery inside him, deep, where the alcohol couldn't reach. He told himself to get away from it, go back to the bunk, but he sat frozen on the spot, aching from the maudlin words and predictable harmonies.

He hugged his knees and squeezed his eyes shut. The night breezes had grown chilly and his clothes were damp from the bushes brushing against him, but still he stayed and listened and drank until the tears dribbled down his hard cheeks and the lump in his throat melted away.

"HELLO, FRANK." Charlotte set aside her needlepoint.

"Hello. Ida inside?"

"Yes, she is. Oh! This is your day to go to church," she exclaimed.

"Yeah." He twiddled a worn gray fedora between his fingers. Except for that item, his dress was the same as always, a tidy blue shirt, sagging overalls, cloddish black workboots.

"We happen to have quite a nice choir in the Episcopalian, too, you know, and a very fine organist. We're not as picturesque as the Baptists, of course, but you might be interested." Charlotte rocked casually and shaded her eyes against the sun, looking up at him.

"Well, I guess I'll go inside." He attempted a smile but it came off as more of a scowl. He flushed with annoyance and ducked into the cool dark hallway.

The kitchen was bright and fragrant with pot roast, spinach, and buttermilk biscuits. Idabelle was fussing at the stove, her huge hindquarters directed toward the door.

"Almost ready, Missus," she drawled.

"Take your time."

"Oh, Mister Frank!" She wiped her hands on her voluminous apron. "Seems like everything been going wrong today that could. But the minute I set this food on the table we'll be on our way."

"Okay, I guess we got time still." Frank leaned against the doorframe with the hat hanging from one finger.

"Want to have a bite of something while you're waiting? There's plenty enough food here."

"I already ate."

"Well, here I go. Just be a minute." She took a platter of meat in one hand and the creamed spinach casserole in the other and bustled into the dining room. She made a second trip with the rolls and butter and the water pitcher, balancing it easily.

"That's that," she said, removing the gay apron. She hung it behind the door, smoothed the somber gray shift over her bulky hips, rolled down the sleeves, and buttoned the tight white cuffs. She covered her neat oily braids with a fussy black straw hat and took up a matching bag.

Frank clapped the hat on his head and held out his arm. Ida delicately grasped his elbow with her fingertips and laughed like a girl, showing gold and ivory teeth. They had to turn sideways to maneuver out of the kitchen and again to pass through the front door.

"I guess we be off now, Missus," Ida said listlessly. "Everything done."

"Does Mr. Chapman have his glass of milk?"

"Yes, Missus. First thing I done."

"Oh, fine," Charlotte said primly. "Well, then, run along, you two." She picked up her work and lowered her burning face until

Frank and Ida reached the hairpin turn, then she went inside to see that her guests were happy.

Ida and Frank continued down the warm dusty road, moving carefully as each misstep caused Ida's sturdy hip to collide embarrassingly with Frank's hard thigh.

"This the street, Mister Frank," she said at last, steering him around a corner.

He frowned slightly, thinking he was familiar with the area but recalling no church there. Then Ida tugged his sleeve again.

He stared mulishly at the structure before them, a whitewashed garage squatting on a scrubby plot.

"This the church," she insisted. "They must be about to start."

He noticed that there were neat striped curtains in the unpainted top row of windows across the old garage doors and the path that led around to the side was lined with painted stones and marigolds. Suddenly a swell of voices reached their ears and Frank followed Ida to the door.

"We missing the beginning," she muttered and clucked her tongue.

The door at the side was topped by a large gold-painted cross and a sign that read "First Corinthian Baptist Church of Christ." The harmony of human voices unaccompanied reached an angelic pitch, then dissolved into fervent syncopation.

Frank's jaw dropped.

"There's plenty more inside," Ida urged, holding the door, beaming proudly.

"WELL, I GUESS it must've been *something* to get you all worked up, Frank." Neil put his carving aside and rocked gently, grinning up at Frank. "Think you'll go back again?"

"Sure. Next week." He threw himself into the other chair and rocked vigorously, but jumped up the next minute to pace again.

"Say, Frank, remember that prayer meeting we ran across in

Virginia when we had the reunion at Uncle Ed's? Just after my Mamie passed away? Maybe you was too little to recall that, but they sure know how to kick up a ruckus, them Baptists."

"It wasn't like that, Gramps. It was real musical."

"Well, myself, I got enough of churchgoing when I was a young kid to last me. But I guess if you enjoy it—why not?" He picked up one of the little curved knives and shaved away at a groove, smoothing and defining it.

"Think Music Masters is open Sunday?"

"I sure doubt it, Frank. Nothing open today but the diner and the gas station, I think."

Frank fetched his tool kit from the hall closet and sprawled with it on the floor. He dug out the tape measure and a grimy pad of paper and took a pencil stub from his front overall pocket.

"I'm starting to wonder," he began slowly, "what kind of thing I ought to build for this record player. Can't just leave it all over the floor like this." He stroked his dark jaw and frowned.

"What do you got in mind? Shelves or something?"

"I thought of shelves. Shelves wouldn't take two minutes to put up once I had the wood, but I'm thinking more about a kind of long open cabinet, maybe, to hold the records, with the stereo on top and the records down below . . ."

"Them records don't even fill up one carton, Frank," Neil pointed at it with his foot and chuckled.

"There's gonna be lots more. We're gonna need plenty of storage space soon, and I gotta plan it now." He started to measure the length of the wall with his tape.

"Well, that'll be something. Mind if I play us a record while we work? How about the Carters?" Neil found it easily in the small collection and turned on the machine.

"You know, this 'Wildwood Flower' they do was one of your grandma's all-time favorites. Lots of different artists done this one. Used to play it myself on the banjo, but I like it better with the autoharp, like this." Neil sat back in his rocker, closed his eyes, and folded his hands over his belly. "I like the words."

"Holler if you need anything," said Frank. He closed himself in his room.

After a while, Neil dozed. The sun was warm on the back of his neck. His head lolled forward and he breathed noisily through his mouth. The record played itself automatically, again and again. Dusk fell.

Neil awoke in the dark with music playing and had a moment's confusion. The songs were all tangled up with his dreams, but he could recall nothing more than an indescribable sense of loss.

His neck was stiff and his stomach growled. He guessed that Frank must have gone off somewhere, leaving the record to repeat like that, but on his way to the bathroom he saw a stripe of light under Frank's door.

"You in there?" he called softly.

Frank swung open the door and blinked down at the old man. He had his mind on other things and waited impatiently for Neil to speak.

"You been here all the time, Frank . . ." He tried to see past the overalls to the papers spread out on the floor.

"Want something?"

"No, nothing special. I just woke up. Figure I'll fix a bite to eat, turkey sandwich or something. Want me to make one for you?"

"No, I'll take something later."

Neil cleared his throat and flashed a smile. He could think of nothing more to say and made his way down the dark hall to the moonlit kitchen. Once he got the light on, he hurried back to the living room to turn off the music.

I T WAS ANOTHER clear fresh morning with brine and roses in the air.

Neil sat in the backyard on a small folding chair, a nursery catalog open across his narrow lap. He had a marking pen poised to circle the serial numbers of trees and flowers and vegetables he might want for his garden.

The catalog made him greedy with its exotic selections pictured in full color. As far as he could tell, there wasn't a thing that couldn't be grown in this sunny, warm state. He was enchanted with the photo of living bamboo and imagined a stand of the fast-growing plants in the shady corner of the yard. Another spot was already reserved for an almond tree. He had warned Roscoe that he was less interested in a harmonious layout than an exciting collection of oddities.

The backyard as it was had one graceful mimosa in the lower corner by the driveway and a privet hedge along the property line. There were inconspicuous evergreen shrubs against the walls of the house, and all the rest was scrubby grass and thriving clumps of onion weed which Neil and Roscoe were planning to attack before the planting began.

Roscoe had long ago achieved the desired effect in his own yard and its upkeep alone was not enough to keep him occupied. His neighbor's untouched land provided the long-missed challenge. He could only guess at what Neil had in mind, but relished the idea of growing all manner of strange plants without the common standard of beauty to concern him. He imagined a sort of Garden of Eden with its divine Cultivator gone slightly mad. He turned over to Neil his most extensive catalog with instructions to circle anything that interested him; they would make the final selection together.

Neil heard the phone ring inside and rose wearily, doubting that he could reach the kitchen in time to answer, but to his surprise it continued to ring, ten, eleven, twelve times.

"Gramps. Were you asleep or something?"

"No, I was out back in the yard, Frank. Say, this is gonna be some garden we're gonna have. It'll really knock your eye out, Frank."

"Gramps, listen. I just sent a truck up to the house. Remember Ida's brother Ike? It's his truck. Show him to the living room and tip him five bucks and make him take the money, okay?"

"Oh, boy! What're we getting now, Frank?"

"Three more rockers. And lumber."

"More rocking chairs, you say?"

"It's the best thing for listening to music. Look, I got to go. I'll be there around lunchtime."

"Okay," Neil sighed. "See you later."

He wandered into the living room and tried to imagine the scene—five rocking chairs facing a wall of stereo equipment and record cabinets. He wondered if he could persuade Frank to add a small table or two, maybe a rug, a few pictures on the walls.

No sooner did he start back to the yard than an old panel truck slowed in front of the house. A dark and dusty black man leaned his head out the window.

"Hey, friend, is this Frank Diggory's house?"

"Yup. Are you Ike?" Neil shaded his eyes to watch the truck turn and back into the driveway in a cloud of smelly blue smoke.

"Frank sent this stuff. He tell you 'bout it?"

"He just called me."

"Okay. Say, I remember you now. From up there." He jerked his head toward the hill behind them.

Neil smiled and stared in fascination at the man's yellow eyeballs and yellow gap-toothed grin. His thick lips were deep purple, wet and pink inside, and his nostrils were nearly as wide as his mouth.

Ike opened the back doors and set to work. His arms were round and powerful with just a few springs of hair. The skin was gray with cement dust and the elbows were so worn and callused they reminded Neil of rhinoceros hide.

Neil watched him lift down the three chairs; they looked comically out of place on the drive, as though they were stranded there. Their style was frumpy Early American and reminded Neil of Emmie's favorite pieces in Belle Plaine.

"Better show me the way first," said Ike.

Neil led him through the kitchen to the living room and he sized up the two doorways with a professional eye; the cumbersome rockers would have to go through on their sides.

Ike took care not to chip the doorways or scratch the chairs as he carried each one into the house. Seeing him work so hard, Neil felt that five dollars wasn't enough. Then Ike made his first trip with an armload of lumber and his bald head became dotted with perspiration. By the next trip, the beads had merged to form streams down his neck. He mopped his skin with a soggy bandana and flexed his arms.

Neil offered him a glass of lemonade, which he gulped gratefully, and then a ten dollar bill, discreetly folded.

Ike held up his yellow palms. "No need, man. Frank done paid me already beforehand."

This was news to Neil, but he was ashamed to withdraw his huge tip. "Well, he wanted you to have this extra. Please take it." He smiled weakly.

"Well, okay, then. I ain't too proud for that." He laughed and headed back to his truck with a rolling, bowlegged walk, and Neil realized that the man was older than he looked.

The living room was a sight with the three new oversized chairs. Ike had lined them up along the windows with the other two and piled the lumber in the far corner. It was good-quality wood. Oak, Neil guessed from the smell.

He poured himself a glass of lemonade and returned to his nursery catalog out back. The chair was now in the shadow of the house and he dragged it forward into the sun to get the soothing warmth on his back and neck. He flipped through the pages to find his place and came upon a picture of Brussels sprouts spiraling around a queer thick stalk. He had always guessed that they grew out of the ground in rows, like little cabbages. It was funny, he thought, to have been a farmer his whole life and know so little about the subject as to need lessons from a rose grower.

He sipped his cold drink and circled a few more numbers— dwarf banana, lily of the valley, Italian broad beans, white asparagus, Persian melon, Golden Bell peppers, spaghetti squash—and the catalog dropped from his hand and he dozed.

The taxi pulled into the driveway and Frank emerged, staggering to the house under the weight of a cardboard carton. He returned with a few dollars for the driver and removed a second box, lighter than the first.

He stood in the center of his music room and looked down at his row of rockers and they were fine. He turned to the opposite wall and imagined the long, adjustable cabinets that would hold the stereo set and the growing collection of records. His hands itched to get started. He looked at the cartons of records on the floor, only the beginning of the collection he envisioned, and he felt giddy with excitement.

He was still standing, unable to decide where to begin, when he heard the honking of a car in his drive.

"Hey, Frank," yelled the driver. "Hey, you left your checkbook in the back seat. Lucky I saw it before I got another fare. You never know about people."

"Thanks, Lou. See ya."

The taxi backed out and cruised away.

Neil came around the corner of the house, stepping uncertainly, rubbing his eyes.

"You all right, Gramps?"

"Oh, sure, fine. Just had a little nap out back. Heard a car horn and it woke me up. Funny," he mused. "All the trouble I got sleeping nights and then in the daytime seems like every time I get comfortable, next thing I know I'm fast asleep. Sure wish it'd work the other way. Anyway, you'll see what I'm talking about when you get to be my age, Frank."

"I like these new rockers."

"Yeah, they seem okay." Neil stood in the doorway and tried to get used to the odd-looking room.

"Did you sit in 'em yet? They're real comfortable."

They sat in the new chairs, bouncing around to try out every inch and rocking on them as if they were toys. The padding felt good against Neil's spine where it bowed slightly.

"This is so comfy I don't know if I can get up!" said Neil. He stopped rocking and eased himself onto the edge, but when he tried to stand the chair moved out from under him and he would have fallen had Frank not grabbed his arm.

"Whew!" His heart drummed in his chest. "I think I better stick with the old ones, Frank. These new ones are too deep and too low for me, more your size. If I just had me a pillow for my back, these old ones would do me fine." He moved down the row and sat in a familiar chair to calm himself.

"Sorry, Gramps. I'll get you some cushions then. You just had to ask."

"I didn't think of it before. I'm asking now."

"Anyway, now we got plenty of room for company to call."

"That's right, son. Company." Neil was pleased.

"Well, I'm gonna fix us some lunch and get to work on my cabinets."

"Sounds good to me."

Neil followed Frank into the kitchen and waited patiently at the table while Frank peered into the icebox, checking his supplies.

"There's some boiled potatoes, sausages. Want hash browns with sausage and apple?"

"Okay with me."

"Anyway," Frank began, taking down the cutting board, "this thing I'm gonna build, it ain't like a regular cabinet, see. It's gonna have partitions in it that you can move around. It'll run all across the back wall there." He broke up the sausage meat in the big black skillet. "But even so, that space is gonna fill up pretty fast." He added a chopped onion to the pan. "So someday, I'll have to add another row on top of that." He cored and chopped two apples. "Now, all this time I can move around the partitions and keep everything in order so I can find any record I want." He sliced the cold potatoes and added them with the apple to the sizzling pan, then dusted the mixture with cinnamon and nutmeg. "I figure I'll need some kind of cross-reference soon." He turned and scraped the food. "Gotta keep track of everything, who wrote the songs, who sings 'em, and like that." He leaned back against the counter, arms folded, waiting for the potatoes to brown, inviting his grandfather's reaction.

"Well, well," Neil began cautiously. "This sounds like some collection you're planning. Is it every kind of music or what exactly?"

"No, just real country stuff—bluegrass and fiddle music. That's all I want. I like the old stuff the best. You can buy re-releases, you know."

"That's what I like, too. Good picking, good old tunes."

"I ordered loads of stuff, but it comes in a little at a time."

The potatoes were brown and he divided the sweet-smelling hash onto plates and sat with Neil to eat, but he could barely taste the food, hardly chewed it, and was finished in minutes. He left his plate to soak with the skillet and disappeared into the music room.

Neil was still eating and trying to picture the cabinet as Frank described it. He heard the sound of the lumber being hauled around and sorted and the toolbox clanking as it yielded its contents. He moved his chair around to give himself a view through the doorway; so long as he didn't come into the room, it wouldn't bother Frank to have him watch.

"**W**ELL, I'VE LOCATED Frank's source," Roscoe chuckled as he handed over a plastic jug of hard cider.

"We got wine here, if you want it," said Neil.

"No, no, I quite like the cider for a change."

"Oh, okay. Frank!" he called. "We got company!"

"Where is he?" asked Roscoe. "The music room? I'd like to have a look anyway." Roscoe crossed to the doorway. He had on a fresh white shirt for dinner, his hair was neatly wet-combed, and he smelled pleasantly of bay rum.

Frank was sprawled on the floor sorting through his records. There were only sixty-odd so far and he was disappointed at the measly look of them in the wall-length unit. Also, he had already run into difficulty in trying to alphabetize them, deciding whether to take the letter of the artist's name or the album title as many of the albums were collections. There was an urgent need for a cross-index system to keep track of everything, and the time to organize was now, before it really got out of hand.

Roscoe looked quietly on as Frank frowned and grunted to himself. At last he spoke up.

"This is fine workmanship, Frank. I'm quite impressed." Roscoe drew nearer and brushed the smooth finish of the wood with his fingertips.

Frank scrambled to his feet, towering over Roscoe, to examine his own work through the eyes of another.

"It all adjusts down here, see," he mumbled. "These dividers go right out to the ends."

"Well, that'll hardly be necessary for a while yet," said Roscoe.

"No, soon. I got loads of stuff ordered from Music Masters. I'll need all this room and more." He frowned and punched his thigh in annoyance. "I just need some kind of filing thing."

"What do you have in mind?" Roscoe began. "Because there's a nice old card catalog type of thing down at the bank. It's been just gathering dust in the basement as far back as I remember and if it's still there, it's yours. It's like a library thingy. Could you use that?"

Frank's face brightened. "Yeah. Sounds like just what I need. I could pay for it. . . ." He pushed the bangs off his forehead.

"Nonsense, I'm giving it to you. Come round next week and we'll go dig it out. It's in a big jumble down there, but I'm fairly sure I can find it. I think it'll match your woodwork, too. It's blond wood, if I remember."

Neil was fussing with the table setting, arranging the silver just so. Then he joined the men in the music room.

"Some fine piece of work, eh, Roscoe?"

"Very impressive," he said and turned admiringly around. "Aha! More rocking chairs." His eyebrows rose and he suppressed a smile.

"Two wasn't enough," Frank explained, "when folks come over to visit." He followed Roscoe's gaze around the room and saw, for the first time, how strangely bare it was. He flushed in embarrassment and his pride in the cabinet evaporated. He was angry with himself for being so slow to see it. "I better check on the roast," he muttered unhappily, ducking out of the room.

"I was just saying, there's a filing cabinet, a card index type of thing, down at the bank, that I'm giving to Frank. He seems to be planning something quite extensive, I gather."

"Well, I don't know too much about it," said Neil. "You know Frank and questions. But we're sure having fun with these old records he's picking up. We both go for the old-timey stuff."

"Well, anyway, it sounds like a lovely idea, a sort of music room. I wish my wife had lived to see this. She loved that sort of music, would've gotten a kick out of the whole thing."

"I guess you miss her a lot."

Roscoe's throat tightened but he spoke lightly. "Man wasn't meant to live alone," he said.

"Ain't it the truth," Neil agreed.

He led the way back to the kitchen where Frank stood over the counter, carving the meat. The salad was set out on the table, along with a basket of warm buns and a tub of butter. A dish of candied yams filled the room with a meltingly sweet aroma. Frank brought the platter of meat to the table and they took their seats. There was a fourth plate at Neil's elbow which he filled after taking his own portions, covered with a cloth, and handed to Frank to set on the step.

"Has Neil been telling you about our gardening project, Frank?"

Frank was leaning low over his plate, chewing, eyes blank. He grunted in reply.

"I bet you never cooked up a mess of artichokes, Frank, or Brussels sprouts right off the stalk, did you?" Neil laughed. "We're gonna need a new cookbook around here when my vegetables start coming in." Neil remembered the apple cider and jumped up. "Look here, Frank. Roscoe brought this over. There's a thoughtful guest for you." Neil poured three wineglasses full and left the jug on the table.

"This is delicious, Frank. I've never tasted sweet potatoes quite like these before. Is there some secret, if I may ask?"

"Oh, these yams? He just peels 'em and dunks 'em in maple syrup," Neil piped up. "Right, Frank?"

Frank seemed more than usually preoccupied.

"Just delicious." Roscoe mopped up some of the syrup with a torn roll.

"Well, I got just enough room left for a piece of that burnt sugar cake." Neil leaned back and patted his little belly with contentment. "Frank could win prizes with his burnt sugar cake." He winked at Roscoe.

Frank pushed his chair back and plugged in the percolator. Then he cleared the table and brought over the golden cake, glazed with rum and dotted with raisins, then the cups, saucers, dessert plates, and the cream and sugar. Neil cut hefty wedges of cake while Frank waited for the coffee to stop perking.

"Fabulous cake. You missed your calling, Frank. You should have trained as a chef. You'd have been famous," said Roscoe.

"Frank would rather do a little bit of everything, right, Frank? He wouldn't take to doing the same thing day in and day out."

Frank poured the coffee and started on his hunk of cake.

"You know," Neil went on, "Frank here was too smart to tie hisself down to the land like his grandpappy. Of course, I didn't have much of a choice. Back in them days, everybody I knew was farming one thing or another. Young people didn't just go off and do whatever they had a mind to—they had to help out at home. Then one day you turn around and you ain't young and you ain't just helping out and then you're stuck. Not that I got any regrets. I had a good life," Neil sighed. He mashed a few moist crumbs with his thumb and sucked it clean.

"You got lots of good years yet," Frank stated.

"Well, I'm hoping, but I don't kid myself. You know, Roscoe, in a few weeks I'm gonna be eighty-five years old. That's no spring chicken!"

"Well, we ought to have a celebration, Neil."

"Like a party, you mean? I don't know, Roscoe. I figure God must have forgot all about me and maybe I shouldn't remind Him I'm still here."

"Well, we ought to do something. Eighty-five . . . I wouldn't have guessed."

"Most Horner men do pretty good. My grandpappy lived to ninety-two or so. My daddy died young in a accident, same as Frank's here, so we don't know. Then I had a great-uncle on my mother's side, lived to be near a hundred, but they didn't know his exact birthday. Anyway, this sun out here does me a world of good. I might just last forever. My joints didn't feel this easy for the last twenty years." He flexed his bony arms, hairless with parchment-like skin.

There were footsteps on the gravel outside and Neil half stood to see if Callahan was coming for his dinner plate. He made out the plump shape of Charlotte Springer, walking carefully in high heels, and hurried to meet her at the door. The plate was gone.

"Charlotte, what a nice surprise! Come on in, dear, meet a friend of ours, next-door neighbor." He held the screen open for her.

She looked fretful.

"Oh, I'm sorry. I didn't know you had company." A rosy

80

blush colored her cheeks. "I hate to intrude like this but I'm in kind of a jam . . ."

"This is Roscoe Small. He lives right past the hedge there. And this is Charlotte Springer. Frank and I stayed at her boarding-house for a time, the big place up on the hill."

"Oh, of course. I've heard about Springer's—all good. Pleased to meet you." Roscoe rose and bowed slightly as he took her hand.

"Excuse me for asking, but are you British, Mr. Small?"

"Roscoe. Yes I am, but it's been more than twenty years since I left." He continued to stand because she was standing.

"Well, I usually wouldn't barge in like this except that my car just broke down on the road. I was driving down to my bridge club and the darn thing just *died*. It was only two blocks from here down Campbell so naturally I thought of Frank. I'd be so grateful, Frank, if you'd take a look at it." She smiled apologetically, twisting her handbag strap in her fingers.

Frank stared at Charlotte for a moment, then rose suddenly, took a flashlight from under the sink, and held out his big palm to her.

For a crazy moment she thought he expected to be led to the car. Then she didn't know what to think and wanted very badly to sink into the floor.

"The keys," he muttered impatiently.

She handed them over, still wondering whether to stay or go out to the car.

Neil saw her discomfort and pulled out the fourth chair. "Sit here with us, Charlotte. Try some of the cake. Would you like coffee?"

She phoned the club first, to warn them not to expect her, and joined the men at the table.

She was wearing a flowered shirtwaist with a lace hankie in the pocket and smelled faintly of lily of the valley mingled with talc. Her fuzzy red hair was gathered neatly off her neck in a small twist. She lowered her eyes with Neil and Roscoe watching her so closely, and colored as she ate her slice of cake in small mouthfuls, dabbing frequently at her lips with the napkin.

81

"So," she said between bites, "you're from England."

"Yes, England," Roscoe echoed. Her girlish bashfulness was not lost on him; he was enchanted. "And where are you from originally? Not California."

"Why do you say that?"

"I'm not sure."

"Well, I'm from Wyoming, as a matter of fact. Do you happen to know where that it?"

"Certainly."

She looked at him curiously, wondering how he meant it.

"Well," she sighed, "I haven't once had a chance to go back for a visit. I never get a vacation in my business."

"Do you miss it there?"

She thought for a moment. "Not at all. Do you miss England?"

"Not at all," he laughed.

Frank let the screen door slam on its hinges and shambled past them to the hall mumbling, "Distributor."

"Oh!" Charlotte jumped up. "Is that serious?" she called after him.

He was squatting among his tools, pawing through them.

"Is it serious?" she repeated.

"Nope." He tossed something into the toolbox, buckled the straps, and left through the front door without another glance at her.

She returned to the table, feeling Roscoe's eyes follow her every movement, and flushed again. "Well, it seems to be something in the distributor, that's all," she said airily.

"Aw, Frank can fix a car motor with his eyes closed," said Neil. "He was born knowing it."

Charlotte cleared her throat. "May I ask what you do for a living, Roscoe?"

"Vice-president of the bank, the First Federal. Fancy title for a fairly simple job. What I do for a living, actually, is wear a clean suit, sign my name, offer suggestions which nobody takes seriously, and chit-chat with the local businessmen."

"Oh, I'm sure you're just being modest. It must be a very important job."

Neil looked from one to the other of his friends and saw their eyes lock across the table and felt that, in some way, a burden had been lifted. He mentally kicked himself for not bringing them together sooner—it was a lovely match.

"Hey, you two," said Neil, "why don't we move into the music room. We'll be more comfortable. Charlotte, there's been some changes in there since you saw it."

"Oh, my! More rocking chairs!" she exclaimed, barely masking her amusement. It seemed to her now that she'd always known Frank was a little strange.

"We ought to give these new ones a try." Roscoe escorted her to an Early American rocker and took the one next to it.

"I don't like to use them new ones," said Neil. "Can't seem to get my old bones out of 'em once I get settled. I just stick with one of these. How's about a little music? Charlotte? This is some of the best bluegrass you're ever gonna hear."

Charlotte leaned her head back and laughed prettily. "It's kind of funny, this music."

Roscoe winced at the first twangs of the mandolin, then tried to ignore the music and concentrate instead on the woman at his side.

Outdoors, in the dark camper, Mister Callahan could hear the music begin. It roused him from his dreams with the insistence of a fly buzzing in his ear.

When he first opened his eyes he was muddled, but then he stomped around the small space, shutting the portholes tight and cranking up the front windows, and still the unbearable music was audible.

He flung himself back onto the bunk and pressed the pillow over his ears, cursing to drown out the sound. Finally he took a flat green bottle from under the mattress and slammed out the door, reeling into the black night.

He started down Campbell Road, heading for the beach, when a nightmarish figure loomed up in his path. He nearly dropped the bottle in his panic and ran shrieking into the bushes across the road. When at last he calmed himself with a few slugs of warming booze, he grew angry again and swore out loud as he went on his way. He knew he'd seen Frank go into the kitchen and he hadn't come out again, but then there he was, blocking the road like some demon. Callahan drank as he staggered along through town, grieving for his warm, soft bed.

There was no one in sight when Callahan reached the abandoned refreshment stand. Far away down the beach he could see a campfire burning, and indistinct shouts floated by him on the wind. He swung the plank aside and crawled to safety, closing the entry behind him.

"Goddamn music, goddamn records, fucking hillbilly music . . ." He rocked himself to sleep on the moldy floor with his arms cradling the empty bottle.

FRANK TRUDGED UP the hill, sweating in the sun. He wore the soft gray fedora, by turns, on the back of his head, then clamped firmly down, then pushed back again. He squinted up at the porch and noted without interest the presence of Charlotte Springer on the swinging bench.

She wore a hat too, wide-brimmed, straw, adorned with stiff fabric flowers. The smile she gave him as he approached was distinctly different from the cringing, apologetic ones he'd come to expect.

"Hi there, Frank," she sang out, kicking off with her toes, rocking the bench. "What's your opinion of my new hat, Frank? Tell the truth now, I'm counting on you."

"It's all right," said Frank. It seemed as if she were speaking to someone else.

"I guess I'll just take that as a compliment." She swung herself vigorously till the chains creaked.

"Idabelle inside?"

"She's around somewhere." She waved airily but her eyes were sharp and critical as she watched him lumber across the porch and through her front door. She wondered how she could ever have thought of him that way. It was too absurd.

Frank peeked into the dining room, where the old men were patiently chewing their food. He crossed the hall to the kitchen and was greeted by the spectacle of Ida's firm, lumpy hindquarters as she stooped at a low cabinet.

"Running early today," he said.

"Oh, Mister Frank! I told Missus we was late last week and I didn't mean to be late again. I told her to just round up the gentlemens a quarter hour early, cause that's when the food's going down on that table and if they wants it hot, they best be there." She untied her apron as she spoke and smoothed her hair with yellow palms. She clapped the black straw hat on her head and gathered up her purse.

"Well, today we be the first ones and sit right up front for sure," she said, glancing at the wall clock.

"I came by early especially to talk about something," said Frank. He sat himself at the small round table under the window and gathered his thoughts.

She followed, mystified.

"Here's the thing," he began. "See, I made me a music room. I got everything I need in there, the record player, enough chairs for folks, some records, cabinets and all, but it don't look right."

She nodded for him to go on but her mouth hung open in surprise. She had never heard Frank string together so many words at one time and she struggled to understand what any of it had to do with her.

"Okay, I drew on paper what I want." He fumbled in his front pocket. "See, I always admired that quilt you made for the TV room, with all them houses on it. It's a real fine job. My mother tried her hand at quilting a few times and never did near as good." He unfolded a smudgy paper and flattened it on the table. "You make me these two quilts for my music room and I'll pay three hundred apiece. You can work out the colors."

"Well, let's take a look here." Ida turned the paper around and examined it. "These look real nice, these designs. You sure you want to spend so much?"

He pushed the bangs off his forehead; the kitchen was still warm from the cooking. "I figure it's a fair price," he said.

"Well, this banjo one would be less than three hundred but the other would be more so it works out." She already began to picture the colors she would use and the different techniques. "I think this gonna be a pleasure to do," she said.

"How long do you figure it'll take, about?"

"In a hurry? I could do the banjo one first in two weeks, maybe less."

The banjo design said BLUEGRASS BANJO in the center in fat block letters and was surrounded by two large banjos, a mandolin, and a fiddle. Clumps of pencil marks were evenly spaced around them, representing the grass, Ida realized.

The other design was a blocked quilt, each block filled with a record and each record inscribed with a song title and the performer's name.

The artistic challenge was exciting, and so was the money. Ida had one nephew in the hospital with a bad burn on his arm, and she wanted to buy something special for a niece who was graduating from high school. A portion of the money would go to the church and some would buy her a sturdy pair of shoes. She folded the paper and tucked it into her purse.

"Well, we got a deal, and now I think we best be going." She pushed heavily on the table to raise herself and smoothed the shift over her awesome hips.

Frank followed her whistling "Glory Unto the Lord" slowly and precisely. He calculated that the first quilt would be finished in time for Neil's birthday party. It would be nice to have some decoration. His new awareness of how oddly bare the room was had spoiled his enjoyment of it for a time. He now imagined the room with the quilts hanging above the record cabinet, and maybe a rug of some kind, and the cushions for the two old chairs.

Idabelle held the screen door open behind her, and the sun so dazzled Frank coming out of the dark hall that he walked smack into Roscoe coming up the steps.

"Steady on," Roscoe cried happily, grasping Frank's powerful arms to catch himself.

"What are you doing here?" Frank asked bluntly.

"I'm going to accompany this lovely lady to church and then I've promised her the five dollar tour of my rose garden, since you ask." Roscoe was enjoying Frank's bewilderment.

Charlotte, too, looked on with amusement. He really is a bit backward, she thought with satisfaction.

"Well, we best be going," said Ida. She hooked her hard brown fingers into the crook of Frank's arm and led him away, taking two waddling steps to his one long stride.

Roscoe watched them make the turn and took a seat on the swing beside Charlotte. "What's that all about?" he asked pleasantly.

"Oh," she began, vaguely annoyed, "Ida takes Frank to her church every week. Seems he likes their choir. Anyhow, I think she's a little sweet on him."

"On Frank? You can't be serious," he laughed.

"Is that so ridiculous?" She held a small white purse in her lap and fiddled with the strap.

"Why, no, I didn't mean ridiculous. It's just that he doesn't seem the type. He's sort of, I don't know, *oblivious*. I thought it was apparent." He squinted out at the sunny street, puzzled.

"I guess everyone gets lonely sometimes."

Roscoe considered the truth of the statement and began to swing their bench gently.

"Would you care for some iced tea or coffee or anything?" Charlotte asked. She found herself anxious to get up.

"No, no. I'm fine. Should we be starting out soon?" He glanced at his wristwatch and held it out to her. His wrist was lightly tinged by the sun, sparsely covered with fine brown hairs, nicely defined by bone and sinew. His hand was elegant, well kept but capable.

"We're not in a hurry. We'll leave in ten minutes or so."

"Well, you have a wonderful view," he remarked. "Look here, I'm awfully glad I met you. I can't think why the old boy kept us apart for so long!"

Charlotte laughed with him and blushed, and he took one of her hands in both of his. Suddenly they were quiet and shy. Roscoe stopped swinging and faced her sideways on the bench, and when she could bear it no longer she suggested they start out for church.

87

Frank walked through the Greek-style portico with his hands stuffed deep in his pockets, ducking his head out of habit in the tall doorway. The Greek theme was carried inside the bank as well, but out of scale, crammed with fat pillars and marbled like an ancient bathhouse.

Frank had been to Roscoe's office before. He went past the tellers' cages, bulletproofed by his own hand, to the little door at the rear, and was surprised to find his path blocked by a stout old man in an olive uniform. The man placed a sweaty palm against Frank's chest and rocked back on his heels to look up at him.

"Hold on there, fella. Mind telling me where you think you're going?" he asked with a smirk.

"Roscoe Small. He knows I'm coming."

Frank stepped back, away from the touch, and drew his hands out of his pockets. It looked to the guard like an aggressive move and he felt for the nightstick dangling off his belt.

"You wait here like a good fella and I'll check if he's in." The guard edged over to a vacant desk and used the house phone without taking his eye off the suspicious character. Then he nodded into the receiver and assumed a new attitude.

"Frank Diggory?"

"Yup."

"Right this way, sir." The guard held the door for Frank to pass through. "Last one on your right, sir."

"I know."

Roscoe came out into the hall to greet his guest. He was in his shirtsleeves yet he had an air of being formally dressed. He also had a certain boyishness here at work that took Frank by surprise when he saw it. Despite his ridicule of the job, it seemed to vitalize him in some way; he bounded down the back hallways like a young heir.

"How are you, Frank?" Roscoe patted his back. "I haven't had a chance to look downstairs since we talked but I'm fairly sure I can find the blasted thing. It was in a jumble of rubbish toward the back."

They went down a flight of stairs behind the fire door and Roscoe flipped a switch, illuminating a quarter of the vast basement.

"Follow me."

They passed stacks of dusty furniture, desks, swivel chairs, old-fashioned grilles, and then a clearing with a cot, and a time clock bolted to a pillar.

"How was church, Frank?"

"Fine," he answered automatically, then recalled with a start his unexpected meeting with Roscoe at Springer's. He decided it was none of his business.

"*We* had a lovely time," Roscoe teased. "Charlotte's quite a woman." He smiled over his shoulder at Frank who grunted noncommittally. "You know, Frank," he went on, "in some ways she's the double of my Marianne. Then in others, she couldn't be more different. But I think women are so much more complicated than we are. Don't you agree?"

"I guess," he mumbled. He was taking an unusual interest in the surrounding mess.

"Aha!" cried Roscoe. He darted into a dark corner, toward a sturdy file-card catalog of gleaming golden wood, the type found in grade school libraries everywhere. "What do you think?"

It was better than Frank had hoped. "Fine," he said.

"Now how are you planning to get it home?"

"Well," Frank grinned and pushed back his bangs. "I was planning to borrow your car."

"Oh. That's all right. You can take the car and I'll walk home. It doesn't matter to me."

"I'll come back and pick you up."

"Oh. Fine. Well, there's a garage door back here that leads out to the parking lot. If I can scare up a set of keys, we'll just back the car in and drive her away."

Alone, Frank inspected the cabinet. The drawers were deep, with rods running along their bottoms, and each had a little brass frame on its front. The wood was in good condition with its tough shiny varnish intact.

Roscoe returned waving a key ring, felt his way to the garage door, and managed to open the lock after a minute of good-natured cursing. The fresh air rushed in as though filling a vacuum and the cavernous room was lit by a block of sunlight.

Roscoe backed his Renault down the steep incline and together the men loaded the cabinet into the trunk. To their surprise, the trunk closed over it.

"Well, as long as I'm taking the car, I guess I'll stop by Music Masters and see if any more of my orders came in. Okay?" Frank grinned and tossed the car keys in his hand.

"Be my guest, Frank. Do whatever you like. I'll see you around four, then?"

"Yup." Frank folded himself into the driver's seat, found the release, and pushed it all the way back. He started up the slope, but when the car bumped onto the tarmac the trunk popped open. Frank shrugged and waved out the window and cruised on slowly down Center Street to the record store.

EMMIE HEARD THE CRUNCH of tires on ice in her front yard and trotted over to the kitchen door. Her heart sank as she recognized Willa's car. She felt that she had not an ounce more of encouragement to offer, but when her friend strode up the path with grim tight lips and hollow eyes, she wondered what was up.

She unplugged the iron before Willa tapped a fingernail on the glass, smoothed her housecoat, and answered the door with a strained smile.

"Hello, Em. Busy?" Willa glanced around the kitchen but failed to notice the ironing board and the heap of damp shirts.

"Nothing special. How are you doing, dear?"

Willa dropped into a chair, at the end of her strength, and began to laugh. She laughed until her shoulders shook convulsively and tears streamed down her cheeks.

Emmie hovered behind her, chilled by the weird display, patting her back and feeling thankful that Armand and Marcia were on vacation.

"Come on, dear. You better just tell me what happened. You'll feel better if you get it out." She brought over a box of tissues.

Willa took a deep breath. "We read the will this morning," she said, "Burt finally came down and so we read the will. And guess what—" She blew her nose and dabbed feebly at her eyes.

"What . . . ?" Emmie took the seat opposite and ducked her head to see Willa's puffy face.

"The house went to Burt."

"The house . . . ?"

"The house, my house! Ain't that a heck of a note? After all these years and now I got no home, nothing. I just don't know . . ." She chuckled bitterly and Emmie's skin prickled.

"But that can't be. You *have* to get the house. Burt's got his own place. He won't want the house, right?"

"Got any coffee?" Willa hiccupped and stared around again with vacant eyes.

"I'm out of regular but I got instant."

"Okay." Willa breathed deeply. "Ma made that will a long time ago. Burt and Janice just got married, with the baby on the way and all. They was still at home with us then. And also, I was engaged. Remember I was gonna marry Jerry Markowski, died in the courthouse fire?"

"Oh, right. The fireman."

"Volunteer. But anyway, he had his own place already and Burt was just starting out, so she made up a will to leave him the place. And she never made another one after that or changed it or nothing. So that's it. It's all legal, signed and sealed." She dropped her head to her hands and let out a sob.

"But it's not the end of the world, Willa. Honey, Burt's not gonna turn you out. He has his own place now and his job upstate," Emmie reasoned.

"Yeah, and I got nothing. A couple thousand dollars that gets split between Burt and me. That's all. You know, if it was just Burt, he'd say the hell with it, turn the house over to me. But of course Janice would never stand for it. I never opened my mouth against that woman before, and believe me, I've had a thing or two to say, but now I'm gonna say this—she's a mean, selfish, uppity bitch. Emmie, I feel like I could be turned out any minute with her twisting Burt around her little finger like she does."

"Well, nothing's happened yet. Don't get all worked up in

advance," said Emmie. She brought over the two hot mugs and the carton of milk. "I still wonder, though, why your mother never made a new will. She was ill for such a long time. She had to know how serious it was."

Willa shrugged in annoyance, then tried to think. "Well, first of all, we never knew that she never changed it from eleven years ago. And then, sure, she's been sick with one thing or another for years, but we never thought she was *dying*. It just seems to me that the ones that always got something wrong go on and on, while them that's never sick a day in their life just pop off like that. You ever notice? It's a funny thing." She took a sip of coffee and seemed calmer.

"Well, I just think it's a darned shame, that's all I can say. And if that brother of yours don't know it, he's a bigger fool—" Emmie broke off and glanced sharply at her friend but Willa was sipping wearily, looking over her cup at the heavy white sky outside that promised more snow.

"I never asked how you all are," Willa said halfheartedly.

"Oh, the usual. Getting by. Armand and Marcia sent a card from Mexico. The kids are having fun. They'll be back soon, I guess."

"Any news from Frank?" Willa asked with small hope.

"Oh, yeah. I did have a card from Pop. Let me take a look here. I know I didn't throw it in the trash . . ." Emmie muttered, disappearing into the living room.

Willa waited quietly and tried to assess her own condition. She found she was numb. Her mind stubbornly refused to go forward. And it's probably a good thing, she thought.

"Here we go. You can't make out Pop's writing but look at the picture first."

Emmie handed over a tinted photo of Nelson Beach itself, taken fifteen or twenty years before from the look of the autos in the parking lot. It showed a yellow strip of sand, a thriving refreshment booth, clusters of bright umbrellas, a spit of dark rocks jutting out to sea, and a wide blue ocean dotted with swimmers. It could have been any beach anywhere but chunky block letters across the sky spelled NELSON BEACH, CALIF VACATIONLAND.

Emmie took the card back from Willa's limp fingers and read out, "All fine here. Hope you are same. Making new friends. Getting very popular. We got a permanent guest, Mr. Callahan. Frank bought a record player and made a music room. I'm planting a garden. Regards to all. Love from Pop and Frank."

Emmie checked the front of the card again herself. "I wonder what he means about this guest," she said. "That part's strange."

"Who do you think this Mr. Callahan is? Would they have a boarder or something?"

"Gee, I kinda doubt it. Frank don't need the money and he can't stand folks staying on. Oh, well. Maybe I'll take me a trip out there one day, fly on a plane. Maybe in the spring."

"Maybe I should go out there, 'cept I can't afford it. I could go and be a beachcomber or something." Willa laughed mirthlessly. "There's nothing keeping me here, that's for sure."

"Come on, Willa, you have friends here. Belle Plaine is your home. It'll all work out, you'll see."

"Well, I'm not so sure."

"Well, I'm gonna have another cup. This instant's not too bad. You want more?"

"Why not?"

"GRAMPS!" FRANK CALLED through the screen, hugging a carton full of records. He rested the box on his knee, threw the door open, and held it with his back as he struggled through and deposited this first load on the counter.

"Gramps?" He peeked into the old man's room. It was vacant. So was the bathroom and the row of rocking chairs in the music room.

He unhooked the spring from the screen door and let it hang open while he went back to the car for the file cabinet. He shook out his arms and took a few deep breaths, bent at the knees, hugged the smooth warm wood, and lifted. He lumbered up the path, found the step with his foot, and fitted himself and his

93

burden through the door. He rested in the kitchen, shaking out his arms, then set his cabinet against the short wall in the music room.

He was going back to the car for the file cards when Neil tottered around the corner of the house, rubbing his eyes, pushing up the magnifying specs. The walking stick dangled from his other hand.

"Oh, Frank. Is Roscoe here too?"

"No, I borrowed his car. Come look what I got, Gramps."

Frank led the way inside and stood beaming at the tall golden file card cabinet.

"Well, ain't that something! Just what you wanted, right, Frank?"

"Yup. Now I gotta figure out how to do this. What were you doing out back? I hollered for you."

"Oh." Neil chuckled and shook his head. "I was shining up the stick like you showed me, with that funny-smelling wax, and I put it down for a minute to plan out something for my garden and next thing I knew I'm fast asleep. I sure wish I knew why I can't pop off at night like that, when I ought to be sleeping."

"You don't feel bad or anything, do you, Gramps?"

"Nope. Never felt better. I guess this sea air makes me sleepy, that and my old age catching up to me." He walked stiffly to one of the shallow rockers and sat, resting the stick across the arms of the chair like a restraining bar, and folded his hands loosely in his lap. He looked resigned and feeble, his hair mussed by the wind, his eyes red and droopy.

"Anyway, Gramps, listen. I been thinking all week and I can't come up with anything good. So what do you want for a birthday present?" Frank asked. "I'd rather surprise you, but . . ." He shrugged.

"Hm, that's a good question." Neil rubbed the crust from his eyes and sighed. "While I'm thinking, take a look at this stick and tell me if I can stop rubbing it. You know, the wood's so dried out, the stuff soaks right in, but I think it's pretty good now."

Frank turned the stick in his hands. "It looks okay to me, but you know what you really need, Gramps? Some kind of tip on here or it'll wear down to nothing in no time at all. I got some brass furniture tips in my kit—be back in a second."

Neil could hear Frank digging around in his toolbox in the hall. He rocked himself and thought about his birthday present. There was a set of German carving knives in Kruger's window that looked real nice but it couldn't cost more than twenty dollars; Frank wouldn't go for anything that inexpensive.

"Gimme the stick again," said Frank.

He tried a brass cap on the end of the stick and it was loose. He drizzled furniture glue into the cap, replaced it, and crimped it tight around the wood with smooth-jawed pliers.

"Here, Gramps. Now it'll last forever."

"Thanks, son. You know, it looks better too, kinda finishes it off."

"Did you think of a present?" Frank asked.

"Oh, I don't know . . . How about a motorcycle? No, a surfboard! That would be fun."

Frank stared down at Neil and pushed the bangs off his forehead.

"Lord, boy, I'm just having a little joke. I can't think of a single thing I want that I don't got already, I really can't."

"There's got to be something. Just think about it some more, okay? I want to get you something real good." Frank sat on the floor with his carton and pulled out a few records. "You ever hear of a singer name of Bob Dylan, Gramps?"

"I might've heard the name, but I don't know. Let's see what you got there, Frank."

"I ordered up a bunch of bluegrass stuff that's gonna be real good, but I bought some other stuff to try out. Ralph don't keep that much stock and it's all sorted kinda wrong, the bluegrass in with the folk music and the country-western section—it's in a mess. Anyway I took a chance on a lot of this."

"You know what you ought to get, Frank? There was a fella called himself Uncle Dave something, a heck of a banjo player. Came to the hall in Lyle one summer and played a show, but I know they made records of him, too."

"I got to know his whole name, Gramps."

"It'll come to me. . . . Anyway, he did one tune I'll never forget, played the banjo behind his back, over his head, side to side, never missed a beat of it. Folks were shouting for him to do that number. Sure takes me back."

"May be on one of the bluegrass collections. I ordered a bunch of collections."

"But they didn't call it that at first, you know."

"Call it what?"

"Bluegrass. Just called it hillbilly music. Now you got country music and bluegrass music and they're different."

"I'm getting a lot of that old stuff, though. It's on order. I went through this catalog Ralph got in the store and picked out all the records that they made from old seventy-eight's. I guess you'll remember a lot of that stuff."

"There was a guy, Dalhart his name was, something Dalhart, but I don't know if they got him on records, but we used to hear him on the radio. Lots of folks that didn't have a radio would come listen when there was good shows. That was the Depression."

"Well, here's some stuff they got in for me, got two Hank Snow albums, more Hank Williams, this one's Ernest Tubb, another Bill Monroe, and this Gene Autry. Oh, and I got another Carter Family but it looks pretty new. I got this, Merle and Doc Watson. I guess Merle's his son . . . Hey, did you know Charlie Pride's a Negro, Gramps?"

"Heck, no!"

"It's true. I saw a album of his."

"I just never liked the new country music as well. They got all kinds of instruments that don't seem to belong. Know what I mean, son?"

"They got whole orchestras, it sounds like. Some of 'em."

"I like the old style where you got your five-string banjo and a mandolin or a autoharp, and then a fiddle or two and a guitar. That's all we used to have, the strings."

"Yeah. Well, I was telling Ralph he ought to get his records sorted right. Or else just put it together alphabetical. At least you could find something then."

"Oh! I know what!" Neil cried, hurrying off to his room. He

returned with a heavy old chalk-stripe suit held against his chest. The pants dangled out beneath the jacket. "Here's what I want for my birthday, Frank."

Frank blinked up at him from the floor.

"See, I can't wear my good old clothes here even though they're in perfect condition—just too darned hot here. But what I want is a new suit, custom made, like this one but in a light fabric I can wear. How's that, Frank?"

"You want a suit like that but lighter fabric?"

"Right."

"Just clothes?"

"Yeah, but if that ain't enough, what the heck, throw in a shirt, a nice pair of shoes."

Neil was clearly excited and Frank was satisfied.

"I know a tailor," said Frank. "Knocked up a fitting room for him last month."

"Fine, Frank."

"We could go see him tomorrow, but I don't know if he could do it in time for your birthday."

"That don't matter to me. We'll get the other stuff in the meantime." He hung the suit over his arm and picked up the walking stick. "I think I'll try this out after supper," he said, strutting around the room, tapping on the bare floor.

"Gramps, what time is it?"

"Almost four, I got. But I think I'm running slow."

"Darn. I'm supposed to pick up Roscoe at the bank. Slipped my mind." Frank scrambled to his feet and dashed through the kitchen, shaking the house.

Neil returned his favorite suit to his closet, first admiring himself in the mirror with the jacket under his chin. The style was simple, classic, and could still be worn today if only the material weren't so heavy.

IT WAS A BALMY EVENING, milder than it had been for a while. There was a light mist in the air but no blanket of fog. Neil dropped a cigar in his jacket pocket and set off down the road, tapping the stick beside him. He felt jaunty, like Fred Astaire about to break into a dance routine.

The sun was hanging low over the ocean, streaking the wispy clouds with pink and violet and shading the sky to a delicate green around the edge. The waves foamed silver near the shore, lapping golden sand. You could look at it night after night, Neil thought, and it was always a delight. He took his time, enjoying the sight and breathing in the fresh salty air, puffing out his narrow chest.

He arrived at Center Street in time to see the little shops closing up. He noticed the weary, numbed look on the faces of the men and women as they shut their lights and locked their doors, vaguely worried and dissatisfied.

A shopkeeper isn't that much different from a farmer after all, thought Neil.

When he was a young man, he imagined that the shopkeepers had it made, wearing a nice suit every day, never raising a sweat, handing out credit, cutting it off if they pleased. But now he saw that they were in the same boat, tied down to a deadening routine. It was a shame for people to spend their best years like that. He wondered if Frank knew how lucky he was to have a talent that saved him from the treadmill which otherwise he most certainly would be on. He'd need only look at Armand, who saw the jaws of the trap closing shut on him and was powerless to save himself, with a pregnant wife and no prospects and still a young fella.

He reached the end of the row of shops and turned in to the beach parking lot. There were no stragglers this evening that he could see. The square was empty except for the dozen trash barrels spaced along the edge, overflowing with soda cans and food wrappers. He sat on a railroad tie and removed his shoes and socks, rolled his cuffs, and lit his cigar. He closed his eyes against the billowing smoke and enjoyed the sharp taste. But when he stood to walk, he saw that he had a problem; the cigar was in one hand, his cane in the other. He looked up and down the beach and decided at last to chance leaving the shoes at that spot and pick them up on his way home. He set out for the line of debris running parallel to the water.

There was a lot of the flat brown seaweed with bubbles in the leaves, but underneath he noticed a few flecks of bright green. He squatted, hoping to find beach glass, but it was only a new kind of weed, emerald ribbons that dissolved between his fingers. He pushed on the stick to straighten up; it was a great help.

He heard a shout that startled him, sounding like his name, but he looked around and saw no one and blamed it on his old ears. He heard the shout again, more insistently this time, and made out a small figure waving at him from beneath the eaves of the boarded-up refreshment stand. He walked back up the beach toward it and saw that Roscoe was waving and Charlotte was sitting against the structure, shielding her eyes to watch his progress.

"Hello, you two. What a pleasant surprise!"

"How are you, Neil?" Roscoe patted his shoulder.

Charlotte stood and brushed off the back of her skirt. She smiled awkwardly and stood apart from Roscoe.

"Charlotte, you look lovely this evening," said Neil.

"Neil, it's a good thing you came along. We need a third opinion on something," said Roscoe. "I have suggested several times to Charlotte that she needn't spend the rest of her life running that boarding house, especially if she happens to get a better offer, but she has this notion that she can never give it up."

"I didn't say that."

"Never is such a silly word, don't you think?"

"I didn't say never."

"Help me convince her, Neil. Please." Roscoe put an arm around Charlotte's soft shoulders and pulled her to him. She flushed and turned her face away, suppressing a smile.

"Well, I hate to take sides here, you know," said Neil. "Both of you are my friends." He chuckled nervously.

"I'm not asking you to take sides, Neil. Just tell us what you think," Roscoe insisted.

"Well, what I think is that Charlotte does deserve more out of

99

life than just running the house. Of course she does it real well. Gee, I don't know what to say.''

"Well, I never said I had to keep on *living* there," Charlotte protested quietly. "But I do want to keep it for reasons that maybe only I understand. And what about my guests, anyway? Neil, you know those men have nowheres else to go. All I'm saying is I want to find somebody to take the responsibility of being there every night. Somebody I can count on, that's all.''

"A lot of people do depend on Charlotte," Neil agreed.

"Well, then, find someone, Charl. It shouldn't be so difficult. Right, Neil?''

Neil felt trapped and uncomfortable, eager to be on his way.

"I put an ad in the paper already. Been in for a week but nobody called. I am trying." She pulled away from his side.

Roscoe sighed. "See what I'm up against? Women today are too independent, don't you think, Neil?''

"I think I said too much already," Neil chuckled, backing away. "You two are gonna have to figure this out without any help from me." He waved and started back toward the water.

Charlotte and Roscoe settled back on the sand, leaning against the rough wood shack. Suddenly a figure darted out from somewhere behind them and raced crookedly down the sand after the old man.

"What in the world—!"

"Hmph. That must be Neil's tramp," said Roscoe. "Funny fellow.''

"The tramp?''

"Well, both of them.''

"Wait up," Callahan croaked. "Where did *you* come from?" Neil stopped and waited for his friend to catch up.

Callahan was laughing and couldn't immediately catch his breath.

"I was in there . . . the whole time . . . in the shack." He gasped and pressed his hands to his chest. "I was in there . . .

your pals showed up . . . I could see them . . . heard them talking. They were there a long time . . . didn't know how to get out." He took a few deep breaths.

"So, you're up to your tricks again, Mister Callahan, spying on people."

They walked on together.

"I wasn't spying. I told you, they trapped me in there. What was I supposed to do?"

"Well, you're out now." Neil puffed on his cigar and felt calm again. "Say, I got something for you up at the house."

"Is it a surprise or what?" Callahan was bobbing strangely as he walked.

"It's just a suit of mine that I think will fit you fine. It's in perfect condition and all, had it custom made. It's just a little too hot for me out here."

Callahan was wearing one of Neil's old suit jackets that was no longer in perfect condition, and as the old man spoke, he reached up into the sleeves and unrolled the shirt, letting the blue cuffs flap down past his hands. The collar was buttoned but floated around his scrawny neck. He pulled it down in front, exposing crusty collarbones. When Neil next turned toward him, he choked on his smoke.

"All right, all right," he said, recovering himself. "I get the message. I think I can scare up a better shirt for you. Frank's a pretty big fella."

"No, I don't mind the farmer's shirts. I like 'em. I just take off my pants when I go to bed and I got me a nice long nightie." He flapped his arms and the cuffs fluttered like wings.

"Whatever you say," Neil sighed. "Look, why are you hobbling around like that? You hurt yourself?"

"Just got a sliver in my foot."

"Well, let me take a look. Let's go sit on the rocks." He pointed ahead with his cigar.

"It don't hurt." Callahan forced himself to walk evenly for a few steps. "It'll work itself out."

"Don't be silly. Let me look at it." Neil hurried to the spit while Callahan lagged stubbornly behind.

"I keep it clean," he whined. "I pour alcohol on it. When I got extra to spare."

Neil waited patiently at the rocks. Callahan dragged himself over and flopped onto a low flat shelf. Neil leaned his stick against a rock and squatted on the sand. He carefully loosened a mended shoelace and drew off the moldy shoe. The sole was cracked across, a clean break that would gape with every step. Neil had forgotten about shoes and socks when he outfitted his friend and felt a pang.

The foot was hard, mottled brown and purple, swollen and veined at the ankles, as hairless as Neil's. He saw a sore in the arch and put on his magnifying specs to examine it.

Callahan pointed to the ball of his foot. "The sliver's here. That other's just . . . I don't know."

The skin of the arch had cracked and festered. It would need to be disinfected properly at home and bandaged. The splinter was long but close to the surface. Neil took out his penknife and clean handkerchief. Callahan cringed at the sight of the little blade.

"Don't look at me, Cal. Watch the sunset." Neil made a small incision in the hot puffy skin and squeezed out a glob of pus. He squeezed again and Callahan made a pitiful sound. There was a drop of blood under the pus and Neil wiped it gently away with his cloth. He scraped the knife lightly over the raw skin until he picked up the end of the splinter.

Callahan's whole body went rigid. His eyes were tightly shut and his mouth open to reveal small stumpy teeth, rotten gray at the gums.

"We're almost there . . . hold still . . ." Neil held the thick grimy ankle with one hand while he trapped the bit of wood between his thumb and the knife blade, then drew the sliver steadily out of the flesh.

"All right. It's over." Neil pocketed his knife. "Or almost over. Do you happen to have any alcohol on you now?"

"You won't tell Paul Bunyan on me? I never drink it in the camper like I promised, but I need a nip now and then. You know how it is." His hand was poised at an inside pocket.

"Don't be silly, get it out."

The light was fading but Callahan's eyes were luminous in his dusky face and he grinned weirdly. Neil's skin prickled as he watched; it seemed for a moment that Callahan was about to reveal his true nature. Then the moment passed and Neil took the flat green bottle and poured some strong-smelling booze over the hole left by the splinter, to Callahan's yelps of pain.

"I want to do a job on this other thing back at the house. You shouldn't let it go on so long, you know." He handed back the bottle and Callahan recovered his smirk.

Neil tore his handkerchief in half and wrapped a piece around the infected arch and drew on the shoe while holding the bandage in place.

"Got anything like this on the other foot?" he asked.

Callahan shook his head vigorously.

"Well, I'm gonna check it later, just the same." He pushed himself up, leaning on the walking stick. "I guess I'm gonna head home. Want to walk with me?"

"No," Callahan croaked.

"Okay. See you later, then." Neil moved a short way off but turned back. "Look here," he said, "when you need something, like shoes and such, just ask me, for goodness' sake. Do you hear?"

Neil could just make out the crescent of Callahan's smile before he turned and blended in with the purple twilight.

"WE'RE DRIVING TODAY, GRAMPS." Frank stood by the kitchen door, waiting for Neil to come out of the bathroom.

"Wait a minute, Frank. I can't hear you," Neil called out.

He was splashing cologne under his arms. He felt nervous about the physical aspect of being fitted for a suit by a stranger and wore a new set of underclothes, a vest and stiff cotton shorts, for the occasion. He had washed his whole body with elaborate care the night before and in the morning checked his armpits suspiciously. His feet were pink from the pumice stone and he dribbled cologne on his socks as a precaution. He wore his favorite khaki pants and a white shirt fresh from the laundry.

"You okay in there, Gramps?" Frank called from the doorstep.

"Coming, coming." Neil noticed a long white hair peeking out of his nostril and snipped it with the nail scissors. He took one more moment to run a wet comb through his white wavy hair, neatening the part.

"Coming, coming!" He hurried down the hall toward Frank who held the door open.

Frank sniffed like a deer as his grandfather passed under his nose. "We're taking the camper," he said. "Got to run it now and then, keep it charged up."

"Oh, gee. I hope Mister Callahan won't be bothered," Neil said timidly. He knew that he walked too slowly for Frank.

Frank settled behind the wheel and Neil joined him up front, watching anxiously as Frank made an over-the-shoulder inspection of his invaded territory. The bunk was sloppy and a dirty fork was stuck to the tabletop, but all else seemed in order. Frank started the motor and gunned it, then idled for a few moments. The motor was in fine working order and made him proud.

"We ought to take this out in the country some time," he said, pulling out of the drive. "That's why I built it."

"Sure, we could do that," Neil agreed. "Get in some fishing."

"I thought you were gonna bring that suit, get a copy made."

"Well, that's what I thought at first, but then I decided to try something new, see what they got now. I gave that old one to Mister Callahan. It fits him real well and he doesn't seem to mind the heat." Neil shuddered. "Frank, how do you figure a fella gets to be like that? Don't you ever wonder?"

Frank shrugged. He continued silently down Campbell, then cruised along Center Street, looking for a parking spot. There were no legal spaces so he parked down at the beach.

"I remember you in that suit," he said at last, shutting off the motor.

"That was a good long time ago. You were just a little fella."

They locked the camper's doors. Frank took no notice of the children gathering to stare at the odd yellow vehicle, but Neil smiled uncomfortably at them and they giggled maliciously when he turned his back.

Frank and Neil walked back along the shady side of the street until they reached the tailor's narrow store front. Frank held the heavy glass door and Neil spotted at once the indestructible dressing booth. Frank's trademark was the fortress-like quality of his work, his use of the sturdiest materials known to man, and the painstaking reinforcement of every job. This dressing room was up to standard.

Kaplan the tailor greeted Frank with a narrow outstretched hand and a mouth full of pins. He next shook Neil's hand, darting nervously forward.

"Well, well." Kaplan rubbed his hands together. "Who's getting the new outfit here?" He straightened his glasses and peered brightly between the two men.

"My grandpa, Neil Horner. It's a birthday present."

"Eighty-five, a week from Friday," Neil added.

"That right?" Kaplan grinned. "My congratulations. Nothing for you, Frank? I'll make you a fine outfit, a nice suit. Beautiful fit for you."

"If I ever find a use for one of them things, I'll sure come to you," Frank said dryly. "Get to work, measure him." He nudged Neil forward.

"Stand over here, Mr. Horner, please."

Kaplan led Neil to a felt-covered block before a three-way mirror and fingered the measuring tape that hung around his neck. He took a good look at the old man, so clean looking, all pink and white, and went to work, taking several measures at a time and jotting the figures on a small pad. "Fifteen, thirty-two, seven and a quarter." Then, "Thirty-six, sixteen and a half, thirty-four and a half." And so on, until every important statistic was recorded.

Frank watched the proceeding with the impartial interest he took in any sort of project. He seemed to be storing the information for possible future use.

Kaplan led Neil to his worktable and pushed aside a bolt of seersucker to make room for his heavy pattern book. He turned the wide pages slowly, anxiously checking Neil's expression, until they reached the end of the men's suits.

"You didn't see *anything* you like, Mr. Horner?" Kaplan's thin lips crinkled up in an uneasy grin.

"No, I saw a few things. Go back."

They started from the beginning and Neil pointed out the different elements that appealed to him.

"See, I like that sort of lapel," he said. "It looks pretty snazzy. But I didn't want double-breasted. And I like my pockets cut in, with a flap, but slanted down, and I don't see that. You know what I mean?" He chopped at his hips to show the slant.

"Sure, I know. You want a little slanted." Kaplan made a note.

"What do they call that? A slash pocket? Makes a short fella look a little taller, I always thought. And I like my pants cut full. I don't care what they're wearing now, 'cause I just rather be comfortable with a nice pair of pleated trousers. With a small cuff," he added. "But not too small."

"Small, but not too small," Kaplan noted. "What about back vents. The men are taking two vents nowadays, on the sides. Very stylish."

"No, I never did like vents. Just ruins the line of the jacket, in my opinion."

"Well, Frank, I can see it's a family trait that you know what you want exactly. Now let's see what we have. The shawl collar, single-breasted, with no vents at all and slash pockets. Pleated pants, small cuff, say an inch and a quarter. How about a vest, Mr. Horner? I always like a vest with the fuller pants."

Neil looked up at Frank as if he'd already spent his allowance.

"Tell him if you want it," Frank said impatiently.

"Okay, a vest. With two points in front and a watch pocket. Just on one side."

"Here, like this?" Kaplan flipped a few pages in his book and tapped a stringy finger on an illustration.

"I like that. That's nice."

"Now we just need the material and we're in business. Did you have anything special in mind?" Kaplan asked, winking at Frank.

"Actually, I need some ideas. Let me see something light. Maybe linen. Do you have some linen samples? Isn't that what they wear in the tropical countries?"

"Well, linen's not really your lightest fabric. We have some light blends that are easier to—"

"No, no blends. Show me linen."

Kaplan handed over the fat little sample book and glanced uneasily at Frank; pure linen was one of his most expensive fabrics. But Frank had lost interest at this stage and stared restlessly at the sunny street outside.

"Well, I hardly know if I dare," said Neil, "but I found what I like. This one here."

"But this is pink," said Kaplan softly. "Maybe you can't see it right in this light . . ."

"I see it. Anyway it says here 'Sunset Glo' and that's what I want."

"Well, I never made a man's pink suit before. But it's your birthday." He laughed uneasily, wishing that Frank would intervene. "Your Grandpa has real unusual taste, Frank. Want to see what he picked out?" Kaplan called.

"Make him whatever he wants. Here's a hundred for advance," said Frank, peeling five twenties off a roll of bills.

"Let me just write this up for you . . . one hundred in advance . . . just a minute . . ." Kaplan poked around in his drawer for the order book, clucking his tongue.

"That's okay. We done business before." Frank waved at him and turned to the door.

Neil shook the tailor's narrow hand again. "How long do you figure?"

"I'll be calling you for the first fitting in, oh, say three weeks. Maybe a little sooner. Bye-bye now."

"Bye now," Neil echoed.

HE WAS ON HIS WAY out the door, tool kit in hand, when the phone began to ring.

"Mister Frank? I got the first one finished last night, the banjo quilt. Want me to drop it by on my way home tonight?"

"No. I'm coming up right now. Don't go anywhere," he said, unbuckling his leather work belt. He reached up to the high shelf of the cupboard and took a fat wad of bills from a cream pitcher there.

"I'm just gonna be doing a little baking and Missus is out at the

107

mall for a few hours, so come on up and see it. I think you're gonna be real pleased."

"I'll bring the rest of the money plus the advance on the next one. Bye." He dumped the belt and the tools in the hall closet on his way out the front door.

The sun was high and hot. By the time he reached the broad porch of Springer's, rivers of sweat were gathering at his temples and flowing into his collar. He nodded to several old fellows rocking patiently in the shade and let himself into the cool dark hall.

"Ida!"

"In the kitchen."

She grinned at him, craning her head with difficulty over her lumpy shoulder. Her hands were deep in a floury ball of dough. She pointed with her chin to the round table by the window. The quilt was folded there, plain side out.

Frank crossed the room in three floor-shaking strides and opened the quilt, spreading it over the table and chairs.

"It's wonderful. Better than I pictured. The colors . . ."

He pulled out the money and set it on the counter in a daze, then went back to admiring his quilt.

"I knew you'd be pleased. My friends and me worked into the night doing the quilting. I wouldn't let 'em stop till we was done." She brought up a deep satisfied laugh that shook her massive bosom and turned back to the dough, kneading more vigorously.

Frank sat at the table to examine the workmanship of the quilt. The stitches were small and even, taken with strong white thread; the fabric was good cotton, with tufts of blue wool spaced across the green ground; the instruments and the lettering were in a pleasing proportion to each other and to the whole area, improved by Ida's slight adjustments in his design.

"Listen," he began, "I didn't tell anyone else so far, but I'm planning to make a birthday party for my grandpa. It's gonna be next week, Friday."

"A birthday party! Well, well. How old Mister Neil gonna be?"

"Eighty-five. You can come, can't you?"

He turned the quilt over and admired the negative design, the

108

neat white stitches on the plain green backing; every aspect of the quilt was a delight.

"I'd be real pleased. Can I bring something? Help out with the food maybe?"

"No, I don't need any food. It's gonna be a surprise party. I want this quilt to be a surprise. I'm gonna hang it on the wall in the music room, but not till Friday."

"Oh, yes? Well, I still like to do something to help. What about other decorations, balloons and such?" She pulled a greased muffin tin toward her and began to pinch off pieces of glossy dough, roll them into balls, and drop them by threes into the cups.

"That would be fine. Can you get off early and help set it up?"

"Hm, let me think . . . I guess you're inviting Missus to come," she asked with raised eyebrows. Frank nodded. "See, we be serving about six-thirty, but if Missus lets me serve at six, I could be at your place soon after."

"No, this is the thing. I want to get Gramps out of the house for a while, send him somewhere with Roscoe, I guess. Then they'll be back around suppertime, six-thirty the latest." He pushed back his bangs.

"I know. I'll come down and set up *before* dinner, then do my work here, then come back down in time for the surprise."

"Okay. I'll telephone you as soon as he's gone. So you hang onto the quilt and bring it Friday."

"I won't forget." She pushed the full muffin tin away and pulled the empty one over. "If you think of anything else before then, give a call."

"Okay, thanks. I better get off to work. See you."

THE EVENING MIST had cleared away. Frank looked out from his kitchen door, past the hedge to Roscoe's porch. When his eyes adjusted to the dark, sure enough, he made out Roscoe's reclining form in the chaise longue. Frank reached for the jug of cider, quietly closed the screen door behind him, and pushed through the hedge, hoisting the jug in silent greeting.

"I came by earlier and you were out," he said, climbing the steps. He settled himself on the empty chaise.

"I took Charlotte up the coast for dinner. I know a wonderful seafood place. They make a ciopinno that's out of this world." Roscoe sighed with contentment. "Would you like a glass for that?" he asked, too lazy to budge.

"Nope." Frank took a slug from the jug. "I want to work out something with you," he began.

"Oh, this sounds serious," Roscoe said cheerfully.

They lay quiet for a few moments, staring out at Frank's little house, the camper, the black shadows that were trees, the sliver of moon, the pinpoint stars.

"It's just a favor," Frank began again.

"Go ahead. Shoot, my friend. You'll find me very agreeable tonight."

Frank hesitated, bothered by Roscoe's tone. "I want you to do something with my Gramps on Friday. After you get off work. I'm making him a surprise birthday party."

"What fun," Roscoe said dreamily. "What am I to do with him?"

"Well, I was thinking you could take him shopping. He was never out to the mall, I don't think. Anyway, I need a few hours to get set up. And I need to use your kitchen Friday, get started on the cooking and stuff."

"The door's always open. Now, what about Neil?" Roscoe swirled the ice in his glass and hummed tunelessly. "Oh! I have a thought." He reached for the Scotch and poured himself a shot. "I was planning to buy Neil some gardening equipment as a birthday present anyway, so what we'll do, we'll pick the things out together. There's a Sears out there that's not bad."

"I want him out of the house from about four to six-thirty."

"Hm, it's quite a short ride. I don't know how much I can stretch it out . . ."

The constant drone of insects swelled unexpectedly and then subsided. The night sounds were different out here. These insects sounded more robust and their song was underscored by the rumbling ocean.

"I promised Gramps some new shoes and a shirt to go with this suit we're getting custom made. Could you get stuff like that out there?"

"No, I know a much better shoe store, just before Beauville on the Interstate. I'll take him there first and then we'll find a nice shirt at the mall and the equipment at Sears. How would that be?"

"Okay. I'll bring you some money before then."

"Not necessary. Reimburse me," Roscoe murmured. "Now, tell me about this party. How old is Neil again?" He slumped lower in the chaise and breathed in the scent of his roses mixed with salt air. His eyes closed and a dear face loomed up before him.

"Gonna be eighty-five. And just as fit as men I've seen half his age."

"Oh, absolutely." Roscoe felt for the bamboo table, set his drink down, and folded his arms.

"I didn't fix on the menu yet. There's six of us, Charlotte, Ida, you, Callahan, and me and Gramps."

"Do you think he ever misses the rest of the family?"

Frank shrugged impatiently in the dark.

The face in front of Roscoe transformed itself until he was seeing Marianne as she looked before her illness. She was smiling at him and he suddenly felt a kind of peace descend, as though his plans with Charlotte had her blessing.

"Guess I'll turn in," said Frank.

Roscoe was silent. Frank leaned over him and peered into his face, smooth and composed with a faint smile. The whites of his eyes were visible through his lashes. Frank rose carefully and tiptoed down the steps and across the drive to his own quiet home.

"SOMEBODY JUST DROVE UP. Look and see who it is," said Neil.

Frank pushed his chair back and stood to see out the window to the driveway. There was a big dark-green van behind the camper, and a uniformed driver was walking to the door with a package under each arm and a clipboard poised.

"Delivery," said Frank. He met the man at the door.

"Neil Horner?" the driver read off the clipboard.

"Yeah, he's here.

"You want to sign this?" He handed over the board and a pencil, then traded them for the two parcels, one flat oblong, the other the size and shape of a shoebox.

"Can you see who they're from, Frank?" Neil tore a piece of toast and wiped up some egg yolk from his plate.

"Both from Belle Plaine. This here's Mom's writing. This must be from Armand." He set them in front of Neil. "Want more coffee?"

"Half a cup."

Neil shook each package in turn and hefted them. They were both fairly heavy but neither jiggled inside.

"Well, open 'em up. They're just birthday presents."

"I'll open 'em. Just don't rush me, Frank." He ripped the paper off the fatter box to reveal the commercial packaging of a shower massage. "Well, what the heck do you suppose this is for, Frank? Can you make it out? What kind of birthday gift is that, a big shower head or something?"

"I know what this is, seen these things advertised. It sprays the water at you in spurts. To massage you or something. Pretty dumb present to send."

"Yeah, it does seem like a darned silly present, even for an old antique like me. Well, I guess they run out of ideas. Oh, here's a card. 'Happy Birthday, Pop. We're digging out from the worst blizzard in thirty-five years and thinking of you in sunny Cal! Many happy returns. Love, Emaline.' I remember that last blizzard she's talking about. Whole half the side of the barn caved in from the weight on the roof. Near broke us, that winter did."

"Oh, good," said Frank, examining the oversized fixture. "You can set it for a regular shower. I'll hook it up later if you want."

"Oh, boy," Neil chuckled.

Frank stacked the breakfast things and began washing up at the sink. His heavy tool belt clanked against the cabinet below.

"Who'd you say this other was from? Armand?" Neil shook it again, cocking his head.

112

"Open it up, Gramps. I can't tell any more from the outside than you can."

"All right, already. I'm just trying to get a little enjoyment out of this, if you don't mind."

"Just open it up before I'm late getting downtown, that's all." Frank dried his hands on his thighs and leaned on the table till it groaned.

Neil tore the brown paper off a striped gift box. He lifted the lid, then a wad of tissue paper. In a protective nest of crumpled paper lay a blue-and-white chessboard made out of stone and a plastic bag containing the matching carved figures. The board was small, not much larger than a place mat, and backed with felt. The men were of a standard design. The stone appeared to be dyed and lacquered. There was a card.

" 'Happy birthday, Grandpa,' " Neil read. " 'Picked this up in Mexico for you. It's real quartz. I know Frank knows how to play. I used to beat him all the time when we was kids. Love from Armand and Marcia and Richie and Becca.' That true, Frank? He used to beat you at this?"

"He wouldn't play if I didn't give him one now and again." Frank turned the little stone pieces in his hands. "I'll teach you sometime, if you want."

"Yeah, okay. But just don't let me win on purpose. I hate that stuff. Rather lose fair and square."

"Don't worry, you will."

"Well, I guess I'll write my thank-you's, get 'em over with," Neil sighed. "Do we got any of them picture postcards left?"

Frank hunted through the junk drawer by the sink and came up with a card picturing a bustling sunny Center Street with the obligatory glimpse of the ocean in the background. He brought Neil the card and a ballpoint and went back to drying the dishes.

"Let me see. I'll just address it to the Diggory Family and take care of everyone at one shot." They both laughed. "Let's see now . . . 'Thanks for the fine gifts.' " He printed the words as he spoke. "How about this, Frank—'Now I won't be a dirty old man.' Little joke." Frank shrugged and Neil went on, clamping the pen in his fingers as if it were a crayon. " 'Frank says he's going to teach me as best he knows how to play chess. Thank you

113

all. Hope all are well.' I'm running out of space. Can you think of anything else?''

"Nope."

"Neither can I. 'Love, Pop.' If we got a stamp around here I can mail this thing right off. Just hate leaving thank-you's hanging over my head."

Frank fished in the drawer and came up with a book of stamps that he tossed onto the table.

"Wait a second. If you're walking down, I'll go with you. Just as far as the mailbox." Neil stood and smoothed his pants. His walking stick rested in the corner by the door.

"All right, but let's go now. I don't want to be late."

"ARE N'T YOU GONNA be late, dear?"

"Who cares. Sharpe's in Rochester today." Armand reached for another muffin. He broke it in half and slathered the inside with margarine. He was already full and leaned back in his chair, his belly swelling over his belt. "What are you doing today, Marcia?"

"Bridge club."

"Well, you better not come home crocked again, hear?" He leaned toward her and sprayed crumbs in her face.

"I wasn't drunk that time, I—"

"Shut up. Mom, get the kids cracking their books today when they come home from school."

"I already told Becca she could go home with her friend for supper," said Marcia.

"Then you just un-tell her. I want those kids to start doing their studies like they should. I don't want to see no more reports like them last ones, hear?"

"For goodness sake, Armand, they're just children. Becca needs to play with her friends. Reading ain't the only thing, you know," said Marcia. "And stop taking everything out on me and the kids and your mother."

"She's doing better already, Armand," Emmie broke in. "I sat with her last night and she read me *Hansel and Gretel* all by herself and did very well.''

"All right, Mom, but I'm talking to Marcia here. I want you to start keeping them home more and watch 'em do their school work. You ain't got a whole hell of a lot else to do, God knows.''

"All *right,* Armand,'' Marcia snapped. She gathered up the few plates and cups and brought them to Emmie at the sink. With her rigid back toward her husband, she grabbed a dish towel and began to dry what Emmie washed, her lips pinched in a hard line.

"Well, I guess I'd just as soon be at work as home sweet home,'' said Armand, spitting out the word "work'' as if it were a curse. He snatched his parka from the row of hooks and dragged it on over his suit coat, grunting in discomfort, then slammed the kitchen door behind him.

Marcia let loose a torrent of tears the moment he was gone, and fled the room, leaving Emmie to finish the washing alone with a sick knot in her stomach.

The phone began to ring and Emmie prepared herself to tell a lie in case it was the store calling for Armand. She dried her hands and picked up the receiver with a shaking hand.

"Hello,'' she said timidly.

"Mom, it's Frank.''

"Oh! Hello. What a surprise! Is anything wrong? Is Pop okay?'' Her heart drummed again.

"No, he's okay. Why I'm calling is I'm making him a surprise birthday party on Friday and I want you to call here around eight o'clock, call collect, say happy birthday and all, put the kids on the phone, and Armand.''

"Wait a second, eight o'clock there would be—eight, nine, ten o'clock here. Could we make it earlier, on account of the kids, say seven o'clock your time?''

"Oh. Okay.''

"So how've you been, Frank?''

"Fine. We're fine.''

"So you're making a party for him, huh? You and Pop got a lot of friends out there?''

"Yeah, I guess.''

"Did Pop get our presents yet? We sent stuff . . ."

"He just got 'em yesterday."

"Well, what did he say? Did he like 'em? Is he there with you, Frank?"

"He's out back. He sent you a card. Look, I gotta go. Don't forget about Friday, Mom. Bye."

The phone went dead in Emmie's hand. She took the pencil from the memo pad and marked Friday on the wall calendar, printing "9:00—call Pop."

FRANK ENTERED THE BANK warily. Three list-less tellers were conducting business behind the bulletproof partitions, several townspeople were filling out pink, yellow, and blue slips at the counter, but the guard was nowhere in sight. Frank walked between the fat pillars to the little back door and no one made a move to stop him.

He knocked on the wall outside Roscoe's open door and Roscoe looked up in annoyance from a desk littered with correspondence and documents. His face brightened when he saw Frank filling his doorway.

"Come in, come in. You're a welcome diversion, Frank." He shook his friend's hand and sat down in his springy chair, offering Frank the armchair opposite. He loosened his tie, locked his fingers behind his head, and leaned way back. "So how are the secret plans progressing?" he asked.

"Fine," said Frank. "But there's one thing. I been trying to talk to Callahan about being there, but every time I come near he runs off." Frank shrugged. "I never did nothing to him."

"Hm, he never got over seeing you come for him with that monstrous gun of yours, I imagine."

"Well, but he could see that I didn't have it on me these times and he still runs off. He's a little, you know, cracked."

"Well, what are you going to do, Frank?"

"I figured to ask you to ask him." Frank flashed a grin. "He knows who you are, probably. He knows everything that goes on. The thing is that you gotta get him to come inside the house. He never will when I'm there, but it's no good if he won't come in for the party. That's what you gotta talk about."

"Convince him that you're basically a harmless fellow?"

"You know what to say."

"All right. I understand the problem. I'll take care of it," Roscoe promised.

Frank's brow smoothed over. "There's one more thing—I need to borrow your car."

"Certainly." Roscoe fished the keys out of the jacket hung up behind him and tossed them on the desk. "Do you mind if I ask you a personal question, Frank?"

Frank shook his head and listened.

"Why have you never purchased your own car? Not that I mind, but I imagine you can afford one."

"I already got a car," said Frank. "There's a bum living in it."

"I see. Well, anyway, what are you up to today?"

"Music Masters got in some more of my orders so I'm picking that up, and then I'm gonna do all my grocery shopping for the party. Then I won't need to borrow the car again tomorrow."

"Well, well." Roscoe chuckled; Frank was making deliberate jokes today. "Is there anything else I can contribute to the festivities?"

"Nope. Everything's all set."

"I've already taken the liberty of putting in a supply of champagne. The good stuff, Frank."

"Oh. That's all right. And take care of Callahan tonight. He usually don't get to the camper till after dark."

"I know. I'll speak to him."

"I better get going. Want me to pick you up after work?"

"No, no, I'll walk."

"See you later." Frank saluted with the keys in his hand and ambled out of the bank and around to Roscoe's reserved parking space in the lot.

R OSCOE BEGAN TO WATCH for Callahan when Frank set the dinner out on the step, steaming under a fresh cloth, and he soon saw a hunched darting figure seize the plate and bolt for the camper. He allowed the man a decent amount of time to enjoy his meal, then strolled down the path and up his neighbor's drive, and rapped smartly on the camper door.

There was no response. He knocked again.

"Who's that?"

"It's Roscoe, from across the way. May I come in and talk?" He squinted back at the street, feeling foolish and out of place.

There were faint rustlings within. Then the door swung open.

Roscoe ducked through the doorway and nodded pleasantly. Callahan took a seat at the little table while Roscoe admired again the cleverly designed interior, the compartments of all sorts, the ingenious use of space, the overall sturdiness of the thing.

"May I sit?" Roscoe smiled as he slid onto the bench across from Callahan. He already felt very much in danger of saying the wrong thing to the sensitive tramp.

"Well? You got something to say?"

"Yes, ah, you are aware, aren't you, that it's Neil's birthday tomorrow?"

"Course I'm aware," Callahan bristled. "I'm aware of plenty. If I wasn't aware of it why would I have a present all wrapped up for him, huh? You ain't telling me any news, that's for sure."

The rush of words was accompanied by an angry spray from Callahan's mouth but Roscoe was careful not to draw back. He could just make out the shape of a sneer in the dim moonlight and the man's azure-blue eyes glimmered uncannily.

"That's fine. I'm delighted to hear it. Now the thing is, there's to be a surprise party in his honor, and it wouldn't be complete unless you were there." All right, I've said it, thought Roscoe.

"Now where the hell else would I *be?* I do happen to live here, you know."

"But I mean in the house. Inside. They want you to take your dinner at the table with everyone else, you see."

"Who's 'they'? You said it was a surprise party. You think I'm a fool? I know who sent you—the farmer!"

"Who? Oh, goodness, yes, but it's for Neil that he wants you to come. You can understand that. Frank doesn't mean you any harm. I promise you."

"Huh! Not much he doesn't. You seen that cannon of his? He'd just as soon blow my head off as look at me." Callahan squirmed with excitement on his bench.

"That's simply not true! Look, why do you suppose he especially sent me to invite you to the party? So he could blow your head off? Use some sense, man." Roscoe immediately regretted being drawn into dangerous ground and tried to speak reasonably. "Look," he said, "Frank has no wish to hurt you. He wants you to come to the party as a friend of Neil's. That's all."

Callahan smirked and pulled his dinner plate close. There were a few green beans left, shriveling in cold gravy. Callahan began to eat them one by one, using his fingers in preference to the fork. Roscoe got the distinct impression that this was somehow a hostile act and watched with growing puzzlement.

"Well, shall I tell Frank that you refuse?" he asked at last.

"I never said that," Callahan shot back. "When did I say that, huh?" He leaned forward and breathed a sour gust into Roscoe's face.

"Come, come, let's not play games, Mister Callahan. Will you or will you not be present tomorrow night?" He rose to indicate that the discussion was at an end.

Callahan bowed his shaggy head. "I wouldn't miss it for the world."

"Excellent. Be sure to be at the house by six-fifteen, no later."

Callahan laughed unpleasantly.

"Come on, you can figure it out. Be there when the others show up." Roscoe cleared his throat.

"That's right! I'm no fool."

Roscoe closed the door on Callahan's skin-chilling cackle.

R OSCOE PARKED BEHIND the camper and called for Neil through the screen door. After a moment he let himself in. He peeked into the bare bright music room and found Neil dozing in a chair, a thread of spittle sparkling between his lips. Roscoe heard an amplified scratching and saw that a record was spinning on the turntable, having failed to repeat. He lifted the needle and switched off the warm set.

"Neil." Roscoe patted his shoulder. "Wake up."

"Oh, sorry. Darnedest thing . . ." He rubbed his face with both hands and shook his head.

"Do you feel all right, Neil? We do have a date, you know." Roscoe examined the old man's face and noted again how well he looked for his age. Except for the deep grooves that ran from the corners of his mouth to his chin and the pouches beneath his eyes, his face could be that of a man twenty years younger. It was only his jerky movements, mostly his walk, that gave him away.

"I feel fine, Roscoe. I was waiting for you to come and just popped off, that's all. Don't sleep too good, nighttimes," he added. He pushed himself out of the chair and Roscoe reached out as if to steady him. "I'm all ready to go. Frank showered me with money before he went off somewheres, wants me to buy the best of everything."

Roscoe removed his jacket and tie. "I think I'll leave these here and pick them up later." He hid a smile and followed Neil to the car. "You know, I think if we had any sense we'd all wear overalls like Frank. It seems the most practical garment."

They settled themselves in Roscoe's car and he set off for the freeway.

"Believe it or not," Neil began, "I recall the very day my daughter took Frank out of rompers and dressed him in his first overalls. They was hand-me-downs with big rolled cuffs. He looked so funny—it was after Sunday dinner and we had his dad's folks visiting, quite a crowd there was, and Emmie dressed him up in his cousin's clothes. Couldn't have been more than three or so. Well, that little fella looked at us so serious, like *we* was the fools, and I just laughed and laughed till I got a stitch, that's the truth. And the next time Em tried to put him back in rompers he kicked and fought like a little wild thing. Course he was big for his age even then." Neil chuckled till his eyes teared. He dabbed his cheeks with a handkerchief and blew his nose.

"So that's the story behind the overalls, is it? Still, he stuck to them all these years," Roscoe mused.

"That's Frank."

"Hm . . . I'm taking you to a marvelous store I know, just before Beauville, for the shoes. Then we'll head back to the mall and make Sears our last stop."

"You know, no amount of teasing ever got through that thick hide of his," Neil went on.

"That's all right. He's true to himself."

Neil looked out at the landscape sliding by. He'd glimpsed this area the day he arrived by bus from the airport, but it had been dusk then, almost dark by the time they reached town, and he'd never been back since. The air was hotter inland, the land was scrubby, more golden than green under the strong rays of the afternoon sun. They passed a few acres of gnarled stumps laid out in rows, dead-looking but obviously tended. Roscoe identified them as grapevines.

"How about that!" Neil cried. "I would never've guessed they grew like that. Could we still get us some for the garden, do you think? Or is it too late?"

"Too late," said Roscoe. "By the way, have you given any thought to your gardening kit?"

"Nope. To tell the truth, I'm kinda counting on you to help me out. See, I could pick you out a first-rate harvester or a combine or whatever, but when it comes to hand tools I'm a babe in the woods. Ain't that a heck of a note? And me a farmer all them years."

They laughed together.

"Don't worry, you're in good hands."

Neil closed his eyes and let the wind cool his face. Roscoe turned up the radio to hear the news. They passed a group of youngsters on horseback and, farther on, a row of fast-food restaurants. Then a large green sign spanned the highway, reading "Beauville—6 Mi. Route 24 Keep Right. Chesterton—19 Mi." Roscoe drove past the turnoff, and with Beauville looming ahead, he turned into the large, nearly empty parking lot of Crown Shoes Manufacturer's Outlet.

"Here we are."

Neil was surprised by the plain, cinder-block facade. "This the store?" he asked doubtfully.

"It's an outlet," said Roscoe, pointing out the sign. "It's a very good line of shoes and we'll be able to spend plenty of Frank's money, don't worry."

They entered at a side door to be greeted by a blast of arctic air and a pear-shaped young man with a bristling ginger moustache.

"Good afternoon, gentlemen," he yodeled at them. "Is there anything special you're looking for? We have some terrific new casuals, large selection of low boots—you name it and I'll find it for you."

"We're interested in a pair of dress shoes. Right, Neil?"

"Oh! We have the latest in dress wear, patent pumps you're going to love. Just take a seat and let—"

"No, no, now just hold on," Neil called. "Listen to me a minute and then we won't go wasting each other's time, okay?"

Roscoe and the salesman stared at Neil with equal surprise.

"Now," Neil began, spreading his hands, "I want a nice pair of wingtips, but not the ones with the big thick sole. Reddish-brown, nothing too showy, but something I could wear for any occasion. You go find me something like that." He sat in the offered chair and smiled primly. "Eight and a half, narrow."

"Oh. All right, I'll be right back and show you what we have, sir." The young salesman waddled away mumbling, "Wingtips . . . wingtips . . ."

Roscoe sat beside Neil and together they gazed at the rows of white boxes stacked from floor to ceiling. A rolling ladder at the far end was being employed by the young man inspecting style numbers and pulling out boxes. He returned with five of them clutched to his chest and an uneasy grin.

"I think you'll find something here, sir." He knelt and uncovered his selections, pulling open the tissue liners.

"Those two don't look like leather," said Neil indignantly.

"It isn't, sir, it's the finest man-made material, guaranteed to never lose its shine for the life of the shoe."

"Son, I am perfectly capable to shine up a pair of real leather shoes, thank you." He waved the two pairs away and peered down at what was left.

"Well, this is a lovely wingtip," the salesman suggested.

"Do you know your business, young man? That's a brogue or an oxford maybe, but it ain't no wingtip. Is there a more experienced man here?" Neil craned around in annoyance.

The salesman flushed and looked to Roscoe for assistance.

"I think what my friend means," said Roscoe, "is that type of shoe, I'm sure you know it, with the perforations around the toe, a slightly more elegant shape. Isn't that it, Neil?" he coaxed.

"The perforations?"

"I didn't think I'd have to draw him a picture," Neil grumbled. "He's supposed to know these things in his line of work."

"Do you have what we want?" Roscoe asked the unhappy young man.

"Are these . . . I don't know . . ." He held out a box to Roscoe.

"Ah, look here, Neil. These aren't at all bad." Roscoe removed one shoe from its tissue and held it in the light. It was a glossy, genuine leather shoe, properly perforated, a fine example of a wingtip.

"That's more like it. Only I asked for a redder brown, oxblood, something like that. This color reminds me of cow dung, looks almost green." He turned the shoe over to examine the sole.

The salesman stood by, fidgeting uncomfortably.

"Well, do you have what I want, or don't you?"

"Oh! Certainly, sir. I mean, I'll go check that for you." He hurried down the aisle, his head hanging low.

"Neil, you're an absolute terror. I've never seen you like this," Roscoe chuckled.

"These young people nowadays are in a business and don't even bother to learn their job. Imagine not knowing a wingtip from a plain oxford, calling yourself a shoe salesman. They need a good shaking up."

The salesman returned reluctantly with only one box. He opened it and stood well back.

"Aha!" Neil cried. "Not bad at all."

"That shoe's practically red, Neil." Roscoe was surprised.

"Well, it ain't oxblood like I asked for, but it's a pretty color just the same." He examined the printing on the box. "Ruby, it says here. Well, are you gonna help me on with these, young man?"

The salesman drew up his slant-fronted stool and removed Neil's shoes, then fitted on the ruby wingtips. Neil stood and walked a few paces, then called for a mirror.

"What do you think, Roscoe?" he asked, parading before his friend.

"Very smart. Unusual color, though. Are you certain they'll fit into your wardrobe?"

Neil sat down and offered his feet to the demoralized young man.

"Wait and see," said Neil with a wink. "How much?"

The salesman gulped. "Sixty-nine ninety-five plus tax."

"Wrap 'em up."

"YOO-HOO! FRA-ANK!"

Frank dried his hands on Roscoe's threadbare dish towel and lumbered down the hall. He stood on the porch and shaded his eyes. Across the hedge he saw Charlotte peering through his kitchen door while Idabelle listlessly unloaded shopping bags from the car.

"I'm coming," he called through cupped hands.

The women waved gaily. He vaulted the railing, pushed through the hedge, and gathered up the bags.

"Park in Roscoe's driveway when you come later or it'll ruin the surprise."

"Of course, Frank. I was planning on it," Charlotte answered calmly.

He preceded the women into the house, peeking into his armload of bags, and pulled out Ida's quilt.

"First things first," he grinned.

They followed him into the music room where the toolbox lay open on the floor. He dug out four clever little clips and attached them to the top edge of the quilt. He brought in a kitchen chair and climbed onto it, holding the quilt against the wall. When he judged it the right height, he marked one corner, then hammered in a nail, slanting into the mark. He hooked the clip over it and held out the other corner, marking the spot when it looked straight. He hung the quilt by the corners and hammered two more nails in between to hold up the edge, then stood back to admire the effect. The green cotton background with the tufts of blue wool "grass," the navy block letters, the gray-and-white banjos with red strings and frets, the brown fiddle and mandolin, all gave a lively focus to the plain beige room.

"That's not all," said Frank, bolting out of the house.

"I must say, Ida, it's a lovely piece of work."

"Thank you, Missus," she drawled coolly, still smarting from Charlotte's takeover of her job as decorator.

"I'm just not sure about the color of that yarn." Charlotte pressed a finger to her cheek and cocked her head in thought.

"Couldn't very well print 'bluegrass' crost the top and then make 'em pink," she answered in a huff.

"Well, anyway . . ." Charlotte sniffed. She brought the other bags from the kitchen and proceeded to unpack, piling streamers, balloons, party hats, a printed paper table cloth and napkins, and a gift-wrapped box onto the rocking chairs.

Frank returned, out of breath, hugging an enormous bright bundle to his chest. He shook it out on the bare linoleum. It was an old-fashioned oval rag rug containing every color and texture in its braided rings. Next he fetched red corduroy cushions for the seats and backs of the original two rockers and tied them in place. He stood in the doorway to take in the whole scene. The room looked cheery and comfortable at last.

"Why, this is a fine rag rug, Frank, a real hand-done one," said Charlotte, stooping to finger the edge. "Where did you ever find it?" There were real wools and flannels in this rug, not like the new dime-store versions, plaids and checks and stripes, braided and sewed.

"Garage sale. Got it cleaned up."

"My, my! It looks real homey in here now," said Ida.

"I'm gonna bring over the cake and stuff from Roscoe's."

"You go right ahead and do what you have to do," said Charlotte. "Ida and I'll take care of everything in here. We're the decoration committee." She smiled at Idabelle who narrowed her small eyes and grumbled unintelligibly.

Frank set off for Roscoe's kitchen, where two oblongs of chocolate cake were cooling and the beef was roasting. He brought the cakes first and set the oven to preheat before carrying the heavy roast between oven-mitted hands. Next he brought the fruits and vegetables, then the champagne, and last, the ingredients for the cake's decoration.

Meanwhile, Charlotte and Ida were busy constructing a canopy of streamers in the music room that radiated out from the center of the ceiling to the walls. Charlotte had selected green and yellow streamers, and pink and white balloons. She stood on a kitchen chair beneath the center point, taping each new strip of paper to the ceiling and handing Ida the rest of the roll. It was Ida's job to unroll it until she reached the next spot on the wall, drag her chair over a foot or so, and tape up the other end when Charlotte was satisfied that the spacing and the droop were just right.

It was tiring work for Ida to climb on and off the chair. Also, she hadn't come as a servant but as a friend of Frank's, and now that Charlotte had taken over, Ida was rebelling in the only way she could imagine, growing more mulish by the moment.

By the time the canopy was finished, Charlotte felt exhausted from the strain of watching her maid trudge sullenly back and forth. She had been tempted to trade places with her, but once Idabelle got into one of her moods—passive resistance, Charlotte called it—she could no longer be counted on to use her sense.

Next, the women sat in the rockers and blew up balloons. Charlotte advised Ida to stretch each balloon before blowing, to make it easier on the cheeks, but Ida received the information with dark indifference and proceeded to blow her balloons to a noticeably smaller size than Charlotte's.

When the floor was covered with a shifting sea of pink and

white, Charlotte cut lengths of string and tied them to the knots of a dozen balloons and gathered the strings into a fat knot. She found a tack and a hammer in Frank's kit, climbed onto her chair, and tapped the tack through the strings and into the ceiling.

Ida wandered into the kitchen while Charlotte hung smaller bunches in the corners of the room and taped the remaining balloons along the walls. When Charlotte's job was done, she joined Ida in the kitchen to watch.

Frank had spread raspberry preserves on one cake layer and topped it with the other. He smoothed a white boiled icing over the top and sides and worked it with a wet knife till it formed a smooth, glistening surface. He beat more powdered sugar into the rest of the icing and divided it into three small bowls. He colored one portion pink, another blue, and the third green. He took a pastry bag and fitted a star point into the nozzle. He worked quickly and surely, extruding a fluted blue border around the top of the cake, then did the same around the bottom. He scraped out the bag, changed the tip, and turned out startling pink rosettes within the border. Next he used the flat tip to connect the flowers with green ribbon stems and leaves, and, with blue icing and a round tip, printed *HAPPY BIRTHDAY GRAMPS.*

"WELL, ARE YOU SATISFIED with your purchases, Neil?" Roscoe rolled out of the vast, emptying parking lot onto the service road, accelerated on the ramp, and joined the traffic on the highway. The back seat of his car was piled high with the gifts.

"So far, I'd say this is the best birthday I ever had," said Neil.

"How do you mean?" Roscoe glanced sharply at him.

"Well, all this here . . ." Neil ran his eye greedily over his loot. "My suit I got coming . . . Hey, there are them little grape trees again. Are you sure we can't get some for the garden?"

"Well, we could grow table grapes, I suppose, the type that takes a little trellis or something. But I suggest that we get our first crop safely in the ground before we make any additions. We'll have a better idea of things then, eh?" He turned and grinned but

Neil's eyes were closed. "Whoa! You're not going to sleep on me, are you, Neil?"

"Oh, sorry. Driving in a car always makes me sleepy. A wagon keeps you wide awake but a car always puts me right out."

"Well, then maybe you should take a little catnap. We're still fifteen minutes or so from home."

They rode the rest of the way in silence except for an occasional sputter from the old man. They were driving toward the sunset, over the foothills to the shore. The air blew cooler through the vents and began to smell familiarly of brine. It was refreshing after the stagnant air of the valley.

"All right, birthday boy. Time to rise and shine," Roscoe patted Neil's knee.

"Oh! We're here?" He rubbed his eyes and blinked around in the dusk.

"Very soon."

They were climbing the hill, twisting slowly, and on either side the houses were lighting up from within like jack-o'-lanterns. Neil looked behind him at the violet sky over the ocean and the rosy sun dipping below the horizon.

"Well, I hope that boy fixed something good for dinner. I feel famished," said Neil. "And if I don't see my favorite chocolate cake after dinner I'm gonna scream and holler and throw a fit."

Roscoe again tried to read Neil's expression and thought he glimpsed a little smile. "Is Frank certain to know about this cake of yours, Neil?"

"He better. They been making me the same one as far back as I can remember."

They pulled into the driveway, and when Frank heard the tires on the gravel he dashed out the kitchen door. The house behind him was dark.

"Did you get the stuff?" he called.

"Absolutely everything," said Roscoe.

Frank gathered up an armload of wrapped gardening tools and hurried back inside. Roscoe followed with a few smaller packages, and Neil lagged behind, clutching his shoebox.

Inside, only the counter light was on, but Neil saw the empty space where the table should have been and turned to Frank expectantly. Frank led his grandfather to the doorway of the music room and snapped on the light.

"Surprise!"

"Happy birthday!"

Neil stood gaping at the beautiful sight, too much to take in all at once: the gently fluttering canopy of streamers and balloons, the table gaily set, Ida and Charlotte in bright party dresses, even Callahan lurking in the corner wearing the old chalk-stripe.

"Whew! I don't know when I've felt happier," said Neil. "Thank you, Frank. Thanks, everybody."

"Did you bring the champagne?" Roscoe whispered to Frank.

"Yup, in the icebox."

"And the glasses?"

Frank nodded toward the table.

"This is for you, Neil, and many happy returns of the day." Charlotte presented Neil with her wrapped gift and kissed his cheek.

"Thank you, dear," he murmured, still gazing around.

"I got you something too." Callahan rushed forward to press a lumpy object into Neil's free hand, then retreated to the far corner keeping his eye on Frank.

"Thank you, Mister Callahan! Hey, Frank, can I open this stuff now? I don't think I can wait."

"Go ahead." Frank brought the packages from the kitchen and arranged them on the floor around Neil's rocker. Neil took his seat and the others drew chairs around for a better view. Roscoe stood behind Charlotte, his hands resting on her shoulders. Callahan hung back, slouching against the wall.

"Well, now, this here's from Charlotte." Neil began to shake the box, then caught Frank's eye and tore the paper. The box was from the men's store at the mall and beneath the tissue paper was a cashmere vest, cool dove-gray, cable knit down the front. He held it against his chest and it seemed to fit.

"It's so good and soft! Thanks so much, dear. This is gonna come in handy," he said. "And this one's from Mister Callahan," he announced.

The object was covered in striped paper that appeared to have been salvaged from someone's garbage. It was taped together

129

with small bits of electrical tape. Neil peeled these off and stared in puzzlement at the gift. It was a mud-colored, wart-textured shell of some kind. He was searching for something to say when everyone called for him to turn it over. The inside was like nothing he'd ever seen, glossy as a pearl with the most delicate pinks and violets and blues and greens all swirled together. He turned back to the sorry-looking outside again and then to the wonderful inside.

"It's an abalone shell!"

"Ain't that something! Why, if I saw this lying out on the beach I'd pass it right by, might even give it a kick. What do you know!" he laughed. "Where did you get such a thing, Cal?"

Callahan narrowed his eyes at Neil as if to say he expected better manners of him.

"Well, you didn't find it, did you, Callahan?" Roscoe called across the room.

"Stuff like that don't lie around for folks to put in their pocket," Frank muttered.

"He couldn't have bought it," whispered Charlotte.

"That's okay. I don't need to know where it come from. It's a real fine gift and I thank you very much, Mister Callahan," Neil said.

"I made you this here," said Idabelle, offering a small white box. "I recall it's your best flavor."

"Then it's got to be . . . hazelnut fudge! Did I guess?"

"Uh-huh." She crossed her arms over her shelflike bosom and hugged herself.

"Then I ain't even gonna peek inside. I'll just wait till you all go home so I won't have to share it around."

"Ida made that quilt there. Did you see, Gramps?"

"Good Lord! Everything looks so different I didn't see what's what when I first came in. It's a real beautiful job, Ida, real fine. And look here! A rug, too!" he cried. "You didn't make this rug, did you?"

Ida shook her head and giggled.

"I bought it, Gramps. And you're sitting on some cushions I got."

"That I did notice! Anyhow, it's getting real homey in here finally." He looked around approvingly.

"This next stuff is a present from Frank," Neil went on, "but he ain't seen it yet." Neil winked at his grandson and pointed to the shoebox at his feet. Frank handed it to him. "Now you all tell the truth—anybody ever seen a more beautiful pair of shoes?" He passed the box around and followed it with greedy eyes. "Plus, Frank and me ordered up a custom-made suit that goes with 'em. And I got me a new shirt and tie, the works. Hand me that long flat one, son." He opened the box and displayed a moss-green silk tie to a chorus of oohs and aahs.

Frank set these things aside and held up a long, brown-paper-wrapped implement. "I'll open these for you, Gramps," he said. The first was a shiny steel hoe with a red-painted handle. Other similarly wrapped items were a bulb planter, a rake, a long-handled trowel, shears, leather gloves, and a coil of green hose.

"All these tools and things are from Roscoe," Neil announced.

"Use them in good health, Neil."

"Me and Roscoe are gonna make a garden in the yard, the most uncommon garden you ever seen, right, Roscoe? What all did we order? Banana trees and almonds and artichokes, some kind of melons, them big white lilies, and what else? I lost track."

"Oh, I don't know, Brussels sprouts, snow peas. . . . I've forgotten too," he laughed.

"Well, we'll see when it gets here," Neil said.

The phone began to ring and Frank ducked into the kitchen to answer it.

"For you, Gramps."

Neil hurried to the phone. "Who in the world . . . Hello?"

"Happy birthday to you—" sang two childish voices in opposing keys.

"Hello, kids! What a surprise!"

"Hi, Grandpa! Did you really have a birthday party?"

"I'm still having it, Becca. Your Uncle Frank made me a surprise party. Isn't that fun?"

There was a fit of giggling on the other end and a fight over the receiver. "You're too old to have a birthday party."

"Yeah, Grandpa. Birthday parties are for kids!"

"Now that just don't sound fair to me. You should see us. We're having a real fine time. We got decorations, balloons, and lots of fine presents. . . ."

"You're silly, Grandpa!" More giggling.

"All right, kids, that's enough. Give me the phone, Richie," said Emmie in the background. "Hi, Pop. Happy birthday and many happy returns."

"Thanks, Em."

"Don't mind the kids. They been giggle-monsters all evening waiting to call you. They're overtired."

"I don't mind. How are you all? Everything okay?"

"Oh, sure, same as usual. We all miss you and Frank here. Still enjoying California and everything?"

"More than ever. Yup, we got it real good out here."

"Well, that's fine, Pop. I'd sure like to take a trip out one of these days."

"Oh, sure. There's plenty of room."

"Okay, here's Armand."

"Happy birthday, Gramps. Marcia says same from her, too."

"Thanks, son. Good to hear your voice. How're things going?"

"Same. Working. You feeling okay and everything?"

"Never felt better."

"Well, I guess I'll say good-bye now. Say hi to Frank."

"Sure will."

"Okay. Bye now." The phone went dead.

"Dinner's ready," said Frank. "Go in and sit down."

The places at the table were marked with party hats, a name printed neatly on each. Neil was seated at the far end, Frank at the near end by the kitchen doorway, Roscoe and Charlotte on one side together, Ida next to Frank, and Callahan by Neil, virtually hidden from Frank by Ida's bulk.

"Can I give you a hand in there, Frank?" Charlotte called out, half rising in her seat.

"No. Just everybody take them hats off the plates."

They picked up the shiny pointed hats and, finding no place for

132

them on the table, clapped them on their heads, except for Callahan who kicked his under the table.

Frank came sideways through the doorway with a tray of half melons filled with fat strawberries. He handed out the plates of fruit and mumbled, "Hope you all got a big appetite."

Callahan drew back from Frank's large hand like a snake recoiling to attack, but he was beginning to feel foolish about his fears.

"Wait, everyone. Don't start yet!" Roscoe dashed to the kitchen and returned holding high the first bottle of champagne. "We have to have a toast." He tore off the lead foil, untwisted the wires, and pushed the cork up between his thumbs, slanting the bottle away from the party.

"Hey, it didn't pop!"

Everybody expected a Hollywood-style cascade.

"Champagne doesn't pop if it's opened properly. Wine pops, champagne doesn't," Roscoe informed them, filling the hollow-stemmed plastic glasses.

He searched his mind for an appropriate toast as he moved around the table, but the few that came to mind sounded as if Neil were going somewhere or had already departed. Roscoe resumed his place and stood with an upraised glass, waiting for the others to join him, then he cleared his throat and looked down at Neil, who beamed happily from face to face, and decided to keep it simple.

"Many, many happy returns of the day, Neil. Cheers," he said and gulped half his champagne.

"Many happy returns!" the others echoed.

"Oooo, it tickles my nose," Ida confided to Frank. "I drank sparkling wine before but it wasn't like this."

"What a nice champagne, dear," said Charlotte, brushing Roscoe's arm. "So nice and dry."

Callahan drained his glass.

"Well, let's dig in, folks. Looks real pretty, Frank," said Neil.

"Like a magazine picture," Charlotte added.

Frank lowered his head and scooped the fruit rapidly into his mouth, then used the extra time, while the others caught up, to

133

ready his next course in the kitchen. He sliced a good portion of the roast at the kitchen counter and poured off the juices into a gravy boat, then arranged the meat and candied potatoes on a large platter, and buttered individual dishes of asparagus. Before he had a chance to clear the table, Ida bustled in with a stack of plates and melon rinds.

"Might as well bring in something, not to waste the trip," she said, taking the tray of vegetables as Frank preceded her with the platter. She distributed the asparagus while Frank served from the head of the table.

Roscoe refilled the champagne glasses, then stood again, waiting for everyone's puzzled attention. "I hope Neil won't feel we're stealing his thunder," Roscoe began, clearing his throat. "It's no secret, I'm sure, but this is to make it official—show them, dear." He took Charlotte's hand and she rose, blushing at his side, while he displayed the diamond on her finger. "We haven't worked out all the details yet but we will, we will." He kissed her softly on the mouth and sat.

"Look at that thing sparkle!" cried Neil. He raised his glass in the air. "To a wonderful couple. Here's to a long and happy life together." He looked at them through brimming eyes and then glanced down the table at his food-shoveling grandson and wanted very badly to shake him.

Ida showed her teeth in a broad grin and leaned forward to see the ring, murmuring congratulations.

Callahan cackled unpleasantly and drained his glass. He went back to spooning up potatoes and meat from the pool of gravy in his plate.

"This roast is so tender, Frank, I wonder how you do it," said Charlotte. "Cuts like butter!"

"It's a beautiful dinner. You must have worked all day," Roscoe said with a wink.

Frank's whole attention was focused on his meal. First he finished all his vegetable, then his candied sweet potatoes, and then the meat. He had eaten that way, one food at a time, ever since he could feed himself, Neil recalled, and he felt a pang for the strange man who was his own flesh and blood.

"So, you two pick out the date yet?" Neil asked.

"We're up against the same old stumbling block," Roscoe sighed.

"Well, I just don't know what else to do! I have an ad in the paper for someone to live in, but I only had one reply and she wasn't right for the job at all. But I have to find someone—I can't just toss it away. It means too much to me."

"Have I told you to do that?" Roscoe asked gently.

"I'm sure nobody wants to hear all about our problems, dear."

They ate silently for a moment until Roscoe spoke brightly. "Love will find a way, never fear."

Charlotte giggled and squeezed his arm.

"Anyone need more?" asked Frank.

Ida held out her plate. "I'll take an extra candied sweet. You do put me to shame with your cooking." She laughed and shook, straining the fabric of her dress.

"I wouldn't mind another slice of that excellent beef. Rare, if you have it, thanks," said Roscoe.

Neil leaned over and whispered to Callahan, "Would you be wanting more of anything? I'll ask for you."

"Naw. My throat's dry, though."

Neil reached for the champagne bottle and poured what was left into Callahan's glass. "All gone," he announced.

"Not so fast, my friend!" Roscoe jumped up and brought another bottle from the kitchen. "And there are three more after this, so drink up, everyone." He uncorked the bottle and refilled all the glasses.

"Charlotte," said Neil, "tell me, how are the old boys doing up at your place?"

"Well, quite a few of the fellows you knew have moved on."

"Really? Moved on?" he echoed, eyes widening.

"Oh, no, no! Not that! A few just got to be too much to handle with their health problems, you know, and went back with their family or into a nursing home. Mr. Reese couldn't manage the stairs. Mr. Jamison had to leave too. He's in a home near Chicago, near his son. I feel so badly when that happens, but I'm just not equipped."

"How about that! Jamison gone. It must be pretty quiet up there, huh?"

"Well, there are some new ones. It never stays too quiet for too long. Did you know Ernest Blatty? No? He was a sweet man . . . Anyway, it must be all your years of farm living behind you that keeps you so fit. I think that's a healthy sort of a life for people, like my daddy and his ranch."

"Well, maybe. But the old farm life is disappearing fast. Ain't that right, Frank? Now, you take my other grandson, Armand, Frank's little brother. See, we had to sell off our land when we couldn't compete with them corporation farms moving in. Held out long enough to get a decent price and then we sold. Now Armand earns his living selling heavy equipment there in town. The same thing's happening all over the Midwest, small farms being ate up by the corporations. Am I right, Frank? Plus, we was already down to just one crop! It wasn't like the old days when a fella grew everything he needed on his own place and sold off the extra. That was back in *my* granddaddy's day. I remember him real well, my granddaddy, lived to be ninety-six years old."

There was an awkward silence while everyone mentally subtracted eighty-five from ninety-six and got eleven.

"He moved the whole family up from Texas in two covered wagons back when he was a young fella," Neil added wistfully. "There was an old photo but I don't know where it got to."

"Everybody done?" asked Frank.

He was answered by satisfied groans all around and began to clear the table. Ida rose to help and since Frank didn't protest, Charlotte felt obliged to help as well. The whole job was quickly done and Frank sent the women back to their places. He stayed behind to prepare the dessert.

There were eighty-five little candles within the fluted blue border and one extra in the middle of the cake for good luck. He plugged in the percolator and brought to the table six each of cups, saucers, and cake plates, along with a cake knife and the creamer and sugar bowl.

"This is the part I been waiting for!" Neil shouted at him.

In the kitchen, he lit the candles, then snapped off the lights in the music room and rushed to get the cake in his hands. He appeared in the doorway to a round of applause and paraded slowly around toward Neil while the party sang "Happy Birthday to You," Charlotte and Ida adding their clear sopranos to the uncertain tones of the men.

"Blow out the candles! Only one breath, Neil!"

"Make a wish first, make a wish!"

"No, I don't wish any more," Neil said. "Since I turned eighty I always say a little prayer instead." He smiled and closed his eyes briefly. Then he took a deep breath and began to blow steadily and economically at the tiny flames but managed to extinguish only half of them. Charlotte leaned forward to help him finish, and they applauded again in the dark.

Frank felt his way to the door, lit the room, and mumbled something about coffee.

"What's under all this fancy icing, I wonder? Do you think Frank made this himself?" Neil asked.

"I know he did! Ida and I watched him this afternoon."

"Where does that boy learn these things!" cried Neil. "I could never figure it out and I lived with him all his born days, except for the time at your place, Charlotte. And I swear I never once saw anybody take him in hand and show him and teach him. Never."

"Let's get these candles out of the way. This looks too good *not* to eat!" Charlotte laughed.

Callahan pushed his chair back against the wall and guarded a fresh glass of champagne, while Roscoe came around to his side and helped Charlotte with the candles, careful not to disturb the design.

"I guess I'm supposed to serve," said Neil. "Pass me them plates, please."

Frank returned with the tall percolator and began to pour coffee.

Neil made a mess of the first slice. He hadn't cut it clean through and when he tried to lift it onto the plate, it tore and crumbled and hunks of icing dropped on the table. The cake landed in the napkin across his lap.

"Well, I see I'm not the man for the job!"

Frank stood over him and cut slices for everyone, ending up with a corner piece for himself.

"Mmmm, Frank, we must get this recipe from you, mustn't we, Ida?"

"Sorry, Charlotte. This chocolate cake's in the family. They never give it out. Emmie used to win a prize every year at our church with this recipe, and there's a *lot* of folks wanted to know how it's done."

"You can have it," Frank said unexpectedly. "I don't care."

"Well, well, there's a first time for everything!" Neil noticed that Callahan's cake was untouched. "Anything wrong?" he whispered.

"I can't eat this stuff," Callahan muttered. "Hurts my teeth. I'm still thirsty, though." He grinned like a death's head at Neil.

"More coffee?" Frank mumbled.

"I wouldn't mind some more of that champagne," Neil said, winking over at Callahan as the bottle was handed down the table. He refilled Callahan's glass and his own as well, setting it to the side for his friend.

"Oh, Frank! I've seen that record quilt Ida's working on for you, and, believe me, you won't be disappointed," said Roscoe.

"There's gonna be another one?" Neil laughed. "This place is getting to look real lively, Frank."

"She does do lovely needlework."

"Thank you, Missus."

Frank began to clear again and again Ida jumped up to assist him. They piled the dishes on the tray and Frank carried it to the sink while Ida followed with the remains of the cake. She returned to collect the crumpled hats and napkins and the tablecloth, packing it all into a sticky bundle.

"I want to push the table out of the way," said Frank.

Callahan scurried around the perimeter of the room to reach his corner. Neil took a seat in his favorite rocker, perfectly comfortable with its new cushions, Ida squeezed into the other old rocker, and Charlotte and Roscoe pulled two new ones together and held hands across the padded armrests. Frank carried the remaining rocker to an arm's length from his stereo set.

"Got some good new records here," he said. "Best country music you'll ever hear. The real stuff." He brought out a thick Library of Congress folder and set one of the discs on the turntable. "All original stuff," he said over the twang of a fiddle.

138

"May I see that jacket, Frank?" asked Roscoe. It was official navy blue with a gold seal printed on the front. Inside, he read that the music in the album was an authentic part of American history that might have been forever lost if not for the dedication of the field workers who labored to collect and preserve this part of our musical heritage.

One set of songs described seemed to deal with disasters, wrecks, breakdowns, murder, thievery, and other misfortunes. Then there were the sacred songs, grouped in another album, and love ballads in a third. In the melodies, Roscoe heard again the mournful snatches that reminded him of his own country's traditional ballads.

"You know, Charlotte, I'm real happy for you two." Neil leaned over and grasped her smooth round arm.

"Oh, thanks, Neil. I'm glad you approve." She glanced at his clawlike hand, gnarled and speckled with thick yellow nails, and remembered what she had learned as a girl in her great-aunt's house, that the old love to touch the young. "Maybe you'll give me away when the time comes. There's no one I'd rather have," she said.

"I'd be real honored."

"Hey, Gramps, did you see this? I got a square dance record here, The West Virginia Breakdowners. Some of these dance numbers they used to play at the fairs. Remember that runty fella, Rudi Barns, used to do the calling?" Frank passed Neil the album.

"You happen to be talking about my brother-in-law's nephew," said Neil. "Hey, the calls are printed out on the inside. We can get us a little square dance going! Roscoe, you ever do any square dancing? Charlotte?"

"I've seen it done but I can't think where," said Roscoe. "On television, I suppose."

"Son, roll back that rug and grab your partner," cried Neil. "Come on, Ida. Don't be shy!"

Frank folded up the rag rug and slid it under the table, leaving plenty of wide-open space. Ida heaved herself out of the chair and timidly claimed her partner. Frank changed records and showed

Ida the proper distance to stand away from him in the starting position. Roscoe and Charlotte arranged themselves the same way.

Neil's first few calls brought utter confusion as Frank tried to propel Ida in the right directions and the other couple watched Frank's lead and fell further and further behind. The three beginners crashed by turns into Frank who was buck-stepping with a traditionally grim expression, and Ida surrendered and allowed herself to be dragged through the remainder of the dance. The tune ended and Neil applauded generously from his chair.

"Ready to try another?" he shouted as the record played on.

"We were just beginning to catch onto that one," Roscoe gasped. "Why not give us another try at it? Are you game, Charl?"

"In a minute. Let me catch my breath."

"Okay, start her up again, son. I think we got some natural-born square dancers here!" He laughed with delight.

Frank set the needle back to start and took his place on the floor. Neil called as before, singing out the words in tune, glancing down through his magnifying glasses when he needed prompting, and slapping his knee to keep time. There was less confusion this time, and less dependence on Frank as the leader.

"Now, I'm ready for a rest," said Roscoe, flinging himself into a rocker.

Charlotte dropped down next to him and fanned herself with her hand.

"Frank, why don't you crank the windows a bit. Everybody's in a sweat."

Frank opened the louvers and a pleasant salty breeze freshened the room. He selected another album and rocked to the beat. "Gramps," he said, "Ralph was telling me about a search company down in Los Angeles that gets the original seventy-eights for you. It costs a lot."

"Oh! Gee, I wonder if my old ones are back home somewhere. Are you gonna do it?"

"Don't know yet. Maybe."

"Hey, where's Mister Callahan?" Neil craned around with a frown. "Did anyone see where he went?"

"Nobody was watching him," Frank said with some contempt.

"I saw him in the corner there a minute ago," said Ida.

"Well, I better check the camper, see if everything's all right." Neil left the party and went out into the dark night. A rectangle of light from the kitchen fell across the side of the camper.

"Mister Callahan? Are you in there?" he called softly, tapping on the little door. He pressed an ear to the cool metal and held his breath, but there were no sounds from within. He opened the door and climbed inside. The bunk-bed was lumpy and he felt it gingerly but it was only the blanket twisted up with some clothing.

"Was he at home?" Roscoe asked at Neil's return.

"Nope, not there." Neil was disturbed. He wondered if he hadn't done enough to include his friend once the meal was done.

"I'm sure he can look after himself, Neil."

"It's not that." He let out a sigh. "I think he don't care for our music too much."

"Oh, come on," Frank said sourly.

"I just hope he doesn't go and do something crazy." Only Neil knew how much champagne Callahan had consumed.

"I'm sure he'll turn up," said Roscoe. "Anyway, it's been a lovely party, but Charlotte is beginning to worry about the old boys on the hill, so I'm going to escort the ladies home."

The ladies rose and stood at his side.

"Happy birthday again, Neil. Thank you, Frank, it was lovely." Charlotte kissed Neil's cheek and brushed Frank's arm with her fingertips.

"Yeah, happy birthday. Thanks for everything," Ida echoed.

"Many happy returns, Neil. And we'll start preparing the yard soon, maybe next week, evenings, if you're agreeable," said Roscoe. " 'Night, Frank. Superb meal." He shook Frank's hard square hand.

"My car's over in your driveway," said Charlotte as they stepped out onto the gravel. Roscoe held her arm close to his side.

"Let's take your car, then, and I'll walk home later."

"Good-night, folks," called Neil, waving from the doorway. His frail silhouette was outlined by the yellow light streaming from the kitchen.

141

"That was some party, Frank," Neil said, back in the music room. "You ain't cleaning up now, are you?"

"Just a few things." Frank took the leaves out of the table, turned it on its side, and fitted it through the doorway.

Neil rocked himself and gazed around at the decorations as if taking his first good look at them; the room was transformed, like something in a dream.

"Where'd that fudge get to?"

"You're hungry?"

"I just want a little taste. It must be under that stuff there." Neil waved at the heap of gifts and wrappings in the corner. "It was a little white box."

"I know." Frank found it with no trouble. He pulled his chair away from the stereo to Neil's side and they each took a piece of the creamy nut-filled fudge. It was so sweet it almost hurt at first, but then their mouths filled with saliva and it was delicious.

"I'm still thinking about Callahan," Neil sighed.

Frank scowled and took another piece.

"I sure got some fine presents, didn't I?"

"Yup."

Neil took a second piece and bit it in half. "That's nice, about Charlotte and Roscoe. You know, she asked me to give her away. Hey, maybe Roscoe will ask you to be best man!"

Frank shrugged.

"They make a sweet couple, I think. But I guess everyone can find the right person when their time comes. Every pot has a lid, they used to say."

Frank made no reply. He stared and chewed.

"Well, I guess I'm ready to turn in. Thanks for making me this party, Frank. It was really something. Well, good-night."

Neil took a last look at the festive room and shuffled off down the hall. He undressed in what little moonlight shone through the windows and hung his clothes over the back of the chair. He crawled between the sheets and gazed out at the black trees and the patches of starry sky and remembered that Callahan was out there, alone, with too much champagne in him.

F RANK GATHERED TOGETHER the breakfast dishes and took them to the sink. He soaped his sponge and began to wash. Neil noticed he was wearing the heavy tool belt.

"Who you working for today, Frank?"

"Just doing some favors, rehanging a door at Ida's church, helping Ike get his truck going. Think the points are shot."

"Well, that's real nice of you, son."

"Can't work without his truck," Frank mumbled. He grabbed a towel and wiped each dish.

"I'm thinking I might walk into town with you, if you're not in too big of a hurry. I'll just be a minute." Neil got up from the table, but instead of heading back toward his room as Frank expected, he went outside.

He knocked on the camper door, then put his ear to it and listened. He let himself in and everything was exactly as it had been left on the night of the party.

Neil went to fetch the walking stick from his room. Frank was squatting in the hallway, checking his toolbox, adding some automotive tools and subtracting tools he was sure not to need. When he buckled the straps and looked up, his attention seemed to rest on the carved stick.

"Ready whenever you are," Neil said brightly.

Frank led the way through the front door and down to the street. He had to slow his walk to accommodate the old man and the toolbox was a dead weight in his hand instead of swinging along as an extension of his arm. Neil marched stiffly at his side, tapping with the stick, head thrust forward, turtle-like.

"Going down to the beach, Gramps?"

"There and around. Why?"

"I thought that stick of yours was just for the beach."

"No, not only, Frank."

"Look how you're walking now, all bent over."

"I gotta see where I'm going, don't I?"

They continued on in silence. Neil frowned down at his feet, trying to place them straight with each step, avoiding the ankle-twisting stones and ruts in the road. Frank scowled around at the sunny day, the chirping birds, the whistling breeze, the neat little houses.

They heard Frank's name called and turned to see a frowsy colorless woman trotting out of her house to meet them. She was clutching a faded housecoat to her throat.

"Frank, that garage door thing is acting up again. Do you think you can look at it sometime soon?" She blinked at the little old man. "Oh, hello."

"Hello," said Neil. He noticed that the woman's face was slick with a clear face cream.

"What's it doing?"

"Well, the timing just went crazy. It closes so fast I'm afraid to drive in there, you know? I press the button and then it shuts so soon I'm afraid to drive in."

"I can stop by later, four or so."

"Oh, thanks a million. See you later. Bye," she said to Neil, and dashed back indoors.

They walked on faster than before and Neil struggled along without complaint.

"Look at that!" Frank cried out. "You're depending on that stick. Next thing, you won't know how to get around without it!" He stopped in his tracks and glared accusingly.

"Well, and what if I *do* need the help? I need my glasses more and more, I don't hear like I used to . . ." Neil walked on a few paces but Frank stuck mulishly to his spot. "I'm old, Frank," Neil called over his shoulder. "Old!"

Frank caught up to him with a few long strides. "But you been acting older since last week, like that birthday give you ideas or something. Numbers ain't nothing, Gramps."

"I know that. Look, I'm not complaining, I feel fine. But I like this stick. I made it for myself and, damn it, I'm gonna use it! And I ain't gonna argue any more."

"I don't want to argue either."

"Just don't tell me I ain't old when I know darn well I am."

"All right, forget it."

A car pulled up beside them and tooted.

144

"Oh, hello, Charlotte." Neil went over and leaned in her window. "How're you doing?"

"Oh, just fine. How are you all?"

"Fine, fine. Feeling my age, according to Frank, here."

"Why don't you two hop in and I'll run you into town if you're headed that way."

Neil went around the car and slid in beside Charlotte. Frank heaved his tool kit into the back seat and climbed in after it, barely squeezing his knees in behind the front seat.

"So what are you two up to?" asked Charlotte, cruising slowly down Campbell.

"Well, Frank here's going over to Ida's church on an errand of mercy and I'm just going to town for a look around."

"Then we'll drop Frank off and go on together. You'll have to direct me, Frank. I always seem to miss that turnoff when I give Ida a lift." She tried to catch his eye in the mirror but he was staring sourly out the window. She wasn't certain he'd even heard and was surprised when he pointed out the turn.

They bumped along the rutted road up to the low white garage and Frank jumped out of the car and charged around to the side of the building without a backward glance. Charlotte made a three-point turn, yanking the steering wheel around.

"What's he doing there?"

"Rehanging a door. Just as a favor," he added. "You know, Frank's usually a kind-hearted fella in his own way. He just acts a little grumpy sometimes."

"Oh, you don't have to apologize for him," she said. "I know he doesn't mean anything by it. I think he's shy."

"Yeah, that's it exactly," Neil said, relaxing.

"What are *you* doing today, Neil? The beach is liable to be pretty crowded for you . . ." They could see the shops of Center Street up ahead.

"I didn't want to say before, but really I'm planning to look around for Callahan. He still ain't turned up and I'm kind of worried."

"But surely a person like that . . . Well, he's had a lot of years of looking after himself, you know." She drove slowly, looking for a parking spot.

"I know, I know, but I can't help feeling something might be wrong. You can let me out anywhere along here." He was already peering into the alleys between the buildings that they passed.

"Well, I have a thought. Why don't I pick up a few things I came after at the drugstore and the five and dime, and then we'll drive around together and look for him. We can cover a lot more territory in the car."

"Oh, fine! That would be a big help."

When she failed to find a space on the street she circled around at the bank and drove back to the beach parking lot. It was as crowded as predicted. Neil had seldom seen it so lively. It was hard to imagine that Callahan could find a hideaway in the frenzy of the afternoon.

"Do you want to come along or wait here?"

"Wait here."

She wiggled her fingers at him before disappearing around the corner.

He walked to the edge of the parking lot and then across the few yards of sand to the ramshackle refreshment stand. He looked for cracks in the wood and tried to see inside, cupping his hands, smelling the decay.

"What are you doing, Mister?" asked a small boy with blue lips and a towel around his quaking bony shoulders. His nose was dripping and he wiped it with the length of his forearm.

"I'm looking for a friend of mine." Neil smiled down at the child.

"Who's that?" he asked suspiciously.

"Hey, maybe you seen him around. He's a fella about my size, probably wearing an old wool suit. He's a hobo, I guess you'd call him. You know what I mean?"

"A bum?" The boy smirked. "Did he steal something?"

"No, no, I said he's my friend." Neil turned again to the rotten wood. "Son, can you see in there?"

"There's nobody there. That's been closed since I moved here." The boy kicked contemptuously at the boards and ran away.

Neil looked down the beach, shading his eyes against the glare, and saw that the sharp black rocks were alive with scrambling children. He returned to the car to sit and wait.

    "I REALLY APPRECIATE THIS," Neil whispered as he climbed into the front seat. He pulled his door closed, wincing at the noise, and ducked his head as they passed his house. The music room was brightly lit and Roscoe saw Frank inside, moving around with an armload of records.

"What's Frank up to tonight?"

"Trying to get his catalog in order. Which is no small job." Neil chuckled, then coughed to clear his throat. "You know, he fills out about a dozen cards for each record, who's the artist, who wrote each song, the different albums they're on, stuff like that."

"Sounds very systematic."

"Wouldn't be surprised if that collection gets to be worth something some day. Them old seventy-eights we're getting, anyway."

Roscoe drove smoothly down the winding road, enjoying the glimpses into warmly lit kitchens along the way. The mist had cleared and a half-moon was rising in the light sky beyond the hills.

"Thing is, he got a system for marking the albums to go with the catalog that I can't make out to save my life. Don't even try, just try to remember where my favorites are on the shelf."

"Hm, I suppose."

"Is it far to go?" asked Neil.

"Not very."

"Roscoe, you mind if I smoke my cigar? I brought along an extra if you want it." Neil held it in front of Roscoe's face.

"Oh, I think not, thanks anyway. But you go ahead. I like the smell, actually. My father smoked a pipe."

They picked up speed on the Interstate, driving inland over the hills, and Neil craned around to watch the last of the sunset over the ocean. His throat was beginning to sting from the hot smoke. "I must be catching some kind of bug," he said. "I can't enjoy this thing at all tonight." He stubbed the cigar in the ashtray and coughed shallowly a few times, then pulled out a stiff white handkerchief, luminous in the purple light, and spat into it.

"Maybe we should turn back if you're feeling ill. We might try one afternoon when there isn't this nip in the air."

"No, it wouldn't be any use in the daytime. I just got a little cold, I think."

"But what makes you think Callahan's in the train yard, Neil? Not that I mind, but you were so secretive on the phone."

"Oh, I just didn't want Frank to hear. You know how he is about Callahan. Anyway, I remember one time we were talking and he told me about riding freight trains, you know, like a hobo. He liked that a lot, he said."

"Well, as I told you on the phone, this isn't a real trainyard we're going to, not any more."

"Well, Charlotte already drove me all over town and I keep checking the beach and I don't know what else to try. Then I remembered that he's real partial to trains. But maybe it is just a waste of time." Neil looked suddenly downhearted.

"Maybe not. It's not such a hike on foot, you know. It's longer for us in the car. Perhaps he *would* go there if he's so mad for trains."

"That's what I thought."

"There it is, just up ahead."

Roscoe slowed on the shoulder of the road and bumped onto the rutted unpaved lot. Great stacks of oily railroad ties defined the yard, rusted rail littered it. There were half a dozen freight cars leaning back in the tall weeds, standing open. Roscoe shut off his motor but left the headlights on to guide them over the terrain.

Neil zipped his jacket before stepping out into the brisk night air. The wrecked trains looked like fine hiding places and Neil made straight for them. Roscoe followed a few paces behind.

"Mister Callahan? Are you in there? It's me, Neil." He called the same words into the pitch-black depths of several cars. Their floors were level with his shoulders as he leaned into the dank darkness. He was fast losing heart when he heard a rustling in the bushes behind the wrecks.

"Are you in there, Mister Callahan? Please, I only want to know if you're okay and then I'll go." He parted the thorny branches and strained forward to see.

"Hold it right there, buddy." The voice was menacing but broke into a hacking cough.

"Who is that?" called Neil. "I don't want any trouble. I'm just looking for somebody."

"Maybe we'd better go," said Roscoe, pulling lightly on the old man's sleeve.

"Who you looking for?" called a second voice.

"A friend of mine, Mister Callahan."

He heard the muffled laughter of several men and drew back, chilled, the hair on his neck prickling.

"Got no 'misters' here. What's he look like, your friend?"

"He's kind of small, sandy hair. He got beautiful blue eyes. You couldn't miss 'em."

"This your friend or your sweetheart?" There was more laughter.

"Let's go, Neil. He's not here." Roscoe tugged harder and Neil took a few steps back.

"Wait. Listen," Neil shouted. "If he turns up here could you tell him Neil was looking for him? Say that I just want to know if he's okay. His name's Callahan."

"All-righty, Neil," a voice crooned nearby. "Time for you to go bye-bye."

Neil was shivering and allowed himself to be led away. Roscoe helped him into his seat and started up the motor. They bumped over the scattered rails, circling around to get back on the highway, then drove several more miles inland before they were able to turn and head back to town.

"HELLO, I HOPE I'm not late." Neil grinned and leaned his walking stick against the work table.

"Ah, Mr. Diggory, yes, your fitting." Kaplan jumped up from his machine and came around the table extending his narrow white hand.

"No, I'm Horner. Frank's my daughter's boy," Neil explained.

"Oh, sorry. I'll be with you in a minute. Frank around?" Kaplan called from behind the curtained doorway.

"He's doing a job over at the mall. I walked here. That's why I'm a little late." Neil blew his nose on a fresh handkerchief. His throat felt raw after his effort.

"Don't you live way up on the hill there?" Kaplan asked. He brought out a bundle of pink linen, and the sight made Neil's heart quicken.

"It's not that far. I like to walk, anyway, keep active."

"But down is one thing, and up is another." Kaplan shook out the first piece, the trousers. "Step inside there and try these on, please. Watch the pins in the bottom."

He held the door of Frank's vaultlike dressing room for Neil to pass through. There was a full-length mirror inside and a brass door latch and four brass hooks on the wall. There was a low built-in bench where Neil sat to remove his shoes. He stepped out of his khakis and pulled on the pale linen pants. They were nubby but slippery-soft against his bare legs. The bottoms were bunched up with excess fabric and he couldn't fairly judge the fit.

He unlatched the door and hobbled out. "This material feels wonderful!" he said. "So cool."

"Step up here and I'll fix the cuffs so you can see."

Kaplan helped him step onto the felt-covered block in front of three mirrors. Hundreds of pins glinted around the block on a square of carpet and Kaplan popped a few in his mouth. He straighted the fabric of one leg, cuffing the bottom and securing it with two pins inside, then did the same to the other leg and satisfied himself that they were even.

"So, what do you think?"

Neil turned on the block to catch every angle, frowning with concentration. He looked over his shoulder to see the back and rechecked it in profile; there was a small pucker in the back seam below the waistband.

"See there? It's sort of sticking out?"

"Yes, yes, it's no problem, don't worry." Kaplan made a mark there with a wedge of sky-blue chalk. "Try on the vest."

He held it out for Neil to slip into, then smoothed it down and adjusted the belt in back. He buttoned it for him and felt the armholes critically.

"Feels a little loose here, doesn't it?" Kaplan sighed.

"Is that hard to fix?"

"No, no, that's what the fitting's for." He pinned up the slack.

"I'm real pleased, though." Neil smiled at the tailor in the mirror and then at his own reflection.

"Try the jacket." Kaplan helped him on with it and stepped back to allow him a clear view.

"This is wonderful, better even than I pictured."

"I think I like the no-vents look," Kaplan decided. "It hangs nicely."

Neil turned again on the block and together they admired the elegantly cut pink suit. It was unusual, to be sure, but on the old man it looked fine. Kaplan was relieved and began to feel some of Neil's excitement.

Neil tried the pockets and was disappointed to find them basted shut. He buttoned the jacket and smoothed it down, then opened it to show off the vest. He craned around to see for himself his unvented back and it was a fine fit, a real piece of workmanship.

"I want to check the sleeve." Kaplan darted forward and pulled Neil's shirt cuff down inside and held his arm out at an angle, frowned, and made a blue slash.

"I love this suit, Mr. Kaplan! I hope Frank's paying you enough for this," Neil laughed.

"Don't you worry about that part, Mr. Horner. Frank and I, we're both businessmen. Now, if you'll slip these off . . ." He took away the jacket and vest, and Neil shut himself in the dressing room.

"How soon, do you think?" asked Neil, handing over the pants.

151

"I have to say two weeks. I'm a little jammed up but I'll get to it as soon as I can. Say, two weeks on the outside. I'll give you a call."

"Okay, thanks again." Neil shook the narrow hand. "I really love what you did."

"Bye, now."

Neil blinked for a moment, dazzled in the sunlight, then walked slowly up the block, tapping his stick on the pavement. He thought he recognized a hunched figure up ahead and hurried on, but when he reached the spot he was alone. He peered down the alley and saw only rows of garbage cans and stacked crates, and beyond that a patch of beach and ocean. He moved carefully through the rubbish, calling the name softly. When he reached the open end, he looked in all directions but saw only playing children and sunbathers and surfboards standing in the sand.

N EIL LAY FULLY DRESSED under his light blanket. He clutched one of Frank's flashlights to his side and shivered with excitement at what he was planning to do. He listened to Frank urinate in the bathroom next door and knew he wouldn't have much longer to wait.

He forced himself to lie still another fifteen minutes after Frank had closed himself in his room, then rose carefully to avoid the creaking of his bedsprings. He tucked his shoes under one arm, felt around in the dark corner for his stick, and tiptoed down the hall.

He sat outside on the kitchen step and tied on his shoes. It was a clear night, but the breezes were damp and he wished he'd thought to wear Charlotte's knitted vest under his windbreaker. He buttoned the tab across the collar and set off down the road.

Every house he passed was darkened, there were no human sounds, no cars passed him on the road. He felt that he was all alone in the world. It was dreamlike, eerie. He tried to cheer himself by humming softly in time to his pace, but it made his throat tickle and he stopped.

When he reached Center Street there was a little activity down the block outside the tavern. A neon light blinked there and men and women leaned together against the cars, laughing in the strange glow. He turned the other way, toward the beach.

He crossed the empty parking lot and sat on a railroad tie to remove his shoes and socks. The breezes blew harder here and wetter. He turned his collar up and walked the cold sand to the refreshment booth.

"Mister Callahan? Are you in there?" he called hoarsely, and knocked and listened. He got down on his hands and knees and felt the boards along the side for Callahan's secret entry. He found the loose board and swung it aside. Training the flashlight inside, he saw bottles and bags and rubbish that looked like Callahan's leavings. He wriggled through the opening onto the damp floor.

He had a note written out and read it once again after pinning it to the wall with four thumbtacks. "Dear Mr. Callahan, I am sorry if you left on account of anything we done. I am worried and I wish that you will let me know you are all right if you see this. You are always welcome back, no questions asked. Your Friend, Neil." He rested against the moldy wood, then dragged himself outside and swung the board back in place.

He set off for the rocks, walking high on the beach, away from the water. It looked forbidding in the night, an enveloping blackness that swept up over the sand, erasing it, and then sucked back on itself leaving a glimmer behind.

The moon hung over the rocks ahead, but Neil couldn't see the man in it. When he was a small boy and his dad told him about the man in the moon, he didn't understand, couldn't see anything like a face in the sparkling surface. Then at school the teacher told them a rhyme about the man in the moon and the children drew real faces in their nighttime skies, but he never saw the face in the moon, only pretended that he did. And when Emmie was small and Mamie held her up to see the man in the moon, Neil looked too, but he still didn't see.

The rocks were slippery with spray. Neil stood at the wide base of the spit and called the name, cupping his hands into a megaphone. It frightened him to make so much noise alone in the night, but he walked farther down the spit, calling out, until the waves lapped at his bare feet. He stumbled in his rush to reach higher ground, wetting his knees and cuffs, then leaned against the rocks to roll the soaked pants legs, thereby wetting his seat as well.

He sighed and shook his head, disgusted with his failure and his carelessness. It was time to head for home. He was tired and felt certain he could pop off to sleep with no trouble tonight. He traced his steps to the spot where he'd left his shoes and socks and sat to pull them on. They were damp too, inside and out.

"THANKS, FRANK. That was good."

"You didn't eat the hash browns."

"Didn't have a big appetite today, but it was good. What're you working on today?" Neil wiped his mouth, then his runny nose, and crumpled the napkin.

"Putting in a floor in a guy's cellar, raising it up. Just hard-packed dirt down there now."

"You doing cement work?" Neil was surprised.

"No, I'm just gonna throw a frame around the whole thing and lay down boards. If they got the order right this time." Frank collected the breakfast things and brought them to the sink. "What're you doing today?"

"I'm not sure. I was thinking I might mess around out back, sort of get the yard ready for when my stuff comes. I'll see how I feel. This cold is bothering me a little."

"You do look kinda squirrely, Gramps."

"Hey, who used to say that, Frank? Your dad, wasn't it?"

"Anyhow, you better take a day in bed." Frank washed the dishes and silver under steaming water.

"I did want to try out them new tools. I'll see how I feel in a bit." He cleared his throat. He wanted badly to cough but controlled himself in front of Frank.

"Just do me a favor and stay in bed today so I don't worry, you hear? And drink some juice. There's apple and orange. I gotta go." He wiped his hands on his thighs, lifted the toolbox off the floor with a grunt, and left the house.

Neil watched from the window, and when Frank was out of sight he went out to the camper to see if there was any sign of Callahan. He hadn't much hope but continued to check every day. Again, there was no reply to his knock, nothing disturbed inside, no note, no sign. As he started back to the house the phone began to ring and he hurried to answer it.

"Hello, Neil. It's me, Charlotte."

"Oh, hello." He broke off. The deep breathing had stirred the congestion in his chest and he coughed into his handkerchief. "Hold on a minute . . ." He coughed again and brought up some clear fluid. The pain seemed to be moving from his throat into his lungs. "Sorry," he said, "I must've got a touch of something. Flu, feels like."

"Oh. I was calling to invite you to come out to the mall with me. I have a few errands and then I thought I'd take you to lunch. There's a new Italian place there with a salad bar and everything, but if you're not feeling well . . ."

"It sounds nice, but I better take Frank's advice, I think, and get back in bed, catch this thing before it gets worse." He pulled a chair closer to the phone and sat, pressing a knobby fist to his ribs.

"Oh, well, we can do it any time. Listen, why don't I stop by with some nice soup and magazines or something. Would you want to borrow a TV set? There's a portable here we never use."

"No, don't go to any trouble. Really, I'll be fine."

"Don't be silly. It's no trouble at all. I'll be by in a half hour or so with the best chowder you ever tasted. Bye, now."

Neil was dizzy when he stood to replace the receiver. It annoyed him to be ill. He'd rarely been ill in his life and had no patience with bed rest and mushy food and coddling. He sighed and got his robe from his room and returned to the kitchen to wait.

Charlotte's car rolled up in a short while and Neil waved from the door with a wan smile. She walked toward him with an enormous stockpot in her hands.

"Oh, Neil, you do look off. Let me feel your forehead," she murmured, setting her pot on the stove. "I know a very good doctor in town. Maybe you should let him examine you."

"I got no use for any doctors. All it is is a touch of flu, one of those twenty-four-hour things, I bet. This soup of yours is gonna do me more good than any doctor."

"Well, let's get you tucked in. I can manage here." She shooed him down the hall and found a ladle, soup bowl, and spoon. She tested the chowder and decided it would take a while to heat up. She let herself into Neil's room and pulled the chair close to the bed. He was sitting up against the pillows and his face was flushed.

"Neil, do you have a thermometer here?"

"I doubt it. Never seen one around."

"Well, will you take a couple of aspirins? You felt a little feverish to me."

"Oh, all right," he sighed. "In the medicine cabinet." He waved listlessly toward the bathroom and Charlotte trotted into the hall.

"Here we go," she sang, holding out the two tablets and a glass of tepid water. "I better check on that soup."

Neil lay back and shut his eyes. It was going to be a tedious day.

"GRAMPS," FRANK CALLED. He dropped his toolbox by the door and lumbered down the hall to Neil's room.

The door stood open, and he saw the old man sleeping against a mound of pillows, bundled up in his robe and blankets. His mouth hung open and the breath rattled in his chest. Frank moved closer, then decided to let him sleep. He backed toward the door, stepping quietly, but knocked into the walking stick which clattered to the floor.

"Oh, Frank. What time is it?" Neil cleared his throat and rubbed his eyes. "Is Charlotte gone?" he whispered.

"I guess. I didn't see her car."

"Oh. She came by to fuss over me. Finally had to pretend to fall asleep and then I guess I really did." Neil began to laugh but a cough cut him off.

156

"Feel any better?" Frank asked, sitting on the bed.

"Oh, I guess. It's just a little chest cold is all. I'll be okay by morning. Charlotte wanted to get her doctor over here but I told her I got no use for them guys."

"Are you sure?"

"Listen, they still don't know how to cure the common cold, right? And that's what I got, so who needs 'em!"

"Want supper?"

"Heck no! I'm so stuffed with soup and tea—in fact I think my bladder's gonna burst if I don't get up this minute." Neil threw back the covers and swung his feet down to the rug. He felt light-headed sitting up, and dizzy when he stood, but did his best to hide it from Frank as he made his way to the bathroom.

"Now I don't know how I'm gonna sleep after napping all day long," he complained, climbing back into bed.

"How about if I teach you chess tonight?"

"Okay."

"I want to make me a sandwich first and get you some more tea."

Neil covered himself and lay back to watch the sky darken outside his window. The constant rattling in his chest made him want to cough, but coughing was becoming painful and difficult to stop. He tried to relax and take his mind off it.

Frank returned with Neil's mug of tea and a thick pot roast sandwich for himself. He set the night table between them and brought over the chess set from the bureau. The pieces were arranged incorrectly and Frank put them right with one hand, eating with the other.

"Okay. Do you know how the pieces move?"

"I told you, I never played this game at all."

"Okay, first, all these little guys are pawns. They can move two squares to start but after that they can only move one. They can only move forward like this, but they can take a piece crossways like this." Frank moved a few pieces to demonstrate, then replaced them.

"I hope they all ain't that complicated."

"No, just listen. You need your pawns 'cause they change into

157

other pieces if you can get them all the way across the board."

"What pieces they turn into?" Neil asked, determined not to learn.

"It's your choice," Frank answered patiently. "Any piece that was taken already you can get back that way."

"What if none was taken yet?"

"Don't worry about it, Gramps. You couldn't ever get a pawn all the way across without you lose plenty of pieces first. But there's other stuff more important than that."

"Frank, this ain't my game, I can tell already. Don't we got a pack of cards around here somewhere?" Neil sank back in his pillows and looked sourly at the blue-and-white board.

"No. Tell me what you don't get."

"All right. I guess I got the pawns. What's next?" Neil cleared his throat and sipped some tea. It was loaded with honey and lemon.

"Okay. I'm gonna name you the other pieces. These here are called castles or rooks."

"Two names, now. Lord have mercy!"

"Come on, Gramps, we could have fun with this if you stop interrupting and pay attention."

"Sorry. Go on."

"We'll call 'em castles then since that's what they look like. These next ones are knights, then the bishops, the king and the queen." Frank noticed that his kings and queens were on the wrong color squares and he shifted them around. "Did you get that?"

"Hush up, I think I hear something," Neil hissed. He sat up and leaned an ear toward the window. It was dark outside now and quiet. Then they heard a dog howl.

"That's all it was," said Frank. "Now you say the names of the pieces back to me."

Neil stared up at Frank with imploring eyes.

"Oh, all right." Frank threw down the end of his sandwich and stood up. "You *know* he'll just get scared off again if I go out there . . ."

"Please, Frank. I gotta know."

Frank stood a moment longer, weighing something in his mind, then stomped down the hall and out the kitchen door, letting it slam on its springs. He knocked loudly on the little metal door and waited, disgusted, outside his own camper.

"I'm coming in," he warned.

He opened the door and crouched to enter, sniffing the air suspiciously. He saw immediately that the bunk had been used. On a hunch, he ran his hands under the covers and, sure enough, found a flat empty bottle in a twisted paper bag.

"There you go, Gramps," he said, tossing the evidence into Neil's lap.

"He's back!" cried Neil. "He's really back!" He turned the bottle over in his hands excitedly.

"Left his calling card." Frank snorted.

"You didn't see him?"

"Nope."

"Frank, I gotta ask you, as a personal favor." Neil's voice quavered. "Would you fix a sandwich or something and set it out in the camper for him? I guess we're the ones got him used to regular meals."

"Yeah, yeah."

Frank split another roll, buttered the inside to keep it from getting soggy, stuffed it with chunks of pot roast, and put it on a plate with a ripe tomato and a mound of potato salad. He covered it with a clean cloth and brought it to the camper. He set the plate on the little table and then, before leaving, he peeled two singles off his roll of bills and anchored them under the plate.

N EIL TOSSED AND TURNED in his sleep. He threw off the covers and banged his elbow against the wall and woke with a start. He was drenched with sweat. Even the sheet beneath him was soaked, and he thought of taking more aspirin.

He eased himself out of bed in slow stages, anticipating the dizziness, but on his feet he was still as wobbly as a new calf. He shuffled to the bathroom and leaned his weight against the sink while he hunted for the medicine in the dazzling light. He took two tablets and washed them down with cold water, then splashed a little on his face and neck.

He had to urinate from all the tea and soup, but felt unable to stand, and vaguely ashamed, he sat on the seat. He remained there, gathering strength for the trip back to bed, when the rattling in his chest compelled him to cough into a handful of toilet paper. He spat up some yellowish phlegm and his chest felt momentarily clear, then the rattling resumed. He coughed up some more of the thickened phlegm and his chest felt strained, the muscles, the bones, the lungs themselves. It was a horrible ache deep inside. He reluctantly planned on another day of bed rest, soup, and tea.

He hoisted himself up, pulling on the sink, and rested against the door before lurching through the dark to his bed. The damp sheet felt cool now. His head continued to spin when he lay down, but after a while the spinning stopped and he dozed, uncovered, through the night.

F RANK WAS PUSHING a piece of toast around his plate, sopping up yolk and butter, when Neil stumbled into the room, smiling feebly.

"Phone wake you, Gramps?"

"No. Is it late?" Neil pitched into his chair.

"Not very. You any better?"

"Oh, not too bad. Didn't eat nothing solid yesterday, you know."

"I'll fix you something. What do you want?"

Neil tried to think of something he could imagine eating. "I guess I don't feel too particular. I'll have whatever you had. Something easy."

"Go back to bed and I'll bring in a mess of scrambled eggs and ham and toast. And tea."

Neil rose unsteadily. "Didn't altogether wake up yet," he mumbled. He made his way back to bed and flopped gratefully onto the pillows, his head and heart pounding together.

Soon Frank brought in a tray. The food looked good and

smelled good too, but when Neil took a forkful of egg in his mouth he felt sure he wouldn't be able to keep it down. He swallowed with effort and felt a sweat break out at his hairline.

"Here you go, Gramps." Frank set the tea on the nightstand and moved it closer to the bed.

"Delicious, as usual," Neil said weakly, taking a small bite of toast.

"Ida's coming by with the other quilt. Be here any minute now. She said she did the quilting with her friends from church in a day and a half." Frank grinned down at Neil and gently swung his arms. "Well, if you need anything, holler. I'll be around."

"Okay, son." Neil took another small bite. "Could you just crack this window before you go? I feel kind of stuffy without a window cracked."

Frank leaned across the bed and pushed the sash up an inch and a half. Then he left the room and Neil heard him walk to the front door to watch for Ida.

He tried another forkful of egg and gagged on it. He listened for Frank, then tilted his plate into the window's opening and slid the eggs and ham out into the shrubbery. He nibbled the toast and sipped his tea.

He first heard Frank calling out the door, then the slam of the screen, and it reminded him of the old days in Belle Plaine when the boys were still small and watched for him and their dad to return from town. It would be the dead of winter, with snowdrifts as tall as a man and temperatures below zero. Instead of risking a breakdown in one of the trucks, they'd hitch up the two old horses and bundle up real good, leave at daybreak, be back by dusk.

"Gramps! Look at this!" Frank yelled from the hall. He arrived breathless in the doorway behind the upheld quilt.

It was a blocked quilt, each square appliqued with a black record and a different-colored label embroidered with a song title and the singer's name. The blocks were separated by strips of red for a windowpane effect and a wide blue strip bordered the whole. The quilting stitches outlined the records and blocks. The border was stitched in a diamond pattern.

Ida stood shyly behind Frank while her work was admired.

161

"It's just beautiful," said Neil. He cleared his throat and reached for a tissue.

Frank flung the quilt across Neil's bed and Ida followed him into the room.

"How you feeling today?" she asked.

"Oh, not too bad. A little achey." He allowed himself a cough and brought up more phlegm. He spat into the tissue while Frank examined the underside of the quilt.

"Missus gonna ask me for a report." Ida smiled down at him. His skin looked blotchy and drawn.

"You tell Charlotte that one more day in bed ought to see the end of this. And some of the credit has to go to that chowder of yours."

She ducked her head and grinned broadly.

Neil felt suddenly tired. He stopped trying to appear lively and let his eyelids drop.

"I think Mister Neil wants his rest," Ida whispered to Frank.

"Oh. Well, I'm gonna hang this up. I got a big piece of wall's been waiting for this." He folded the quilt sloppily and crossed the hall to the music room. Ida closed Neil's door quietly behind her.

"WATCH OUT! Get back! Get away from there!"

Frank heard the weird shouts as he slowly awoke in the dark. He held his clock in the stripe of moonlight shining through the curtains and saw that it was after three o'clock.

"It's going the wrong way!"

There was more that he couldn't make out. He threw off his covers and tiptoed to his grandfather's door. He put his ear to the wood and held his breath.

"Whoa!" More garbled words.

Frank turned the knob and let himself in. He saw that Neil was uncovered and as he drew near, the old man opened his eyes and looked straight at him, greatly agitated.

"It's just me, Gramps. What's the matter?"

162

"He's hurt bad!" Neil clutched Frank's pajama sleeve.

"Nobody's hurt, Gramps. You had a bad dream is all."

Frank tried to settle him back down on the pillows. He brushed the damp hair off Neil's hot forehead with his wide palm.

"You're running a fever. Just lie still. I'll get you something."

Neil lay rigid, staring intently at the ceiling, and seemed to be listening to something. Frank backed out of the room and fetched two aspirins and a glass of water from the bathroom.

When he returned to Neil's side, the old man's eyes were closed and he appeared to be sleeping. Frank covered him with the blanket and leaned across the bed to close the window's small opening. He went back to his own bed and lay awake a while, listening, then dozed off.

"YOU JUST STAY PUT. Don't stir for nothing, hear?" Frank laid his fan of cards on the bed and stomped to the kitchen to see who was pulling up the driveway.

It was a big green delivery van. The uniformed driver hopped down from the cab and strode around to the back of his truck, taking no notice of Frank on the doorstep. Then he approached with a clipboard of fluttering papers.

"This the Horner residence?"

"Oh, yeah," said Frank.

"I got three parcels here for you. Sign, please." The man handed Frank the clipboard and a pencil. He looked Frank up and down and figured him for paid help. "Want to give me a hand with it, buddy?"

Frank followed to the rear of the truck and the man handed him down two long, rough wood crates and a burlap-wrapped tree. Frank set them aside on the grass and the driver bolted shut the double doors, hopped into his cab without a word, and drove away.

Frank dashed inside. "Gramps! Your stuff came. The stuff for the garden—it's here." He stopped in Neil's doorway as the old man pulled himself up and grinned weakly.

163

"The stuff came?" he echoed.

"All them bulbs and seeds and stuff. There's a tree, too." Frank came forward and touched Neil's forehead. "Are you sure you feel okay? You still feel feverish to me."

"One more day of this and I'll be fine. All these covers is why I'm hot." He threw the blanket aside and let his eyelids droop.

"I'm gonna fix you another cup of tea. Then you drink your tea and I'll bring them crates around back and unpack everything so's you can see."

As soon as Frank left the room, Neil began to cough. It wracked his chest and his eyes brimmed from the pain. He spat thickly into a tissue and lay back, exhausted.

Frank returned with the mug of tea but Neil appeared to be sleeping. His hair was damp and his cheeks flushed. Frank set down the tea and backed quickly out of the room.

He dialed Springer's. Charlotte answered the phone.

"Frank, is anything wrong?" she asked, surprised.

"Well, it probably ain't nothing, but I'm thinking maybe Gramps ought to see that doctor of yours."

"Oh, of course. Would you like me to phone him for you?"

"Yeah."

"Should I tell him a particular time or just say as soon as he can?"

"Soon as he can. Bye." Frank hung up the phone and started out the door when he heard Neil's shouts.

"What happened?" He ran to the old man's side.

Neil stared wildly about. "It's falling the wrong way!"

"Gramps! You're only dreaming." Frank sat on the bed and grasped Neil's frail shoulders. "Wake up, Gramps. You're okay."

"What? Where did they all go?"

"Nobody's here. Just you and me. You had a bad dream, that's all." Frank pushed him gently back on the pillows. "The doctor's gonna be here soon."

"Yeah! Get a doctor!" He became excited again.

"Okay, he's coming. You just drink that tea and I'm gonna bring your things 'round back. You watch out the window."

Frank carried the heavy crates and the tree from the front yard to the back. He could see his grandfather a few feet above him, gazing at the sky. Frank ran to get his hammer from the hall closet, then waved it at Neil to get his attention.

"Okay, Gramps, here goes the first one." He pried up the boards across the top of one crate. Inside were layers of rich dark peat cushioning the bulbs and shoots and little plants. "Well, there's lots of different things in here but I can't tell which is which." He turned back the peat and tilted the box so Neil could see. "Oh, here's an invoice, anyway. Hold on a minute and I'll tell you what we got here." He took the pink slip out of the clear plastic envelope and studied it.

Neil began to cough. He coughed and leaned forward, pressing his hands to his aching ribs, and couldn't stop himself. Frank watched in horror as Neil began to gasp, falling back, his face an angry red, hands feebly gripping the air in front of him.

Frank dashed to Neil's room and thrust his fingers into the old man's throat to clear his windpipe and drew them out, coated with pus-colored phlegm and blood. He tossed the pillows behind him on the floor to lay Neil flat and covered his gaping mouth with his own. He pinched the nostrils closed and began to breath into his lungs, deeply and desperately, feeling for a heartbeat with his free hand.

He stopped for a moment to put his head to the bony chest, but he couldn't be sure if it was a heart he heard or the pounding of his own blood in his ears. He continued breathing into the unprotesting lungs until his own felt ready to give out. Only then did he race to the phone and shout instructions to send an ambulance at the startled operator. Again he breathed for the old man, not daring to stop, fooled by the beating of his own pulse.

At last he was pulled off the body by an ambulance driver and a paramedic. Frank was shaking and mute. He could barely make out their white forms through his swimming eyes. The paramedic listened to the old man's chest and punched the area of his heart several times. He shook his head. The driver went outside, familiar with the routine.

"I'm very sorry," the man said to Frank. "Are you a relative?"

"He's my grandfather," Frank rasped. "Get him to the hospital."

"There's nothing anyone can do for him. I'm sorry."

"Doctor's gonna come."

"But it's too late. Look, are you alone here? Is there a friend you could call, someone to stay with you?"

The driver returned with the stretcher and together, he and the paramedic rolled the light body onto it, covering him with a white plastic sheet. They carried him to the waiting ambulance and Frank followed in a daze. The driver strapped the body securely in the back while the other man approached Frank with a clipboard.

"Can you give me your grandfather's name?"

"His name . . ." Frank echoed.

"Can you tell me *your* name?"

Frank was silent, his brow creased. "His name is Neil Horner," he said slowly.

"Okay, good. Are you coming in with us? You don't have to."

Again Frank struggled for words.

"Look, I can see this is a bad time for you. I think you better stay here and drop by the hospital tomorrow. Is there anyone I could call to come and stay with you?"

"No."

The paramedic was reluctant to leave. His driver was calling to someone across the hedge.

"This is Mr. Small, says he's a friend."

"Okay, good. Do you think you could stay with this man for a while, Mr. Small, until he snaps out of it? I don't like to leave him alone like this."

"Yes, yes, of course. But can you tell me please what happened, Doctor? We thought he just had a cold or flu or something. It seems incredible!"

"Well, I could take a guess that whatever it was developed into a nice case of pneumonia. Do you happen to know how old he was exactly?"

"He just turned eighty-five." Roscoe brushed furtively at the corner of his eye and swallowed hard. "Good Lord! He was so fit for a man his age."

"Even so, at eighty-five any little cold or illness can turn into something really nasty." The paramedic slapped his thigh with the clipboard and glanced back at the large, desolate man on the walkway. "We'll be taking the body to Beauville Presbyterian. Can you bring your friend in tomorrow to answer a few questions?"

"Yes, certainly."

The men climbed into the ambulance and drove slowly and silently away.

Roscoe shook his head and wiped his eyes again. His throat stung as he pushed through the hedge and walked slowly to his stricken friend.

"YES, HELLO. Uh, a friend of mine was brought in yesterday afternoon . . . Neil Horner, his name is."

"Can you tell me the attending physician, please?"

"No, no, you see, he died. I was told someone would want to talk to us. That man is his grandson," Roscoe said quietly. The nurse followed his pointing finger and saw a large man in denim overalls blocking the door to the lobby.

"One moment, please." She checked a ledger, found the information, and paged a doctor by telephone. A tall thin man in street clothes soon hurried toward the desk.

"I'm Dr. Summers. Are you a relative?"

"No, just a friend of the family, Roscoe Small." He shook the doctor's hand. "This is the grandson, Frank Diggory." He waved Frank forward from his post; he moved like a sleepwalker.

"Follow me, gentlemen. We can talk in my office."

The doctor set off down a wide corridor, stopped abruptly, and threw open the door to a small anonymous office, modern and bright. The desk was too large for the room and squatted diagonally across one corner. The doctor took his seat behind it and the two men drew up chairs to face him.

"Now let's see what we have here," the doctor muttered, glancing over the report on his blotter, his fingers lightly joined to

167

form a steeple in the air. He frowned at the page and cleared his throat.

"Now, Mr. Horner is your grandfather, correct?"

"Yeah," said Frank. He spoke just above a whisper and stared down at his large hands. The smooth dark bangs fell forward and hid his face.

"Eighty-five, hm . . . Can you give me the name of your family doctor?"

"Didn't have none."

"They recently moved here from the Midwest. Minnesota, I believe." Roscoe looked encouragingly at Frank.

"We do like to have a brief medical history," the doctor said. "Mr. Diggory . . . ?"

"What."

"Can you provide me with a medical history? Or the name of your doctor in Minnesota?"

"He never took sick before."

"Never? Was he ever examined by a doctor, Mr. Diggory?"

"What for?" Frank mumbled.

"Was he . . . a religious man?" the doctor guessed.

"No."

"Doctor, he *did* seem in excellent health. I can vouch for that. It was such a shock," said Roscoe.

"All right. Now, this illness, can you tell me what his symptoms were? Mr. Diggory?"

"Just a cold," Frank began. "He said it wasn't nothing. I told him to stay in bed. He just looked tired, coughed some . . ."

"Was he in any pain? Was there any delirium?"

Frank fretted and twisted his fingers together. "Delirium?" He turned to Roscoe for assistance.

"I'm certain Mr. Diggory did everything possible," said Roscoe quickly.

"He didn't call in a doctor, did he?"

"As a matter of fact, he did call a doctor, but unfortunately, it was too late. He arrived after it was all over."

"Look, this man was eighty-five years old!" Dr. Summers pushed the report aside and tapped a pencil angrily on his desk. "I examined the body and it was obvious to me that your grandfather had an advanced case of pneumonia. His lungs were *clogged* with fluid. The expectorate was *full* of blood. He *must* have been in pain. He must have coughed quite a bit! He must have had a high temperature and delirium and yet you waited, how long? before calling a physician? You know, we treat pneumonia very successfully these days with penicillin." There was an edge of bitter sarcasm in his voice.

"He said he was getting better. . . . I didn't know."

"Of course not. You, sir, are not a doctor."

"Just one moment," Roscoe broke in. "I wonder if I might speak to you alone, Doctor. Frank, why don't you wait in the car and I'll finish up here." He waited while Frank got to his feet and shambled out of the office. "Now look here, Doctor, my friend is extremely upset just now. He was terribly close to his grandfather, unusually so. I'm certain that he took the best care that he knew how—"

"But his best was not nearly as effective as a few good shots of penicillin would have been," the doctor answered peevishly. "I'm sorry, but I am sick and tired of this ignorant distrust of medicine. I face it all the time. We're here to help people and we *can* help if we're called in before the patient is stone cold!" He threw down the pencil in disgust.

"Well, I'm sure you're right, but my friend is an individual, not the representative of an attitude and just now he's under a terrific strain and cannot defend himself against your remarks. Now, if there's nothing else, I'd like to go out to him. I'll call the undertaker and all—I know how this part goes. Good day."

Roscoe found his way out to the parking lot. Frank was leaning against the car with his head down and his arms folded.

"Get in, Frank. Everything's all right." He slammed his door and Frank climbed in beside him. "Listen to me, Frank. That doctor in there's got a chip on his shoulder. He doesn't know you, but I do, and I know that you did your best for Neil always. He was very old," Roscoe said slowly. "He had a happy life. Think about that." He started his motor and pulled onto the ramp.

"He was saying it was my fault."

"He would have died anyway, Frank. Pneumonia kills old people. And besides, they would have taken him away to a

169

hospital, a strange environment, hooked him up to a lot of tubes and machines. I'm certain this was for the better.''

"But there was a chance. . . .''

"Thoughts like that are slow poison, Frank, they eat away at you. Neil was a happy man. You did just fine.''

They drove the rest of the way in silence. Frank looked down at his lap and shook his head from time to time as if to chase away a bothersome thought. Roscoe used the time to make a mental list of all that had yet to be done.

"Here we are.'' Roscoe pulled up behind Frank's camper and they sat a moment in the sputtering car. "Come on,'' said Roscoe. Frank followed him into the empty house and perched on the edge of a chair, waiting for Roscoe to tell him what to do next.

"Where do you keep the phone book, Frank?''

"In the pantry.''

Roscoe found the book and ran his finger down the short column. "Frank, I'm going to call the undertaker down on Center. He's no better than the rest, but no worse. Is that all right?''

"Go ahead.''

"After that, I think someone should call your mother. I'll do it if you want me to. I imagine she'll fly out for the funeral. In fact, maybe you'll want to bury him back home.''

"No, bury him here.'' Frank looked up. "I'll call Mom.''

W HEN FRANK STEPPED OUT of the house he nearly stumbled over an empty plate left like a reminder on the kitchen step. He set the plate inside on the counter and went on his way.

He walked swiftly down Campbell, letting the steep grade propel him forward. One hand held a shopping bag, the other was jammed deep in his pocket, and his head hung low. He didn't want to see any friendly people, or neat houses, or swaying trees. He watched the dusty road beneath his feet and let the rhythm of his steps lull him for a time.

He reached Center Street and headed for the tailor's narrow

shop. Someone shouted his name in greeting and went unanswered. Kaplan was pinning a cuff for a customer, crawling around the gray felt box, when Frank walked in. He looked up and froze in alarm at the expression on Frank's face.

"The suit isn't ready yet," he stammered. "I told your grandfather I would call . . ."

"Pack it up. I need it now."

"But it's not done," Kaplan pleaded. "There are a few adjustments . . . Couldn't you come back tomorrow?"

The customer closed himself in the dressing room. Frank never glanced at him. He was staring in the direction of Kaplan's head but his eyes were unfocused.

"Pack it up and tell me what I owe," he said.

"Can't I at least take the basting out?"

"Let the undertaker do it. My Grandpa's dead."

Kaplan trembled behind his curtain, folding the pink material into a square of brown paper, sneaking peeks at the fierce giant in his doorway, afraid that Frank might challenge him on the color of the suit. But Frank waited silently, seeing nothing. Kaplan brought him the parcel and put it in his arms.

"What do I owe?" he asked gruffly.

"How much?" Kaplan stalled; it was such expensive fabric, but the work wasn't complete. He shrugged and tried on different expressions as he debated with himself.

"Just tell me the same as if—" Frank frowned and kicked his foot and Kaplan realized that the sooner he gave an answer, whatever it was, the sooner all this would be over.

The customer reappeared in his other pants and handed Kaplan the new pair. "How soon, Kaplan?" he asked.

"Friday?"

"Before lunch?"

"Okay, before lunch."

The man had to detour around Frank to reach the door.

"Let me see. Ah, here's your receipt!" Kaplan snatched up a scrap of paper from his work table. "One hundred sixty makes us even," he said and sucked in his breath.

Frank took a roll of bills from deep in his pocket, counted out twenties and dropped them on the table. He started for the door.

171

"I'm real sorry, Frank. My condolences."

Frank stopped to listen but neither turned nor spoke, and continued on his way. Kaplan pulled out a soggy handkerchief and mopped his forehead and neck and sagged against his shelves.

Frank strode through town with the brown bundle and the bag, his head down, watching the tips of his workboots on the glinting pavement. Someone tried to stop him to talk but he jerked his shoulder roughly from the friendly fingers. He walked on to the end of town, past the bank on its grassy plot, to a squat, red-brick building with boxes of geraniums on every white windowsill.

He let himself in and noticed with revulsion that the place was air-conditioned. He stared around at the too-white walls and the too-dark woodwork and wondered for a moment if he was in the right building. There was a fussy antique desk isolated on an island of carpet on the parquet floor, but no one was there. He approached it just the same and waited awkwardly.

A formally dressed man came out of a doorway, brushing his palms together, and turned down the corridor.

Frank called out. "Hey!"

"Sir? May I be of help?" The man wore a stiff smile as he looked Frank up and down. A messenger or workman of some sort, he thought.

"You the undertaker?"

"I am the director here, Mr. French." His smile grew tighter.

"This here's the suit I want to bury my grandpa in. In here's a shirt and tie and shoes to go with it."

"And the name of the deceased . . .?" The man accepted the bag and parcel with a small bow.

"Neil Horner. You got him yesterday. From the hospital."

"Ah, I see. Just let me make a note of that name." He found a marking pen in the desk drawer and wrote the name on a slip of paper. "May I offer my deepest sympathy. This must be a trying time for you." The director extended a cool hand but Frank failed to notice it as he turned and left.

172

"**M**RS. DIGGORY?" A pink-faced, neatly dressed man was waving as she came down the ramp. "Mrs. Diggory?"

"Who can that be?" wondered Willa, close behind. "I can't see Frank anywhere."

"This man must know," said Emmie. They threaded their way toward him through the arrivals area.

"You must be Frank's mother." The man smiled kindly and took her hand in both of his. "I'm Roscoe Small, Frank's neighbor."

"Oh, of course," she said, as if that explained everything. "This is Willa Peterson. Where's Frank?"

"Ah, well, he's at home just now. He wanted to meet you himself but I insisted that he rest," said Roscoe. "He's awfully despondent. We're going to have to be patient with him." He cleared his throat.

"Oh, well, of course! He was so attached to Pop," Emmie said, trying to conjure up the picture as she spoke.

"Well, we had better find your bags." He flashed an impersonal smile at the younger woman, wondering if she were another relative or someone just met on the plane. He escorted Mrs. Diggory across the wide linoleum floor to the escalator and the Peterson woman trotted along behind.

There weren't many pieces left on the carousel and Emmie and Willa quickly located their luggage. The guard checked their stubs and Roscoe wrested the suitcases from them. His car wasn't far from the door. He led the way, expecting the second woman to speak up if her destination was other than Frank's house, but she followed quietly and climbed into the back seat. Roscoe stored the bags in the trunk, made sure everyone was comfortable, and cruised smoothly out of the parking lot and onto the highway heading toward the shore. The lights of the airport twinkled prettily behind them in the purple dusk.

"Did you have a pleasant flight?"

"Oh! This was our first time on a airplane," Willa spoke up. "I can hardly believe I'm here."

"We had some trouble when we switched planes, somebody said it was a bomb threat. I guess they check those things out pretty good." Emmie giggled nervously.

"Oh, Em, I don't think that man knew any more what was going on than we did."

"Well, that's certainly bad luck on your first flight," Roscoe chuckled.

"Excuse me for asking, but you're English, aren't you?"

Roscoe glanced at Willa in his mirror. "Still shows, eh? Actually, I've lived here a good long time, more than twenty years."

"And you still have your accent!" Willa exclaimed.

"Well, it takes work, I suppose." They were climbing the hills now, following a snake of red taillights that stretched as far as the horizon. "Is my window blowing on you too much?"

"Oh, I don't mind. It feels nice. It was five below back home when we left, right, Em?" They were still swathed in shapeless woolen coats.

"I do want to tell you, I'm so awfully sorry about your father, Mrs. Diggory," said Roscoe.

"Oh, thank you. Could you tell me how it happened exactly? Frank wasn't too clear on the phone."

"There's not much to tell. It started as a simple cold and developed very quickly into pneumonia. At his age, that's not unusual. . . ." Roscoe shrugged.

"And he died at home?"

"Yes, well, it was so sudden, you see. I know Frank did everything in his power."

"But he never went into the hospital? It seems so queer. You'd think they would've made him go into a hospital at his age."

"Well, it's just that he seemed so fit and it happened so suddenly. I know it's difficult to understand, but believe me, it would be just awful if you expressed these doubts to Frank, Mrs. Diggory." Roscoe's heart was sinking. "He feels badly enough as it is, and as I say, he did his very best."

"Oh, of course," Emmie quickly agreed.

174

"Anyway, your father was quite a fellow. I was very fond of him. I'll miss him."

Emmie hesitated just a moment. "Don't you think Frank would be better off coming home with us, now that Pop's gone?"

"Well, not really. I mean, why?"

Emmie and Willa looked at each other, astounded.

"He doesn't have anyone here!"

"I wouldn't say that. He has a clientele for his work, friends, a home," Roscoe explained. "I really don't think it's even crossed his mind to go back." He was beginning to understand; this was a delegation come to reclaim Frank.

The sky was dark when they reached the underpass, but the moonlight sparkled over the wide water and the women caught their breath.

"The ocean! The Pacific, Em! Well, what do you know!" Willa slid over on the seat, cranked her window down, and let the salty air blow across her face.

They watched, transfixed, as the waves lapped the narrow beach below the cliffs. The sky was filled with stars over the gently curving horizon and the moon was a fat yellow slice. They passed through a few towns along their way, and the women asked with mounting anxiety if each was "it." By the time Roscoe was able to answer yes, Emmie was stiff with apprehension and Willa was chattering uncontrollably.

"Well, isn't this nice," Emmie said weakly as they wound up the steep hill.

Roscoe pulled into Frank's drive and went back to unload the trunk. The women stood fiddling with their purses, glancing nervously toward the warmly lit kitchen. Then Emmie gasped as the hulking silhouette of her son appeared in the doorway with the unmistakable outline of a shotgun by his side. He hung there, leaning sloppily against the doorframe, mute.

"Frank, look who's here! For heaven's sake, put that thing away and come say hello," Roscoe called with more confidence than he felt.

The dark figure retreated and then returned, lurching forward, emptyhanded. He came close and squinted into Willa's face with an expression of pure disbelief.

"We thought we'd surprise you, Frank," Emmie laughed nervously. "Cat got your tongue? Say hi to Willa."

"Give me a hand here, Frank," Roscoe broke in. He tugged Frank's sleeve, pulled him around to the trunk, and stuck a suitcase in his hand.

"What's *she* doing here?" Frank asked loudly and accusingly.

"Be quiet, will you," Roscoe hissed. "Come on, everyone. Let's go inside. You can offer us a cup of coffee, Frank," Roscoe said cheerily, fooling no one.

He led the way, with the women following close behind and Frank lagging, but inside, Frank dropped the suitcase, trudged off to his room, and slammed the door.

Roscoe located the percolater and the can of coffee. His face was red with embarrassment and he was glad to have something to do, measuring grounds, setting out cups and saucers, finding the sugar and cream.

The women perched at the table, perspiring in their coats, downcast, close to tears.

"There are some nice honeybuns in here," said Roscoe, his head buried in the icebox. "Honeybun, anyone?"

"We just had dinner on the plane," said Emmie mournfully.

"Well, I'll just put a couple on a plate and you can help yourselves if you like." The coffee stopped its merry perking and Roscoe poured it and reluctantly joined the grim little party.

They sipped in silence. Emmie and Willa listlessly broke the buns apart and took dainty bits with their fingers until they were all gone. Roscoe itched to get back to his own home, to call Charlotte and prevail upon her to come down and spend the evening, to fix a nice drink and put his feet up.

"I'd better see what Frank is up to," said Roscoe. "We'll get you settled in here." He forced a smile and ducked into the hall, rapped on Frank's door, and waited.

The door flew open with unexpected violence and Frank glared down at Roscoe, swaying slightly. The front of his overalls hung down unbuttoned; it was strange and shocking to see.

"Frank, I think you ought to take over here, show your mother and her friend where to put their gear. I'd like to go home soon."

"There ain't room."

"What are you talking about? They're *out* there, waiting!" Roscoe gestured helplessly.

"Mom can sleep in Gramps's room but I got no place for the other."

"I'm flabbergasted." Roscoe took a step back; he smelled some sort of alcohol on Frank's breath. "This is astonishing behavior."

"You tell 'em."

"I will not! If you really intend to be so rude, so unkind, you can just tell them yourself. I'll have no part of it."

Roscoe turned on his heel and walked stiffly down the hall feeling Frank's angry presence behind him. The women rose, open-mouthed, as he marched past and out the door.

H E MADE STRAIGHT for the telephone, dialed Charlotte's number, and her sweet voice came on the line, slightly breathless.

"It's me, Charl."

"Did you just get back? I was waiting."

"No, no. I've been at Frank's. He's behaving abominably. I'm totally disgusted. Can you still come down? I'll pick you up if you'd like."

"No, don't. I'll be down in ten minutes."

"Hurry, love."

Roscoe busied himself in the living room, collecting empty glasses from the end tables and rubbing at the rings they left. On his way to the sink he heard a faint but continuous knocking on his front door. With a sinking heart he went to answer it.

Emmie and Willa stood together on the porch, their cheeks wet with tears, hands filled with luggage. He felt suddenly exhausted.

"We hate to bother you," Emmie began.

"It's all my fault!" Willa sobbed.

"Come in, it's all right. Come in." Roscoe took their bags once again and they followed him inside, dabbing at their red noses. "Now sit down and tell me please what this is all about. I haven't understood a thing since I picked you up."

177

The women huddled on the couch and he brought them tissues from the bathroom, then sank down in his armchair.

"I just don't understand that boy! My own son . . ."

"It's my fault, Em. I was stupid to come. He don't want to see me one bit!" Willa cried.

"Then you're no relation to Frank?" Roscoe prodded gently.

"No!" Willa wailed. "A friend, or so I thought."

"We thought he'd be *happy* to see familiar faces," Emmie explained. "We thought he'd come back home! There's always a place for him," she said between hiccups.

"You didn't mention this idea to him just now, did you? Because he's in no state to think about the future, I don't imagine."

"Mention it! We didn't say boo, did we, dear? He just came right out and said I could take Pop's room but there wasn't no place for Willa." Emmie slid her arm through her friend's. Willa flushed and her eyes welled up.

"He said the same to me," Roscoe murmured.

"Well, I stood right up to him and said if there's no place for Willa then there's no place for me either."

"And what did he say?"

" 'Suit yourself,' right, dear? 'Suit yourself' to his own mother. I'm so ashamed I could die!" She burst into fresh tears and hid her face in a wad of tissues.

Willa patted her back and cooed comfortingly. She turned to Roscoe and said, "All this is my fault. I should've known better. I mean, Frank was never the most outgoing person, but still I feel like such an idiot. He must hate me to act like this."

"I'm sure it's not that he *hates* you, but he's really under a terrific strain. He's just not himself right now." Roscoe glanced at his watch; more than ten minutes had passed.

"I don't belong *here,* I don't belong *there,* I wish I was dead!" It was Willa's turn to sob and Emmie smoothed her hair and said, "There, there."

Roscoe heard his front door slam and stood. The women looked up with wild eyes and clutched each other in terror. Roscoe's heart ached for them.

178

"Darling, at last!" Charlotte flung herself into Roscoe's arms but his reaction was off. She followed his gaze to the dowdy women on his couch and stepped back. "Oh! I didn't know."

"Darling, this is Mrs. Diggory, and Willa—I'm sorry, I didn't catch your last name."

"Peterson. It doesn't matter," she said miserably.

"This is Charlotte Springer, my fiancee."

"Springer . . . ?" Emmie squinted at her through puffy eyes.

"I run the boarding house where your father stayed. Frank, too, for a short time. Their first home in California." She forced a smile, alarmed at their tears.

"We're having a bit of trouble with Frank tonight. I mentioned to you that he hasn't been himself lately," said Roscoe.

"You know what?" Emmie broke in. "I could almost swear he'd been drinking! I really do believe so."

"It's possible. Anyway, Charl, he's been rather inhospitable, and the ladies are in need of lodging." Roscoe and Charlotte studied one another's eyes.

"Well, the attic is empty," she began. "Oh, it's not really an attic," she assured them. "We just call it that. It's a big old room on the top floor, too many steps for most of my guests, a big L-shaped room with a view of the whole town, the beach and all. We can move another cot in there and you'll be real comfortable."

"There now, isn't that a stroke of luck?" Roscoe became jolly.

"Darling, let's load up my car and get everyone settled in right away."

"This is really too kind of you," Emmie said to Charlotte. "I hate to be so much trouble."

"No trouble at all. It's the least I can do. I was awfully fond of your father. It was such a shock."

"Well, let's get this show on the road," said Roscoe.

THE PHONE HAD RUNG many times before Frank hauled himself out of bed and staggered into the kitchen. It was late morning and the sun slanted brightly through the window, magnifying the sharp pain in Frank's head. He cleared his throat into the receiver before muttering hello.

"Mr. Diggory? This is Mr. French, director of Boxwood Funeral Chapel . . . ?" He paused for recognition.

"I hear you," said Frank. He pulled over a chair and dropped into it.

"Well, sir, do you *know* what was in that package you brought us yesterday?"

"My grandpa's suit."

"That suit happens to be pink."

Frank paused. "Pink?"

"Pink!" cried the director. "Now will you tell me what I'm supposed to do with *that?*"

"Dress him up in it and bury him," said Frank. "He picked it himself, he must've liked it."

"It'll look absolutely absurd."

"Anything else you got to say?" Frank could see Roscoe through the door, marching purposefully across the driveway.

"Indeed there is. The gentleman I first spoke with could not provide us with information regarding the religion of the deceased."

"Never had none."

"Nevertheless, you'll be wanting a service of some sort."

Frank thought this over. "Nope. I guess not. No thanks."

"But if you eliminate the service, there's nothing. Just the burial. The viewing, which I shudder to think of, and then the burial." His voice rose petulantly. "It's almost barbaric!"

"Sounds fine to me." Frank motioned Roscoe inside. "Anything else bothering you before I hang up?"

"Bothering *me?* Not at all. We'll see you later then. Good day, sir." The phone went dead in Frank's hand.

"Well, Frank, who are you menacing now?" Roscoe couldn't suppress a wry grin.

Frank joined him at the table. "Seems Gramps picked himself out a pink suit for his birthday present, so that's what he's gonna be buried in."

"Is that all?"

"No service."

180

"What do you mean? Nothing at all?" Roscoe was aghast. "Frank, do you think that's quite fair to your mother? The funeral is for the living, you know, not the dead."

"Gramps never had no use for churchgoing in his life. And no preacher out here ever clapped eyes on him, and I ain't paying no stranger to say nothing over him when he's stone dead and don't know the difference."

"Well, I think you're wrong," Roscoe said quietly. "Would you care to know where your mother and her friend found refuge last night?"

"You want coffee?" Frank asked sourly, busying himself at the counter.

"They're up at Charlotte's, Frank. And I think that was a rotten way to behave. I mean it."

"Well," Frank drawled unpleasantly, "I'd just like to know what business it was of Willa to fly all the way out here when she wasn't asked and nobody's kin besides."

"I imagine your mother asked her, Frank, which should be enough." Roscoe was beginning to feel he was talking to a child.

"Then it's her business," Frank muttered. He set out cream and sugar and waited across the room for the coffee to finish perking, showing Roscoe only his broad back.

"What about this afternoon?"

"What about it?"

"Well, Charlotte will be bringing your mother and Willa. You may ride with me, but I want a promise from you first that you'll be civil," he said. "You're not the only one who loved him, you know."

Frank was glaring at the shiny pot, his jaw clamped tight and his arms folded across his chest. At last the coffee was ready and he poured two cups.

"Thanks," said Roscoe. "It's set for four o'clock, so I'll come by for you at three-thirty. I have to show my face at the bank for a couple of hours at least." He thought as he sipped. "Actually, you know what I think I'll do? I think I'll plant that almond tree outside his window. Do you mind?"

Frank was staring into his cup. He shook his head no, but Roscoe couldn't see his face beneath the smooth dark bangs.

"Then I'll be by earlier to do that, and then clean up a bit, then we'll go." Roscoe looked gloomily at Frank's rumpled shirt and softly worn overalls; he didn't know if Frank even owned anything else. Well, thought Roscoe, that's the least of it.

"IT LOOKS A BIT weepy, I'm afraid," Roscoe said, brushing the soil from his hands. "I think it might perk up, though, with proper watering. I've got to change and wash up. I'll just be a few minutes."

Frank stood inside his kitchen door, quiet and withdrawn. He looked dully out over Roscoe's head and Roscoe stepped back to try to put himself in Frank's field of vision.

"You'll be ready to go?" Roscoe prodded.

Frank looked down and kicked weakly at the doorframe.

Roscoe hurried through the hedge and into his house. Frank didn't stir. His battered gray hat was within arm's reach on the counter. He looked out again at the brilliant sky, and the rustling of the leaves seemed louder than every other sound. He smelled the sour salt air and felt it on his face. All the days were the same now.

Roscoe pulled up behind the camper and tooted his horn. Frank reached behind him for the hat and wandered outside as though under a spell. Roscoe leaned over and threw open the passenger door. Frank climbed in.

Roscoe was wearing his most somber suit, a navy pin-stripe. He had attached a black ribbon around one sleeve. He could smell a touch of mildew under his cologne, a funeral smell.

They drove in silence to the chapel and Roscoe felt a shiver as he parked behind the waiting hearse. They were standing in the sun when Charlotte parked a half a block back. The women hesitated in the car, frozen in their gloomy dresses, then Ida heaved herself out of the back seat and made for Frank, hugging him around the middle to weep on his chest.

Roscoe motioned to the others and they came timidly forward, clutching small nosegays like protective charms. Their dresses, too, smelled of disuse. Charlotte pulled Roscoe aside.

"Didn't you try to get him to change?" she hissed, her nails biting into his arm.

"Truthfully, no, Charl. In the big scheme of things, it didn't seem to really matter."

The blast of cold air inside was sickening at first. Mr. French glided toward the party and led them into a small white chapel where rows of dark pews, divided by a wide aisle, faced the platform. And on the platform lay the open coffin, raised to viewing level by some device concealed in folds of white satin. There were fat bunches of chrysanthemums around the bottom, laced together with bunting.

Frank was the first to stand over the coffin, gazing down with an eerie smile, admiring the suit on the old man. It looked wonderful somehow. Frank took a seat in the first row and the others approached the coffin by turns.

Emmie recoiled in horror at first and glared furiously at her son, but he was unreachable. She looked back at her father, bent close to him, and lightly touched the wavy white hair. He seemed so peaceful, almost like he was dreaming of something pleasant. She retreated to a nearby pew and cried soundlessly into a plain hankie. Willa patted her back and cried with her.

After several minutes had passed, the women began to peer around the bright little room, wondering what was next. Mr. French and his assistant entered with eyes downcast, from a side door. They bolted the coffin shut and stripped away the satin and flowers below to reveal a folding metal frame on casters. When they began to maneuver it down the step, between the pews, Roscoe stood and smiled wanly.

The others were astounded.

"What's going on!" Emmie cried. "Where's the funeral!"

"Frank didn't want a religious service," Roscoe whispered apologetically. "I'm sorry. I tried to reason with him, but, well, you know Frank."

"But you can't just stick a man in the ground without a word!" she shrieked. "It's . . . it's indecent!" She burst into fresh hot tears. "This whole thing is a nightmare," she sobbed.

"Look, if it would help, I could say a few words at the

cemetery. Would you like that?'' He took Emmie's arm and steered her down the aisle.

''You're such a kind man,'' she hiccupped, blotting her cheeks and blowing her nose.

The director and the assistant were having trouble outside; Roscoe's car was too close to the back of the hearse and they couldn't even lower the tailgate. Roscoe backed up the car. The coffin was successfully loaded. The men and women separated and the procession rolled ceremoniously out of town.

The cemetery seemed unnaturally green in the sunburnt countryside. The neat headstones stretched back as far as the eye could see, some plots adorned with fresh bouquets, others trimmed with stones and small shrubs. The motorway wound in graceful curves to the appointed site. The party left the two cars, and the women grouped around the ugly hole while Roscoe and Frank helped the professionals load the coffin onto a pulley system over the grave. Mr. French waited disgustedly for Frank to give him the go-ahead, but Roscoe stepped forward and cleared his throat.

''Uh, I have a few words I'd like to say . . .'' He got their attention and tried to gather his thoughts. ''I didn't know Neil for terribly long, but I can truthfully say he's one man I will always remember, kindhearted, charming, serene, and wise—and a wonderful friend. I hadn't prepared a speech, really . . . I just want to say . . . farewell.''

Mr. French's hand was ready on the crank when Roscoe turned and nodded. He lowered the coffin on the whining pulley, released the ropes, and pulled them through. The women dropped their flowers onto the coffin and moved away from the sight. The assistant summoned a workman lurking nearby, aloof until now, and he began to shovel dirt into the hole. The funeral was over. There was nothing to do but go home.

CALLAHAN HEARD A CRASH. It seemed to come from far away and he tried to weave it into his dream, failed, and rubbed his eyes. He had no way of knowing the time but guessed that it was late. He took a slug, an eye-opener, from his bottle, and listened at the door for a repetition of the noise.

The next crash was almost identifiable and came from the house without question. He could see a light on, not in the kitchen but further back. He tucked the bottle inside his jacket and crept around the rear of the house. He peeked into the old man's room as he passed and noticed that nothing had been disturbed. He checked the farmer's room and it was empty. He scurried past the front door and crawled into the bushes along the music room wall. Light poured out of the windows above him. Two successive crashes made his heart race. Then there was a moment's quiet and he slowly raised his head till his nose was on the window ledge.

Frank sat on the floor facing in Callahan's direction. His long legs were splayed out and he held a sweating green bottle of something to his lips. The ruined stereo set was heaped by the door with the wires tangled into careless knots. One speaker cover had been slit cleanly from corner to corner. There were pieces of broken records, black plastic shards, strewn about the floor, mixed in with torn album jackets. The quilts were piled in a corner of the room, stuffing showing through their seams.

Before Callahan's astonished eyes, Frank grabbed a handful of albums from the cabinet behind him, flung the covers aside, and tossed the records, one at a time, flat on the floor so that they shattered into jagged triangles. Then he took another long pull on the bottle.

It made Callahan thirsty to watch and he drank from his own bottle. The destruction of the music room had his wholehearted approval. He was trembling with excitement, wide awake now.

Frank selected another album, a double set, crash, crash. He took another drink. So did Callahan.

He cackled softly in the bushes and made himself more comfortable, drinking with Frank sip for sip. Frank's face was grim, distorted. Callahan's was ecstatic; he could barely contain himself.

Frank rose unsteadily and Callahan ducked low, his heart pounding. He dared to look up again in time to see Frank aim a mighty kick at the second speaker, splitting the fabric and smashing the delicate insides. He lurched around the room, hunting for still-whole objects and his eye settled on the sturdy filing cabinet. He pulled out the long drawers two at a time, grunting with satisfaction, and flung them at the opposite wall. They spilled their carefully inscribed cards but remained intact, spoiling the wall with corner-shaped dents. When Frank finished with the drawers, he dumped the cabinet on its face and stood panting, glistening with sweat, his arms hanging limply, worn out at last.

He looked at the devastation around him and his eyes were strangely blank. He bent to grab the neck of his bottle, lumbered to the door, and put out the light.

"CHARL, sleeping?"
"Almost."
"Almost doesn't count."

"Mm, you're squishing my arm. Lift up. Okay." Charlotte snuggled closer to Roscoe with her arm cradling his neck. "This is nice," she murmured.

"My dear girl, it should be like this always, every night. It will be as soon as you give up that blasted house and marry me."

"Darling, I'm trying to find someone. I interviewed someone this afternoon."

"And?"

"And she wanted the weekends off. I said I'd let her know."

"Then I hope Emmie and Willa never go back so I can have you to myself. I'm tired of sharing you with those old geezers up there. It's not fair."

"As soon as I find somebody to live in. That's all, darling. Say you understand." She could see Roscoe's face, oval and smooth in the moonlight, smiling sweetly at her. It was happening at last, long after she had given up hope, the thing she most wanted. Then why can't I tell him yes, she wondered.

"You sure you can't get Ida? Under any condition?"

186

"What, you mean more money? It doesn't matter to her. She has to look after her brother's kids. It's more important to her."

"It's important to me to have you as my wife."

"Quiet a second. Did you hear that?"

"It's probably Callahan lurking about."

"Is *he* back again? He gives me the creeps." She nuzzled Roscoe's neck and he breathed in the perfume of her fuzzy red hair.

"Oh, he's all right. Slightly mad, I suppose, but basically harmless. He must miss Neil terribly. It was funny, that."

"Them being friends?"

"Hm." Roscoe began to knead Charlotte's shoulder with his fingers. He found a tight knot of muscle under the soft skin and worked it gently. She relaxed against him, rubbing her breast against his side and sighing when he pressed the tender spot.

"It's not because I don't want to," she whispered.

"I know."

E MMIE MARCHED RESOLUTELY down the hill to Frank's front door. Then her strength flagged and she peered anxiously through the glass before tapping lightly. She waited, holding the screen open with her toe, peering behind her at the road that wound merrily down to the sea.

When Frank failed to appear, she yearned to scurry back up the hill to safety, but dutifully, she went around to the kitchen door and peeked in, cupping her hands against the screen. She called her son's name in a quavering question and gasped as he lurched down the hall toward her. A plastic jug dangled from one finger, his blue shirt was rumpled and dingy, his hair stood up in a cowlick where he'd repeatedly pushed it off his face, and he badly needed a shave. If Emmie had been a stranger, she felt sure she would have made a run for it, but being his mother, she drew herself up, met his eye, and held her ground.

"You coming in?"

"I want to have a little talk with you. It won't take long. . . . I guess you got stuff to do," she apologized, following him to the table. He sat sloppily, stretching his long legs out to the side. She perched opposite.

"Frank, dear," she began with a frightened smile. "I wonder if you thought at all about coming home to Belle Plaine. Where you wouldn't be so all alone. I mean, with Pop gone, it must be . . . I don't know, pretty lonely for you. And everybody's always asking after you, you know, all your old customers . . . It wouldn't take much to start right up again. Where you left off. Frank?"

"What." He stopped glaring at his shoe tips to take a swig from his jug and direct a pitiless glance at his mother.

"Are you listening, dear?" She looked away, flustered.

"I hear you."

"Well, how about it? I think it would be the best thing to be around family and friends, you know? And there's always a place for my boy. What do you say? Will you come home?"

"No."

"But why? Will you at least think about it? Frank?" She waited for a response, and when none was forthcoming she chattered on. "Because, what is there now? You looked after Pop and made a nice home here but now he's gone. It's time you start thinking of your own self and what's best for you." She paused expectantly, feeling that she'd made a good point. Some of the old confidence returned. "Listen, Frank, I was thinking . . . You know that long shed where the coops used to be? You could take it over if you want and make a nice cottage for yourself. It's already got water and electricity. It wouldn't take much work for you. Frank . . .?"

"What."

"How does that sound?" She leaned eagerly forward. "Will you think about it? Just sleep on it, dear, okay?"

"No."

"But what are you gonna do here? You don't want to be all alone?" she pleaded. "Do you?"

"Yeah."

He rose wearily and, without looking back, sauntered out of the room swinging his jug. She heard a door slam and sat a moment longer, composing herself. She noticed something strange on the floor of the next room and went to the doorway to take a look.

Her mouth hung open as she surveyed the scene—broken records littering the floor, file cards mixed in covered with Frank's clear printing, an expensive stereo destroyed, chairs overturned, drawers lying every which way. It looked like the work of a madman. Her skin prickled and she shrank back, listening for his footsteps, feeling behind her for the door. Once out of the house she took off at a trot, panting up the hill.

"HERE WE ARE. Do you take milk?"

"Yes, thanks." Willa stirred her coffee and breathed in its comforting aroma. "I just wish Em hadn't gone all by herself," she fretted. "He's been so horrible this whole time."

"Oh, Frank's all right, really. He'll get over this, but it takes time." Charlotte broke a muffin in half and buttered the inside lightly. "He was awfully attached to Neil, you know."

"Well, but there isn't much time left. I mean, I guess we'll be going back real soon, so if Emmie can't talk sense to him now, then that's that."

"I guess you're anxious to get back."

Willa smiled sadly and shook her head. "It don't make a speck of difference to me. There's nothing but a big old empty house waiting for me. And it ain't even my own. But I shouldn't be bothering you with my problems. You been so kind."

"That's all right, dear. Do you mean to say you have no family back there?"

"Well, I did have. I lived with my mother, took care of her for a long time. She always was sickly. Anyway, she passed away and now I'm all alone. I got a married brother in Duluth. That's way up north."

"I know. Well, what a shame. When did your mother pass away?"

"Oh, almost two months ago, I guess." Willa looked suddenly weary.

"You must miss her."

"Well, I do. I miss taking care of her, that's a fact. I feel so useless now, nobody needs me or wants me for anything." She waved her hands. "I really mustn't go on like this."

"But I understand perfectly. I myself cared for an aunt through a long illness. This was her house. Anyway, it does help to talk about these things, not keep 'em bottled up. I hope you think of me as a friend."

"What a sweet thing to say." Willa put her head down on her arms and began to sob.

"There, now, you just let it all out." Charlotte stroked her shoulder.

"I guess I was kinda sweet on Frank," Willa sighed, wiping her cheeks with a napkin. "Emmie always told me he kinda liked me too, that he just had his ways, you know?" She hiccupped. "And I went on hoping and dreaming. Even when he moved out here I kept hoping he'd come back. Pretty stupid of me, I guess."

"Not at all. You should never regret feeling nice feelings about someone."

"I suppose."

"So now you feel kind of rootless? Like you don't belong?" Charlotte suggested.

"That's it exactly! Just sort of cut loose." She took a sip of coffee and sniffled.

"And how do you like what you've seen of California, our little town here?"

"Oh, it's real nice." She turned obediently to the window behind her. "Do you really have this weather all the year long?"

"Yes, most of the time."

"It must be heaven."

Charlotte took a moment to finish her muffin and organize her thoughts. "Have you ever considered moving out here yourself?" she began casually, her heart beginning to race.

"Me? How could I! I mean, I may not own my own house in Belle Plaine, but at least I can stay as long as I want, rent free. I have just a little money. How could I think of moving anywhere?" She laughed mirthlessly. "I know I said I don't belong, but the truth is, I'm kinda stuck, whether I like it or not."

190

"Hmm." Charlotte's eyes glistened as she studied the woman. "I'm going to say something now that might be none of my business and you just stop me if you want, and no offense, okay?"

"Sure."

"Well, you know that Roscoe and I are engaged . . . ?"

Willa nodded for her to go on.

"Well, there's only one thing stopping us from marrying right away and that thing is this house. I've been running it for a long time now. It gave me my independence and my security and I'm *attached* to it—I could never just sell this place. But at the same time, I love Roscoe and I want to marry him and live with him. See my problem?"

Willa nodded, somewhat mystified.

"I've been desperate to find a reliable person to live here in my place. The duties are very light. The main thing is that this person must be here every night because, you know, the men are all old and things can happen . . . But Idabelle does all the cleaning and cooking and I would still handle the business end—there's really nothing to it. Oh, Willa, you'd be so perfect!" The words burst out. "Just think of the advantages to yourself! It would be more than just a roof over your head. People would be depending on you. It's like a real family here, the men are so sweet. It really is a nice life. And of course there would be a nice salary in addition to room and board. Is this really such a shock?" Charlotte laughed happily at the look on Willa's face.

"I don't know what to think! No one ever, *ever* offered me any kind of a job before. I never thought there was anything I could do that was worth money! Gosh, I can't believe it!"

"But you'd be so perfect for it. Will you think about it, please? I know it's a lot to decide all at once."

"I don't need to think about a *thing*. Lord, I got *nothing* back there, a little bitty savings account and a heap of old clothes that would be too warm for here." She laughed. "I don't have to go back at all! It's the answer to my prayers, that's what it is." She stared around at the roomy bright kitchen and marveled at her good fortune.

"You're positive? You'll take the job?"

"You bet. Boy, will I take it!"

"I can't tell you what this means to me!" Charlotte threw her arm around Willa's shoulders and hugged her quickly.

"What it means to *me!*"

"I'm going right down to the bank to tell Roscoe. I can't wait another minute. Listen, poke around and get the feel of the place, make yourself at home. I won't be too long and we'll talk more when I get back, okay?"

"Wonderful."

Charlotte squeezed her again, pecked her cheek, and trotted out to the car.

"YOU'RE CERTAIN SHE WON'T change her mind?"

"Positive. You should have seen how thrilled she was. It's going to be perfect. Oooo, I'm so happy!"

"Me too." Roscoe pulled Charlotte behind a stout tree and held her close. He looked over her curly head at the featureless rear of the bank across the parking lot and felt that everything in the world was good.

"You know what we're going to do, Charl? Elope. Tonight."

"You're not serious." She pulled back and examined his face.

"Why not? We've waited long enough."

She laughed and kissed him. "You're right." She felt as carefree as a girl.

"I have one or two things to get out of the way here and then we'll pack a few things and take off. We could head for Yuma to get married, and take a few days' honeymoon on our way back. What do you say?"

"Sounds wonderful. Ida can help Willa settle in. I just know this is going to work out. I'm so happy, darling."

"Me too, love. Come, watch me be vice-president." He patted her hip, took her hand, and led her to the side entrance.

"Mrs. Jenkins," he spoke into the house phone, "could you come in here for a moment and bring me that conditional certificate of thingamajig plus a Xerox for us."

"But you said you wouldn't sign it till they showed proof—"

"Just bring it in. I'm sick of the whole thing. I want it out of this office today. I'm taking a few days' holiday." He winked at Charlotte.

"Whatever you say, Mr. Small."

Charlotte watched eagerly, perched on the visitor's chair. She felt proud of Roscoe despite his remarks about his job.

"Are you always so silly at work?" she asked. "Or is it just for my benefit?"

"Silly, did you say? I'll have you remember that your future husband is a very important man."

The secretary let herself in, smiled in a preoccupied way at Charlotte, and waited for Roscoe's signature, her hands clasped primly.

"Mail it off and good riddance. What's next?" He stirred the contents of his "In" box impatiently. "Mrs. Jenkins, is there anything in here that can't wait till next week?"

"I don't think so. The usual load of paperwork for the quarter will be in on Wednesday, but I can get started on it without you if it'll help."

"It will indeed. You're a dear. I'll send you a postcard if I think of it. See, I'm marrying that nice lady over there."

"Isn't that lovely," said Mrs. Jenkins, scooping up her papers and shutting the door quietly behind her.

"Well, Charl, come give me a kiss and we'll blow this joint."

CALLAHAN WOKE PUZZLED. He didn't have that watery-kneed nightmare feeling at all. It had to be something else, something going on in the house. His heart pounded excitedly as he slid down from the bunk to peer out the porthole. There was no light showing, no movement of any kind. The insects sang steadily and the waves broke far away. He considered going back to sleep but instead he slipped the flat bottle inside his jacket and plunged into the cool night air.

He went first to the back of the house and tried to get a peek at Frank's room but the curtains blocked his view. He scurried past the front door around to the music room and again admired the wreckage. It gave him a thrill to remember drinking with Frank that night, secretly, in the bushes. At the kitchen window, he hoisted himself on tiptoes and let his eyes adjust to the deeper gloom.

At first he couldn't make sense of what he saw, Frank slumped over in a chair, huge hands dangling, legs splayed out, a long something sticking out of his mouth, propping him up. The shotgun.

Callahan took a long drink to fortify himself, then, trembling, let himself in and crept near the body, slowly, closer than he'd ever been before. He gently removed the gun and wiped the blood off the barrel with a dish towel. His heart was racing but his hands grew steadier as he worked. He set the gun in the corner and began to clean the gore off the wall with another cloth, by moonlight, not daring to turn on the light. He gagged over a lump of something, a clot of bone and hair, but worked doggedly until the job was done.

He heaped the soiled cloths in the sink and took a break to look for something to drink. Under the sink he found the five champagne bottles lined up, all empty. He removed his jacket and tried to calm himself before approaching the body again. The excitement was almost unbearable.

He lifted one hand, still warm and pliant, and compared it with his own. His hard and leathery hand fit like a child's in Frank's broad palm. Each finger was like a separate, well-made limb. He let it drop and pushed down Frank's eyelids with his thumbs. He stroked the black bangs dipping across the wide forehead and the hair was silkier than he'd imagined. The back of the head was blown away.

He bent awkwardly beside the body and tried to lift it from under the arms but it was hopeless; he didn't have the strength. He rested again, trembling from the feel of the warm body against him, and tried to think.

The floors were smooth linoleum; the chair could slide along. He straightened Frank in the chair and tilted it back, supporting only a fraction of the total weight, and began to drag it through the kitchen and down the hall to the bedroom. He gagged when the

194

broken head lolled against his chest, but made steady progress.

The sun was rising behind the hills now. Callahan parted the curtains to let in the golden light. He leaned the chair back against the mattress, climbed on it himself, and pulled under Frank's arms until only his legs still hung off the bed. It was easy then to arrange him flat out, his head on a pillow, his hands curled at his sides.

Callahan stood back to admire what he'd done. He returned the chair to the kitchen and brought back the shotgun to rest the butt in one lifeless hand with the barrel over the shoulder, like a soldier at arms.

The new light was bathing the body now, and Callahan noticed several days' growth of beard on Frank's usually clean jaw. He found an electric razor in the bathroom and crawled under the bed to find the outlet. The whirring blades were unbearably loud and he made a quick job of it, sloppy around the neck and chin but still an improvement.

He noticed a sturdy laundry bag in the bathroom and dumped out the socks and shorts and shirts. He took two clean blue shirts from Frank's dresser and added a few T-shirts and rolled socks.

Then he searched the old man's room. On the nightstand he found the bone-handled penknife and the heavy gold-colored wristwatch resting in his abalone shell. He added these things to his sack and closed the door behind him.

In the kitchen, he took cans of soup from the pantry, and corned beef hash, tuna, salmon, and ham. He found an opener and stowed it all. In the cupboard he found the emergency money, a thick roll of bills, and pocketed that. He slung the sack over his shoulder and walked out into the road.

The sun hung over the hills, a fat orange ball, lending a pink glow to the sky. In the other direction, the ocean stretched out, rippling and sparkling near the shore, and the wind made a great live rushing sound in the leaves overhead. A little hunched figure moved slowly through the landscape, along the tall weeds by the side of the road, his eyes cast down, searching his path for scraps and parts of things and lost coins.